BOUDREAUX'S LADY

The League of Rogues - Book 15

LAUREN SMITH

INTRODUCTION

Hello Readers!

This book, *Boudreaux's Lady* comes a bit out of chronological sequence from the rest of the League books you may have read so far. This book takes place a few years into the future where the main League of Rogues characters are all happily married and producing adorable future rogues and rebellious ladies.

How did this book come about?

My story ideas can come from the strangest and most wonderful of places sometimes. The idea for *Boudreaux's Lady* came from a unique opportunity. I met author Kristen Proby online after reading her contemporary set romance series about her family the Boudreaux's which is set in New Orleans. In that first book you learn that the Boudreaux family has been in New Orleans for a couple of hundred years and they own a lovely plantation house and there's a great family of brothers and sisters who all have their own love stories within the Boudreaux series.

As I read that first story *Easy Love*, I fell in love with the Boudreaux family and when I learned Kristen was opening up her Boudreaux world for other authors to write in, I came up with the idea of writing the Boudreaux family's origin story. I pitched the idea to Kristen who absolutely loved it!

When I considered what sort of characters would give up their lives in England and move to American in the early 1800s I was inspired to write a gothic- mystery.

The opening scene in the prologue, where a pair of twins were born and the lord of the manor threatens to cast one of the children into the flames is actually based on a true story in England.

Only, in the true story, things were far more gruesome. The lord in reality, tossed one of the babies into the flames since he wanted only one heir to his lands and didn't want to have the problem of twins. But the death of the child haunted him to the point of madness. One night while he rode down the dark road to his home, he was tormented by the sounds of a wailing child and glimpsed a baby in flames which appeared before him on the road. His horse reared back at the same moment he had a heart attack and he fell off his horse and perished on the road, only to be found the next morning, dead and cold.

The true story haunted me so much that it provided the seed from which this story grew. So, dear reader, turn the page and enjoy this gothic-mystery set in my beloved League of Rogues universe.

PROLOGUE
ENGLAND, OCTOBER 1806

The shrieking wind against the windowpanes nearly matched the wails of the young woman in bed. Her body seized with agony, and she cried out as a midwife pressed two hands against her swollen belly.

"Push a bit harder, my lady." Lucy, the midwife urged.

The woman in the bed sank back against the pillows. "I can't."

"You can, Albina. You can." Lucy knew she ought not to be so familiar with the woman, but she'd brought Albina into the world and now she would bring forth Albina's child. Lucy pressed again on Albina's belly, feeling the child shift at last into a better position.

"*Push*, my lady. Push once more!" Lucy encouraged.

Albina dug her fingers into the sheets. Sweat covered

her pale face as she squeezed her expression into a snarl before she relaxed.

Lucy peered between her spread legs. "I see it crowning, my dear. You're so very close. Another few pushes now."

A look came over Albina's face, one of such determination that Lucy was momentarily taken aback.

Albina pushed, her teeth clenched, and Lucy rushed to catch the child emerging from the womb with a white cloth. The babe was quiet. Too quiet. His face a frightening shade of blue. Lucy smacked the baby's bottom, laid it flat on the bed, and pressed on it's tiny chest in a rhythm to stimulate its heart. She even parted it's little lips and tried to clear it's airway, but to no avail.

"It's a little boy," Lucy sniffled. "But...I don't think the wee one made it." She started to set the baby on the bed but gasped as Albina bent almost double, pushing again.

"Another?" Lucy hastened to prepare a fresh swaddling cloth as Albina pushed again. Soon, a smaller child emerged, mewling and fiery tempered, fighting like a warrior to stay alive. This babe's cries were strong and healthy.

"Is he all right?" Albina asked, looking at the baby.

"*She* is very healthy." Indeed, the baby girl was screaming mightily.

Albina reached for the quiet bundle on the bed beside her. "And the boy?"

Lucy's eyes burned as she shook her head. She offered the dead child up to Albina.

"Give him a name. A strong, proud name, my dear. One full of love and he will take it with him to the heavens."

Albina held the baby to her chest, tears streaming down her cheeks as she stroked the baby's cold face and touched his small fingers. So perfect yet gone already from this life.

"Andrew. You are my darling Andrew." She kissed the child's forehead and then allowed Lucy to set him in a prepared bassinet until he could be buried.

"And this one?" She pushed the little girl, still crying, into her mother's arms. "Name her too."

Albina gazed down at the girl, such love and sorrow in her face that Lucy's heart broke.

"Philippa. My little Philippa." Albina's head fell back against the pillows. "Oh Lucy, I'm so very tired. Take care of them both, please." Albina held the baby out and Lucy took Philippa before Albina's arms dropped to the bed. Sweat dewed on the new mother's forehead and her pale skin gave Lucy much to worry about. Many delicate women didn't survive childbirth, and Albina's birth had been doubly difficult.

Lucy jumped at the sound of the bed chamber door crashing open. Lit by firelight, Cornelius Selkirk, the Earl of Monmouth, stared at her and the baby.

"Well? How is my son?" he demanded, casting only the briefest glance at his ailing wife.

Lucy nodded toward the quiet bassinet. "Gone, my lord."

"Gone?" His hard stare shifted between the bassinet and the squirming baby in Lucy's arms. "There were two? What about that one?" He pointed at Philippa, who had stopped crying and had gone very still at the sound of the angry male voice in the room.

"My lord, this is your daughter, Philippa." Lucy did not offer the baby to him. She knew better. Monmouth had a temper the likes of which she'd never seen in a man.

"Damnation! What use has a man for a daughter? I needed a son!" He turned to Albina, who was now white as alabaster.

"I'm sorry, my lord. Your son never drew breath." Lucy attempted to keep his rage away from Albina.

Monmouth pointed an accusing finger at Philippa, nestled safely in Lucy's arms. "Yet that little brat lives?"

"She does. A brave and healthy baby. You should be proud of her."

Monmouth's face took on a frightening reddish hue. "Proud to have another useless female here under my roof?" He spun to Albina again. "By God, woman, you have failed in your only duty. I will not stand for it. I won't!"

When his wife made no reply, he rushed at the bed, shaking her shoulders violently. But Albina lay still, her eyes glassy and unseeing. A pool of blood between her thighs was still spreading slowly, thickly. She'd bled out.

Lucy's heart fractured in her chest. Albina was gone. But perhaps it was a kindness in its own horrid way. The brutish Lord Monmouth had never deserved her, nor did he deserve the child she still held in her arms. Though at least it could be said that when he realized what had happened to her, some emotion other than rage passed through him, if only for a moment.

"Dead... My wife and son both dead." He stared in cold fury at little Philippa. "And *that* creature is to blame." His gaze moved to the fire blazing in the hearth, then around the dark room. Lucy could see a flurry of murderous thoughts passing across his face in rapid succession.

When he turned to face her, her heart stuttered in fear at what he might do.

"The miller in the village. You delivered a son to him, did you not?" Monmouth demanded.

"Yes, two days ago." That birthing had been easy. A stout lad had been born to the miller, Mr. Wilson and his wife, Beth, with no complications. Beth was healthy and hearty like her child.

"You will take a message to them, tonight. I will pay ten thousand pounds for their son. And you will give them that brat in exchange."

"But, my lord, she's your daughter—"

"Do it, or I swear I will throw that child into the fire." Monmouth loomed over her with such dark menace in his face that Lucy did not doubt he would carry out the gruesome threat.

"What are you waiting for?" he hissed.

Still clutching the girl in her arms, Lucy fled the room. In a few minutes, she was in Monmouth's coach being escorted to the miller's cottage two miles away. The night was a bitter cold, with deadly drafts and vicious chills that would steal many a life before dawn. Thankfully the storm which had raged half an hour before had gone, leaving a cloudless night sky by the time they reached the miller's home.

"Thank you, Joseph," Lucy told the driver. "Please wait for me." She knocked hard on the miller's door. After a few moments, a weary young man answered.

"Yes?" Wilson asked. He recognized Lucy, and his eyes widened at the sight of the Monmouth Crest painted on the black coach doors behind her in full view beneath the moonlight.

"May I please come inside, Mr. Wilson?" Lucy asked.

"Yes, of course." Wilson stepped back and let her pass through into the house. Philippa, who had been tucked securely under her cloak, now made a mewling sound and Wilson jolted.

"You have a baby?" He peered down at Philippa.

"Yes," Lucy said quietly.

Beth came down from the tiny set of stairs that led to the second floor of the cottage.

"Beth, you should return to bed." Lucy chastised gently.

"I'm all right, Lucy." Beth smiled and pulled her dress gown closed as she joined her husband.

"What's all this about now?" Wilson asked.

She tried to calm herself. Her hands couldn't seem to stop shaking. All she could see was the look on the earl's face as he threatened to cast Philippa into the fire. "I've come here on a mission of great urgency. The countess of Monmouth died giving birth to twins tonight. The first, the son, was stillborn. The second." She swayed Philippa in her arms. "Survived but is a girl. The earl knows you have given birth to a son. He has an offer for you. It's one I beg you to consider for the sake of the child in my arms."

"What sort of offer?" Wilson and his wife exchanged worried glances.

"Ten thousand pounds if you give him your son to raise as his own."

"What? No!" Wilson shook his head.

"Wait!" Lucy caught his arm. "Please, listen. He will murder this young babe. But if he had a boy to raise, one to replace the child he lost, she will be spared. Think, please. Your son could be raised in a fine house, become an earl, never go hungry or cold a day in his life. And in return, you would have this child to raise as your own and a small fortune to live on. You could start a new life in London, have anything you could desire." She peeled the blanket back from Philippa's face. "She is such a beauty. The daughter of an earl, the granddaughter of a duke."

Wilson and Beth stared down at Philippa, both silent.

"I don't want to give my baby away. He's my little Roddy," Beth murmured.

"What if his lordship let you be his wet nurse?" Lucy hoped she could convince the earl of that at least, given that the child would need a source of milk.

"I..." Beth looked Philippa again. "He would truly kill her? This sweet thing?" She held out her arms, a mother's instinct too hard to fight. Lucy passed her the baby.

"He would."

"How would we know our boy would be safe with him?" Wilson asked.

"I worked at the house for years. Monmouth would dote upon a son, but he sees no value in a daughter, only a burden. She's in grave danger."

"Oh look, Mason. She's hungry." Beth had let Philippa suckle the tip of her index finger and Philippa was clamping on desperately, her little rosebud mouth searching for milk.

"Beth..." Wilson looked torn at the situation he'd been placed in. "He's our boy."

Beth sniffled. "I know but think of what a grand life he could have. Wouldn't he Lucy?"

"Yes, a grand life indeed."

"We aren't to be bought, not even by a man like

Monmouth," Mason said quietly. "He can't simply bully us into giving up our child."

"Mason, we can't let him kill *this* child." Beth held Philippa protectively now.

Wilson sighed, his shoulders drooping. "Fine. We accept, but Beth has to nurse Roddy and we must be allowed to see the boy once a year."

That, Lucy knew, would be a hard bargain. But she would find a way, for Philippa's sake.

"Bring me the boy and I shall take him back to the house to his Lordship."

Wilson climbed the stairs and returned carrying a small squirming bundle. The man held his son for a long moment, and Beth leaned down to kiss the boy's forehead.

"We love you, Roddy. That will never change. Please forgive us for what we have done, but you will be safe and cared for." Beth stroked his cheeks, squared her shoulders, and tightened her hold on little Philippa.

"Thank you, Mr. Wilson. Beth, you saved a precious life tonight. For that you will be repaid."

Lucy exited the cottage and carried the bundled baby boy into the waiting coach. She looked back only once, seeing the face of the miller and his wife standing in the doorway with their new daughter.

Two lives torn from their rightful places in life, but perhaps it would indeed work out best for both of them. Lucy would do what she could to ensure that was the case.

❧ I ❧

"H e doesn't look a thing like me," the Duke of St. Albans grumbled.

Beauregard Boudreaux eyed the older man standing beside him at the back of the crowded ballroom.

"Who, Your Grace?" Beau asked.

"Roderick, my grandson." St. Albans pointed at a blond-haired young man who was dancing with a pretty girl. Beau glanced between the two men, searching for even a hint of resemblance. Roderick had a kind face and bright brown eyes but lacked any resemblance to the Duke. St. Albans, although he was of five and sixty years, was still a fit man with dark brown hair and the clearest gray eyes Beau had ever seen.

"Perhaps he favors the father's family?" Beau studied the young man again as he spun his pretty partner around.

"The Earl of Monmouth? No, he has a coloring similar

to mine." St. Albans crossed his arms over his chest, a strange expression deepening the wrinkles around his eyes and mouth. "My child, his wife, was not fair of color either. She favored me."

"He seems to be a good lad, Your Grace."

"Oh, yes. He is a delightful boy. He has a good head on his shoulders, but I wish..." St. Albans didn't continue his thought. Instead, he turned to leave the ballroom, a look of regret clinging to him so openly that Beau felt compelled to pursue him.

St. Albans had practically raised Beau. As a young boy, Beau had lost his father in France, and he and his mother had returned to her family's home in England, a small manor house neighboring the St. Albans estate. When he was sixteen, he'd started scaling the short cobblestone walls between the two estates and wandered into St. Albans' gardens then down by the lake, where he first met the duke.

Now, at the age of six and thirty, he felt the duke was a friend, as well as a surrogate father. Seeing the duke distressed by the past left Beau unsettled as well.

St. Albans walked down the picture gallery of his home, away from his ballroom, and paused before a row of paintings. A servant at the opposite end of the hall trailed behind Beau and St. Albans, lighting the lamps around them before discreetly retreating.

Beau put a hand on St. Alban's shoulder. "Your Grace?

Are you all right?" The older man glanced at him with a sad smile on his face.

"I'm sorry, my boy. I'm not fit company tonight. I never should have hosted this bloody ball. I thought it might distract me." The wrinkles around his eyes and mouth deepened as he stared up at the portraits around him.

"Distract you?" Beau wasn't sure he was following his friend's words.

"Yes." St. Albans twisted his family's signet ring around on his little finger as he stared up at a portrait tucked in the corner of the gallery.

"It is the anniversary, you see, of my sweet Albina's death. Her mother, God rest her, died when Albina was only six years old, and Albina became my whole world. Then I lost her too."

"Albina died twenty years ago?" Beau must have met St. Albans just a year after the duke had lost his only child.

"Perhaps that's why my heart aches when I look at Roderick. It's not so much me that I wish to see in him, but *her*." He pointed a trembling hand to the painting in the corner.

Beau's breath caught at the figure painted in the oils. The most beautiful woman he'd ever seen sat on a settee, a book resting in her lap and her chin resting in her hand as she leaned against the arm of the settee. Her pale skin seemed to glow like alabaster beneath the moonlight. Dark brows arched above a pair of mischievous startling gray eyes and a sensual mouth made for kisses and witty remarks. The watered silk of her gown had been painted with such perfection that Beau thought, perhaps half madly, that he could reach out and touch the silk, not merely a painted canvas.

"Lovely, wasn't she?" St. Albans said.

"Beyond lovely," Beau agreed. As one of London's desirable bachelors, he'd had the best mistresses a man could have, but all paled in comparison to this vision. Her exquisite face would have made Helen of Troy weep with envy.

"You would have liked her, Beau." St. Albans grinned, even though his eyes were still deeply shadowed with sorrow.

"I imagine I would have, Your Grace."

"She was clever and amusing. So full of heart. And that devil Monmouth stole her away to Gretna Green. She thought she loved him but learned too late he only wanted her for her looks and her breeding. She was not some bloody beast at Tattersall's. She was my child."

Beau sensed his old friend was battling with painful demons of the past and had no idea how to help.

"He didn't keep you from seeing your grandson, did he?"

St. Albans shook his head. "He lets me see the boy, but I thought even after all these years, I would see some small bit of her in him, but I don't. I'm getting old, Beau, and at this time in a man's life, he wants to see some part of himself live on. I fear I won't have that."

"I'm sorry, Your Grace. Why don't we go back to the ball?"

"You go on, my boy. It's time you danced with a few young ladies, is it not?"

Beau didn't want to tell him that he had no desire to dance with any of the young debutantes tonight. To see the dewy hope in their eyes and their proud mothers looking on, hoping to snare him in a Parson's mousetrap. No, he certainly didn't want that. It was nothing more than a painfully artificial and insincere charade which would wound innocent girls when they came to the rude awakening that he would never wed them. But he couldn't tell St. Alban's that. He knew full well that the duke wished for him to settle down and marry.

"If you are to retire for the night, I shall as well."

St. Albans seemed to shrug off his bad spirits somewhat and turned to Beau. "Off to see your mistress?"

"Perhaps," Beau hedged.

"What's this one's name?" St. Albans asked, slight disapproval in his tone.

"Daniela."

"Daniela? Is she an opera singer? A dancer?"

"This one is an opera singer. She was the toast of Italy last year."

St. Albans straightened his shoulders. "Very well. I will

come back down to the ball, but you will dance. You understand? Five dances."

"Two," Beau countered.

"Three, or I'll find you a bride tonight." The duke warned. Beau knew that particular threat was actually well within St. Albans's power.

"Three then, Your Grace," he conceded.

St. Albans clapped a hand on Beau's shoulder. "Come now. You know it amuses me to see all those ladies fall at your feet. You're far too handsome not to make at least a few little women swoon tonight."

With a beleaguered sigh, Beau followed St. Albans back to the ballroom, but he couldn't seem to forget the woman from the portrait. Her amused smile was as though the painter had caught her in a moment of secret delight at some joke. She looked like a woman who lived to love.

But love was a fool's game, one for young men with bouquets of flowers and young ladies who knew not what life held in store for them. Beau decided long ago he would not lose a woman to death. So, he lived in a bachelor's residence and kept a mistress content in a little suite of rooms. He would do that for as long as any man could, but he would never fall in love. He never wanted to endure the pain that so clearly haunted St. Albans, nor did he ever wish to inflict that pain on a wife if he were to die as his father had and leave her alone.

Beau spotted a friend, Ashton Lennox, and his Scottish wife, Rosalind, in the ballroom. Perhaps he could steal Rosalind for one of his required dances.

Ashton nodded to him in greeting. Beau took a step in their direction, but nearly trampled upon a plump woman who'd materialized in front of them. She wore colorful turban festooned with a tall ostrich feather and waved an even more feathered fan in front of her face. St. Albans stood at Beau's elbow, effectively cornering him so he could not get around the woman.

St. Albans cleared his throat. "Beauregard, may I present Mrs. Hamlin? Mrs. Hamlin, this is Beauregard Boudreaux. His father was a French Marquis."

"French aristocracy? Oh *bonjour,* Mr. Boudreaux." She curtsied, her head lowered, allowing the long ostrich feather on top to caress the front of Beau's bottle green waistcoat.

"*Bonsoir,* madame," he corrected gently. The woman blushed and waved over her shoulder at a timid little creature.

"Priscilla, come here and meet Mr. Boudreaux." She waved frantically for the young woman to join them.

Beau kept his patience even though he wanted nothing more than to run for his life. He had been through many such introductions and they always reminded him why he hated such affairs.

"This is Mr. Boudreaux." Mrs. Hamlin presented her daughter to Beau. She had to be barely eighteen, fresh faced, attractive, and a little shy. The pale pink muslin gown she wore was fetching and enhanced the blush in the girl's cheeks.

"A pleasure." He bowed respectably over Priscilla's trembling hand. "I trust your card is open for the next dance?"

The girl somehow managed a frightened nod.

"Good. Shall we?" He led her away to the dance floor but gave a parting look at St. Albans which promised retribution. The duke merely smiled.

Once Beau was out in the center of the dance floor, he began speaking to his nervous partner.

"Miss Hamlin, now is the time where couples engage in conversation. Would you care to converse?"

"I... Yes," she replied.

"Excellent, shall we discuss the weather? Or perhaps something more interesting?" Beau winked at the girl as they passed by one another in the dance.

Priscilla blushed, but when she came back around to him, she was smiling and engaged in the moment.

"Something interesting?" she asked. "What do you mean?"

"Well, how about this. Tell me which of these young bucks would you like to notice you? We can manage to catch their eye if you're game, my dear." He would do the girl a favor. She was sweet after all and clearly quite frightened of a seasoned rake like him.

"Which buck that I...? Oh heavens." She bit her lip and then shot a glance at the young golden haired viscount, Rodrick Selkirk, St. Albans's amiable grandson. The young man was dancing a few couples away. It was only a matter of time in the dance before he and Selkirk would switch partners briefly.

"Very well. Watch and learn, Miss Hamlin."

"Cilla, please." The girl said shyly.

"Not Prissy?" he teased.

Her brown eyes flashed. "Certainly not. I already despise my name and that nickname is no better."

"Well then, Cilla. We shall begin. Tell me what things you enjoy when not dancing with rakehells that would make your mother reach for her smelling salts?"

Cilla laughed in delight at his teasing. "Riding, certainly. I enjoy steeple chase and my gelding is one of the best jumpers in London."

"Indeed? I would most enjoy watching you put gentleman to shame in that regard. Far too many men think they know how to clear a hedge." He twirled with her and their hands intertwined as they spun next to the other partners of the dance.

"I assume you read, embroider cushions, sing, all of that as well?"

At this Cilla shook her head. "I do enjoy reading but haven't the time or patience for the others."

Her honesty delighted Beau. Most women wouldn't dare admit not being a master of those feminine talents.

"My father lets me go shooting when we have small house parties."

"Are you a crack shot?" Beau teased but the girl nodded in excitement.

"I am indeed!"

"My dear Miss Hamlin, you've certainly intrigued me. Watch this, child." He switched places with Selkirk, dancing a moment with the other young lady before he and Selkirk circled one another.

"Damned if I'm not a lucky man. Miss Hamlin is a most delightful partner." The other man shot a glance to Priscilla who looked boldly but briefly at Selkirk, then glanced away, her face still in full bloom of a blush.

"She is pretty," Selkirk mused, somewhat distracted by Miss Hamlin now.

"Not just pretty, the girl is quite unique, not some frivolous bit of muslin you see. She's an excellent rider, a steeple chase expert if you can believe it, and her father takes her hunting. A crack shot, he says. Wouldn't it be rather the thing to have a wife who could actually entertain a man and join him in his pursuits?"

Selkirk's eyes were bright. "Indeed, it would! I hadn't thought a woman might enjoy vigorous riding or hunting parties. What a novel thing." The young man was staring now at Cilla with an intensity that made Beau chuckle inside.

"A smart man would snap her up before someone else does," Beau confided before he rejoined Miss Hamlin to finish the dance.

"There. He's watching," Beau informed his partner.

"Now, smile at me as though you've just conquered my heart."

Miss Hamlin raised her chin and flashed a surprisingly bright smile at him. When the dance ended, Selkirk bowed to his partner respectfully before coming straight to Miss Hamlin.

"May I beg an introduction?" he asked.

Beau nodded. "Of course. Lord Selkirk, this is Miss Priscilla Hamlin."

"Charmed." Selkirk's open, honest face hid nothing as he looked at Priscilla eagerly. "Do you have any dances free?"

"I do, Lord Selkirk."

And just like that, Beau slipped away, smiling smugly to himself. He had only to endure two more to appease his friend, but he intended to be so clever about it that no woman would walk away tonight with any designs upon him involving marriage. No hearts would be broken if he could help it.

A liaison was another matter, however. He grinned at a couple of lusty young widows watching him from the edge of the dance floor. Perhaps tonight held more promise than he thought.

THOMAS WINTHROP, SEVENTH DUKE OF ST. ALBANS, watched his young protégé, Beauregard Boudreaux drift effortlessly across the dance floor. The lad's whiskey colored eyes and dark hair along with his handsome features had made him the highlight of many a young lady's night, yet it was clear none were winning his heart.

"My dear boy..." St. Albans breathed out as an aside. "Marriage is what you need, marriage to a good woman." But that was easier said than done. He knew only too well that Beau intended to never marry. The lad had grown quite terrified of the idea. That was not altogether unsurprising given how he'd lost his father and his mother had to abandon their home and life in France to come to England. The poor woman had never remarried, and the boy had grown up with few friends. Yet, somehow, the boy had found himself at Thomas's door.

Thomas had been bound up in his own grief at the time, having so recently lost his only daughter. He'd wanted the boy to leave him alone, but Beau wouldn't. He kept hopping over the wall between their two estates, finding Thomas and pestering him with questions, or sometimes simply sitting beside him near the lake. Despite Thomas's desire to be left alone, an unlikely friendship had formed, and Beau had become like a son to Thomas. Now all Thomas wished for was to see the boy happily married, settled down and creating a house full of surrogate grandchildren who could come and visit Thomas every day.

Mrs. Hamlin sidled up beside Thomas. "I've been

speaking to some of your guests, Your Grace. Is it true what they say about Mr. Boudreaux?"

"Is what true, Madame?"

"That he's a master seducer. A rake of the worst kind who has bedded half of the most talented singers in Europe?"

Thomas thought about his answer a long moment and then smiled. "Yes, it's quite true."

Mrs. Hamlin gasped in terror. "Good heavens! And he's dancing with my child!"

"Be at ease, Mrs. Hamlin. Look, I believe he has, in fact, rendered aid to your darling child."

"Aid?" Mrs. Hamlin's feather on her turban quivered as she studied the ballroom with a critical eye.

"Is that your grandson speaking to my Prissy?"

"Quite so... Quite so."

Clever boy, Thomas thought. Somehow during the dance, Beau had transferred young Roddy's attention from his own partner to that of Miss Hamlin. Consequently, it gave Beau the chance to escape the moment the dance ended. Beau gave Thomas a self-satisfied look, but Thomas held up a pair of fingers and mouthed, "Two more."

Beau rolled his eyes and captured the hand of the nearest wallflower. Of course. Wallflowers and rakes never mixed well. She would be terrified of someone like Beau: a tall, confident man in his prime, not some silly young boy still learning how to dance.

When the two remaining dances were done, Beau caught Thomas's eye across the room and gave a little bow.

"Cheeky devil." Thomas muttered, but couldn't resist chuckling. "I'll find a way to see you good and settled this year, mark my words. It's well past time you took a wife."

The question was, how would he find the lucky woman that would be Beau Boudreaux's perfect match?

❧ 2 ❧

Philippa Wilson smoothed out the fresh linens of the large four poster bed and sighed. There was nothing more dreadful than tedious work. And given that Philippa, at only twenty years old, was trapped in the dull, monotonous position of an upstairs maid, life at that moment seemed quite unbearable.

"Hurry up, Pippa," Ruth, her friend and fellow maid, whispered as she ran a duster over the fireplace mantle.

Philippa stared at a stack of books on the bedside table. If she could just get a peek at them...surely her master and lady wouldn't mind.

"Just want one look, Ruth. Hold on a moment." She reached for the nearest tome, but Ruth rushed over and blocked her way, holding out her arms to prevent Philippa from touching the table.

"You mustn't. We aren't to put on airs."

"Airs? It's a book. I'm not dressing in their clothes or using their silverware!" Philippa argued.

"That's not how they'd see it." Ruth's exasperated groan embarrassed Philippa. All of her life she'd yearned for something *more*. More knowledge, more experiences, more passion for life. The life of a servant was suffocating. Yet it was the position she'd been born and raised into. Her parents owned a small textile shop on Bond Street; it had its good and bad years, but never quite good enough. So, at eighteen, she'd taken a position as a maid at Lord Lennox's house. The handsome baron and his wife were a wonderful family to work for. But still, after just two years, Philippa felt strangled by living a life in service.

"Come on, Pippa. We have other rooms to finish before dinner."

Philippa's shoulders dropped as she followed Ruth out of the bedchamber. This was not at all how she wanted to spend her day. Ruth walked briskly down the hall, carrying a bundle of used linens. Philippa lingered in the upstairs corridor as she often did, pretending for a brief moment she was a fine lady, waiting for adventure to knock upon her door. She closed her eyes, smiling as she imagined a dashing stranger coming to the door to whisk her away.

The sound of a knocker rapping on the door jerked her out of her daydream and made her duck halfway out of sight.

The butler, Mr. Beaton, answered the door. "May I help you, sir?"

"Lord Monmouth to see Lord Lennox," the man said. "I have an appointment." There was something about his gravelly voice that sent a shiver of revulsion through her. Her heart began to race with a primal fear she couldn't explain.

"Please, step inside, my lord. I will speak to his lordship."

"Thank you." The man who introduced himself as Lord Monmouth entered and the door was shut behind him. He was tall, perhaps in his early fifties, and might have been attractive once, but his face was so harsh that his good looks had withered over time. For some odd reason, Philippa couldn't stop staring at him. She'd never seen him before, of that she was certain, yet something about him drew her out from the corner of the upstairs wall and into the open corridor at the top of the staircase. The man removed his hat and looked around, his grim expression darkening his countenance further. He wore a superfine black coat and a silver waistcoat of expensive silk.

Lord Monmouth. She knew the title. He was an Earl. She wasn't surprised to see him here. Lord Lennox gave the best business advice in London, and even dukes came to the baron for help. No doubt this man had come for the same reason.

Philippa crept closer, pausing at the top of the stairs and rested one hand on the bannister. As if suddenly aware he was being watched, the man's gaze turned up the stairs and fixed on her. Her breath caught as his eyes widened to the size of Lady Lennox's fine blue and white patterned China saucers.

The man gasped, his face pale. "No, you can't be... Not here. It's not possible."

Suddenly he was rushing up the stairs. Philippa froze, her feet rooted in place as he bore down on her. Fear spiked inside her, making breathing impossible.

Lord Monmouth grasped her by the neck. Philippa tried to scream, but the sound was strangled into a gasp. He shoved her against the nearest wall, his large hand squeezing painfully.

"You can't be here!" He hissed, his eyes wild and lips curled in a vicious snarl.

Philippa clawed at his wrist, digging her nails into him as she sucked at air like a fish out of water. But it was no use... Shadows gathered at the edge of her vision, like grim reapers waiting to claim her soul in some terrible nightmare. A long few seconds passed before her hands were too heavy to lift. They dropped to her sides as everything faded into nothing.

A distant shout, heard as though from beneath a deep lake, reached her ears before she was dropped to the ground.

When her vision returned, she saw Lord Lennox dragging a raging Monmouth to his feet. They were arguing, but she couldn't make out the words over a persistent and painful ringing in her ears. Then Monmouth shoved

Lennox hard and fled down the stairs out of sight. Philippa closed her eyes again, and only opened them when she heard someone calling her name. Lord Lennox rushed back to her.

He shouted for his wife and the butler before he knelt in front of her. "Pippa, are you all right?" He brushed her hair aside and when she still couldn't move or speak, he picked her up and carried her to the drawing room at the other end of the corridor, setting her down on the settee.

Lord Lennox's bright blue eyes searched her face. "Pippa, what happened? Why was Lord Monmouth hurting you?"

Lord Lennox's wife, Rosalind, appeared in the doorway with Mr. Beaton right behind her. "Ash? What happened?" The dark-haired lady of the house rushed to Ashton's side and gasped when she saw Philippa's condition.

"Dear Lord! Pippa, are you all right?"

Philippa wanted to die of shame. She'd caused an uproar in her master's house and would surely be cast out without a reference. She rubbed at her throat.

"Give her a minute, Rosalind. Lord Monmouth nearly killed the poor girl." Ashton gently raised her chin with his fingers and examined her neck. His lips pursed and he addressed Mr. Beaton. "Beaton, fetch the doctor. Her injuries could be serious."

She rubbed her throat. Tears burned her eyes as she tried to speak. "I swear, my lord... I did nothing... Lord Monmouth... said I can't be here." Did he think she shouldn't have been standing so visibly when most servants were trained to remain out of sight? But no one flew into a violent rage over that. Yet what else could he have meant?

Rosalind knelt beside her husband and patted Philippa's knee. "It's all right."

"My lady, I'm terribly sorry..." Philippa blinked away tears as they dropped down onto her cheeks.

"Do not apologize," Ashton said in a gentle but firm tone. "I don't allow guests to come into my home and attack my staff. Lord Monmouth is solely to blame for this."

"What did he say to you?" Rosalind asked. "What were his exact words?"

Philippa briefly closed her eyes to replay the awful moment.

"He said... No... You can't be here. Not possible...I fear it's all a bit muddled now."

Rosalind tilted her head. "Such an odd thing to say. You don't know Lord Monmouth, do you?"

Philippa shook her head, but winced as fresh pain jolted the tender muscles of her neck and throat.

"Just rest for now," Lord Lennox said. "The doctor will be here soon." He stepped outside while Rosalind helped Philippa remove the white cap from her hair and unbutton the top buttons on her gown to help the doctor have access to her neck.

"Please don't send me away, my lady," Philippa croaked.

Rosalind raised a brow, and with her next words, her Scottish accent was thick with worry. "Hush now. Don't speak such nonsense. You are a valued member of this household and I don't care what reason or excuse Lord Monmouth gives, he cannot lay a hand on anyone like that. It is his fault, not yours."

Philippa wanted to hug Rosalind, but there were invisible lines between a maid and her mistress.

"Does it hurt much?" Rosalind asked.

"Yes," Philippa whispered. "I believe he wanted to kill me, but I have no idea why."

"Ash will find out. He won't let Monmouth get away without answering for this, his title be damned."

Lord Lennox cleared his throat in the doorway. "Dr. Montgomery is here, Pippa."

A young doctor who couldn't have been more than thirty entered the room. The man smiled warmly at Philippa and his handsome face brightened as he took her in. Philippa blushed in mortification. She knew the effect she often had on men. It had been one of the hardest things about finding employment in a decent house. Many ladies in London would not hire a girl who was too pretty, let alone one with "beauty unparalleled" as one matron had said to her. She remembered how the woman had reached for the small brass bell on the table beside her and rang it.

"It's nothing personal my dear, but I can't have my

nephew see you. He's all set to marry an earl's daughter. One look at you could destroy my carefully laid plans."

That hadn't been the first or last house that had turned her down for employment. For similar reasons, she didn't dare apply for positions at bachelors' residences, where there would be no protection from the advances of an employer. She'd been fortunate to find a home like Lennox House where her master was so clearly in love with his wife that he had no interest in other ladies.

"Would you like me to stay with you, Pippa?" Rosalind asked as the doctor sat on the settee beside her.

"Yes, please." She was grateful for Rosalind's presence. Not that she didn't trust the doctor, she simply felt more secure not being alone. The doctor examined her throat. His hands were warm as he pressed various places on her neck and asked where it hurt. She nodded each time a spark of pain flared up.

"Well, it seems you have some damage to your throat. It will be sore for a while, I imagine." He looked at her face. "Your eyes will be red for a few days; strangulation has that unfortunate effect. You may have trouble swallowing or speaking for long periods of time. Drink lots of warm broth and hot tea. Nothing bitter. Sweeten your tea with honey."

"Thank you, doctor." She reached up to button her gown.

The doctor gave a gentle smile. "If you have need of my services, Miss Wilson, you have but to send for me."

His earnest look created a twinge of guilt inside her. He was neither the first nor the last man to make such an offer, but unlike with many men, she sensed that he meant it kindly and was genuinely interested in her.

I could marry a man like him if I wanted. But she wanted more in life than to be a man's wife. Not a rich husband or a fine house, no. She wanted passion and adventure—two things women in any social class could never have. Why couldn't women have more in life to look forward to?

"Thank you, doctor. Mr. Beaton will see you out." Rosalind saw him to the door and returned to Philippa, concern still filling in her eyes. "Why don't we get you some tea and send you to bed early?"

"I'm so sorry, my lady. I'm still able to work, I promise you," she rasped as she rose from the settee and followed her mistress into the hall.

"You need not worry about that for now." Rosalind patted her arm gently.

Ruth was waiting for her outside the drawing room. She curtsied to her mistress.

"Ah, Ruth," said Rosalind. "Have some tea with honey taken up to your and Pippa's room. She's to drink the tea and go to bed early. Any work either of you have left undone this evening can be finished tomorrow."

"Yes, Mistress." Ruth slipped her arm through Pippa's and they headed for the servants' quarters one floor above.

The room Philippa and Ruth shared was small and cozy, with two slender beds on opposing walls. Bright red wool blankets covered their feather tick mattresses. Ruth had a knack for knitting and embroidery which left the room feeling warmer and more welcoming than an average servant's chamber.

Philippa's side of the room had articles from the Morning Post tacked to the walls detailing various adventures from America or Europe. Lord Lennox always allowed the staff to read the paper each night after he was done with it, and Mr. Beaton had given Philippa permission to cut out the articles she liked out and take them to her chamber. They made for a canvas of excitement she liked to re-read each night.

"I cannot believe that man attacked you. I'm so sorry I wasn't there to help! You're truly all right?"

Philippa unbuttoned her dress and changed her nightgown with her friends help. "I simply don't understand why he did it. I was only standing there."

"Gentlemen are queer creatures and dangerous at times. At least his lordship was there to save you."

"Indeed." Philippa didn't want to think about what would have happened if Lord Lennox hadn't come into the hall. She might be dead, strangled by a man she'd never met before for no apparent reason.

"Rest now. I'll bring tea up in a bit," Ruth said, her face still strained with worry.

"Thank you." Philippa felt quite useless in that moment, a burden upon those around her. She climbed into her bed and pulled her wool blankets over her body.

When Ruth left, she dug out a small pouch out from under her mattress. It held a slender necklace with a sapphire pendant. It had been a gift from her mother when she turned sixteen. She had no idea how her parents had been able to afford it. She brushed the pad of her thumb over the sapphire before returning it to the velvet pouch and slipping it back under her mattress.

Tears soaked her pillow as she buried herself in her blankets and tried to shut out the world around her, even if only for just a few hours.

CORNELIUS SELKIRK, THE EARL OF MONMOUTH, HID IN the mews two townhouses away from Lennox's home. His heart was still racing and blood was still roaring in his ears. Tonight had turned into a disaster. All he'd wanted was to meet with Lennox about some investments. Instead, he'd walked in and seen his doom looking down at him from the top of the stairs.

That doom came in the form of a twenty-year-old girl in a black servant's gown. Though her hair had been covered, there had been no mistaking her. She was Albina reborn. He knew the girl was somewhere in England because he'd allowed the child to live, after all, but he'd paid for the miller and his wife's silence and their move away from his country estate. He'd imagined them in some backwater town continuing their trade, not in

London. So, what was the chit doing in London where anyone could see her and realize she looked exactly like Albina? The mere sight of her had almost killed him where he stood. He thought for a moment he was seeing a ghost.

If someone who remembered his late wife saw the girl there would be no question that she was a Selkirk. His boy Roddy would then be challenged as his heir and Cornelius couldn't afford that. If he hadn't acted so foolishly tonight it was possible she might have gone unnoticed, but now he'd drawn attention to her and it put all he'd worked toward at risk.

He would not let some distant cousin inherit his estate, not after all he'd sacrificed to build it. Remarriage had been out of the question. The doctor had said his blood flow was not strong enough to become aroused and he would likely never have intercourse again. That mattered little to him. His desire for bedding women had died years ago. Yet he hadn't been concerned. He had Roddy. But seeing the girl tonight...all of his old fears came rushing back. He'd acted mad and realized how reckless it'd been to try to kill the girl inside Lennox's house. Lennox wouldn't let this matter be buried and that meant he would do everything possible to discover what made the girl so special.

Now she would have to die. There was no way around it. She was a liability he couldn't afford. There was too much at risk.

Cornelius relaxed when he realized no one was pursuing him. He emerged from the mew and walked to the nearest corner on Half-Moon Street to hail a passing hackney.

"Where to?" the driver asked.

"The Clubhouse on Bennett Street." He settled back inside the coach. The question was how to remove the girl without raising suspicions further. There was one man who could be counted upon to help him, and on a night like this, the Clubhouse was where he would usually find him.

When the coach stopped on Bennett Street, Cornelius paid the driver and walked up to the conspicuous red door that marked the entrance to the gambling hell. He entered the townhouse where raucous laughter and shouts of excitement echoed throughout. Footmen bustled about the corridor and up the stairs, carrying drinks, messages and money between clients. Cornelius caught the arm of a passing servant.

"Is Lord Sommers here tonight?"

"Yes, sir. He's playing the hazard tables upstairs. First door on the right." The footmen rushed off and Cornelius headed upstairs.

Alistair Sommers sat at a hazard table with a buxom woman behind him whispering things in his ear that made the young buck smile. Alistair was only twenty-nine, but the viscount had a reputation that made more seasoned rakes shrink away from him.

Men like Sommers never went to balls. If they did, they never thought twice about compromising any woman they walked past. But Alistair was far more of a threat than simply ruining the reputations of young women at balls. He belonged to a hellfire club called the Devil's Own where men there did not simply play at sinful acts, they committed them. Men died under mysterious circumstances thanks to them, but the Bow Street runners were baffled as to how to tie any of the crimes to the club's members.

"Lord Sommers," Cornelius said. He sat down at a vacant seat after an inebriated young man lost a large sum of money at the table and left.

"Ahh, Monmouth. I'm surprised to see you here," Alistair didn't even bother looking at Cornelius. He was focused on the game.

"I have something that might interest you. For the right price, I hope."

"You know I don't pay for pleasure." Alistair sounded bored.

Cornelius tried not to let his temper be riled. "You misunderstand, Lord Sommers. It is *I* who would pay you. I require a little matter to be dealt with."

Alistair glanced away from the game, curious now. "Oh? Nothing trivial, I assume."

"I think you will be most interested, but I cannot speak of it here."

"Very well. This game has lost its fire for me." He

collected his winnings and brushed the woman away as he stood.

"There's a private room at the end of the corridor," Alistair said. Cornelius followed him to a bedchamber.

"Now then, what's the matter?" Alistair asked.

Cornelius smiled. "A woman. I need her removed. You may do whatever you like with her, but she needs to be disposed of afterwards."

Alistair crossed his arms over his chest. "What woman, and why?"

"She is a threat to my estate, someone who would ruin my son's inheritance. That's all I shall say on the matter."

"Hardly seems like a challenge. What about this woman would tempt me?"

"She's not any woman. She has the face and body of Helen of Troy with lustrous black hair. You know of my deceased wife's beauty"

Alistair was far more interested now. "Men still speak of her in reverent whispers even though she's been dead for twenty years."

"This woman is her exact image." Cornelius felt strangely smug about the girl's beauty even though he was, at that moment, plotting her murder.

Alistair's eyebrow raised. "Any relation?"

"Are you interested?"

"If she's as beautiful as you say, then yes. But why do you wish her dead? Why not have her taken and hidden away somewhere instead? A beautiful woman is a prized asset to most men."

"Unfortunately, her very beauty is what condemns her. Even to hide her away might not be enough."

Alistair's brown eyes glinted with malicious understanding. "Then I am even more interested. Where is she?"

"She's working at Lord Lennox's home as upstairs maid."

"A maid? And yet she is a threat?"

"I will not explain further. It is simply something that must be done."

"Lennox's household is tightly knit and loyal. It will be impossible to bribe my way inside to grab the girl." Alistair stroked his chin and began to pace. "But maids do run errands. Assuming it does not have to be tonight, I will wait for her to leave the house and take her then."

"Excellent." Cornelius relaxed. "Once you have her, send word to me and I will send you one thousand pounds. Half when she is in your possession, the rest when she is dead."

"That's not much for murder," Alistair mused.

"After you see her, you will wish to pay *me* for the time you have with her."

Alistair chuckled. "No woman is that lovely. But we have an accord."

"Good." Cornelius exited the room and left the gambling hell. The fewer people who saw him there, the better. In fact, he intended to go straight home and take Roddy with him to the country to keep suspicion off them both in case Lord Sommers was caught with the girl's body.

There was a brief moment where he felt a stab of guilt at sentencing his own daughter to death, but when everything was factored in and accounted for, she, like her mother, only stood in the way of what truly mattered.

❧ 3 ❧

Philippa felt like a prisoner for the next two days. Her voice had recovered, but the bruises around her throat were still visible. The ugly purple marks formed two dark rings around her neck. Lady Lennox had not wanted her to resume her duties until she felt capable, but after three days of laying quiet in her bed, Philippa needed to be doing something. So, despite Ruth's protests, she'd dressed in her black uniform, bound her hair with her maid's cap, and assisted her friend in cleaning the upstairs rooms.

By early evening she felt more like her old self and was sitting in the kitchens with one of the footmen, Roger, as he polished pair of Lord Lennox's Hessian boots. Their lordship's valet had the night off.

"His lordship finally felt it was safe to leave the house,"

Roger said as he dipped a cloth into the pot of black shoe polish.

"What?" Philippa's hands paused in the midst of folding a linen napkin. "He was afraid of leaving?"

"Afraid of leaving you. Lennox is worried that Lord Monmouth might return. The man has vanished, it seems. Presumably out of guilt, but one wonders. He and Lady Lennox didn't leave the house for the last two days. Lennox wanted to be here should Monmouth return for you."

"That hardly seems likely, does it?" Attacking her unprovoked was one thing, but to continue to pursue her afterwards?

Roger was quiet a moment. "You weren't here, but five years ago the household underwent a similar danger." His brow furrowed.

She knew of what Roger spoke but had never dared before to ask for any details. "What happened?"

"A man named Hugo Waverley waged a private war against his lordship and his friends. One that almost cost them all their lives. Those were dark and dangerous days. There was even an assassin in our midst. A killer was working in this very house alongside us."

"Good lord!" Philippa gasped.

Roger pursed his lips and buffed hard on a large scratch on one of the tall black boots, but his face held a distracted look. "The man had been hired by Waverly to kill Lord Lennox."

"But clearly he didn't."

"No, he didn't. Despite Sir Hugo's well laid plans, his lordship and his friends prevailed. When Sir Hugo died, the threat was gone. We've had a good peace these last few years, but Lord Lennox has that same worried look about him now. He doesn't like not knowing where a threat might be coming from or when it might strike next."

Guilt gnawed at Philippa. If she only knew why Lord Monmouth had tried to kill her, then perhaps Lord Lennox could sort out the matter peacefully. But Monmouth had vanished and the rumor about town was that he and his son had left for their estate a full two days ride from London.

"I wish... I just wish I knew what I did to upset Lord Monmouth." She reached for another napkin, folding it slowly and setting it aside.

Roger suddenly smiled at her. "Perhaps he got one look at you, fell in love, and knowing he could not have you drove him mad. He wouldn't be the first."

"Don't be silly. Men don't act like that around me. *You* don't," she said.

"That's because ladies do not turn my head, or my heart," he answered, though he did not elaborate. It was a dangerous thing to admit to, but Philippa did not pass judgment on such things. Asking a person to control their heart was as pointless as trying to control the weather.

"I don't want to be beautiful enough to drive men mad.

Besides, the madness in Monmouth's eyes was not that of lust, I assure you." She sat back down in her chair, a dark cloud settling upon her shoulders. She didn't want to be beautiful. It only made men want her and other women despise her.

"You are and you cannot change it, so you shouldn't let it worry you."

"Easier said than done, Roger."

Mr. Beaton entered the kitchen and spotted Roger. "Ahh, there you are. I have an errand for you."

"Yes, Mr. Beaton?" Roger set the boots on the table and stood up. Philippa rose as well.

"His lordship is at Fives Court for a boxing match this evening. He wishes to have a message sent to Lord Sheridan at Berkeley's. You may take the coach."

"May I go as well, Mr. Beaton?" Philippa asked. "I would stay in the coach, of course." She would not be allowed in the gentlemen's club for any reason, but that wasn't the point. Getting out of the townhouse, even for a brief period of time, would make her feel normal again.

The solemn butler considered her request with hesitance. "His lordship was worried about you being alone."

"But I would be with Roger and Mr. Lauder." Lennox's coach driver was a stout man in his forties who could certainly hold his own in a fight. Roger had told her over a glass of sherry last Christmas that Lauder used to fight in the underground boxing rings. That was where Lord Lennox found him and offered him employment.

"I'd keep an eye on her, Mr. Beaton," Roger promised. He tugged on his blue and black striped waistcoat, proud like all servants here were to wear the uniform of the house of Lennox.

"Very well but have a care. His lordship is still concerned about Lord Monmouth."

"Of course, Mr. Beaton." Roger gestured toward the way out. "Shall we?"

Philippa was almost bouncing with excitement as they headed upstairs to wait for Mr. Lauder to pull the coach around. She and Roger climbed into the tan and black coach and settled in for the ride to Berkeley's.

"You are my favorite footman," she told Roger gleefully. She peered out of the window as the coach traveled and watched the dust settle over the London streets.

The evening was shaded in hues of deep gold and purple, coloring the structures of the fine townhouses. Philippa loved London at night; it was a beautiful city where the streetlamps glowed and candles in the windows illuminated the lives of the people indoors like shadow puppets.

When she was a child, her father used to hang a curtain near her bed and her mother would hold a candle behind it. He used paper cut outs on sticks and acted out amusing stories for her. She loved listening to her mother sing after each performance. She'd had no other siblings and her parents had made her their whole world.

Philippa bit her lip, a sudden homesickness overcoming her. She had not seen them very much since coming to work here. She was well overdue for a visit.

Roger nudged her with one of his feet. "You all right, Pippa?"

She forced a little smile that she didn't quite feel. "Yes, I suppose I'm just missing my parents. It's been months since I've seen them."

"That's the hardest part of being in service. I became a footman at fourteen and I admit, only to you, that I might have shed a tear or two in those first few months of being away from home."

"I've been here almost two years. I shouldn't still feel like this, should I?" she asked.

Roger's brown eyes softened. "You're never too old to miss your family, especially if you come from a loving home." Philippa looked at his attractive features that were so pleasing to many who visited the Lennox house. Yet he would always be alone. More than ever, she was grateful to have Roger as a friend.

She reached over and patted his knee, earning a soft smile from the footman. "That's true. I hadn't thought of it like that." She peered through the coach curtains again as they stopped in Berkeley Square.

"Stay here. I'll just be a moment." Roger removed the sealed letter from his pocket and headed into the gentleman's club.

Philippa watched the entrance for minute then looked

out the other coach window to watch the people in the square.

A white face, framed frighteningly in the window suddenly appeared before her. She gasped and fell back just as she heard Mr. Lauder yell.

"Oi! Get away from there, you scoundrel!"

The face vanished and the coach door was flung wide open. A man lunged inside and sought her with his hands. She kicked out, screaming as he wrapped his fingers around her ankle. She managed a good heel to the brute's face that sent him sprawling onto the ground.

"Mr. Lauder! Help!" she shouted as she opened the door behind her. The man she'd kicked lumbered back into the coach. She managed to escape out the opposite side, but she found no freedom there. Instead, she fell right into the arms of a second man with a smile as cruel as his face was handsome.

A scream left her mouth as the man's hand roughly covered her lips. Philippa raged and fought, biting the man's gloved hand in the process. When he dropped her, she tried to run, but a viselike grip on her arm spun her back to face him. The last thing she saw was the man's fist headed straight for her face.

BEAU SAT IN A COMFORTABLE OLD ARMCHAIR BY THE FIRE with a glass of brandy in one hand. He studied the amber liquid and puzzled over the night's events. He'd visited Daniela a few hours before and handed her a handsome set of diamonds as well as the deed to a quaint little townhouse he'd bought for her. She would have a lovely home for the rest of her life. Then he'd told her it was time to go their separate ways. She'd been saddened by the news, as had he. With one last chaste kiss goodbye, he'd left. Daniela had been more than a mistress; she'd been a friend. She'd looked upon his face when they'd parted with a bittersweet smile.

"You've changed, my love. You need more than I can give, yes?"

He hadn't wanted to agree with her, but something had changed within him. Ever since he'd spoken to St. Albans at the ball, he'd felt as though he'd be trapped forever if he didn't move forward. But move forward to what? He didn't know.

He only knew that something called to him, demanding that he end this way of life, not that he could say why. Still, he'd never ignored his instincts before.

Now he was at his club alone, drinking and lost in worrying thoughts. He couldn't get the painting of St. Albans's daughter out of his mind. Every time he closed his eyes, he saw the woman's flashing gray gaze, the dark lustrous waves of her hair and her devious smile that promised a man endless pleasures of the body and also the mind. But that woman was dead and gone. It was no wonder St. Albans was still haunted by grief two decades later. His daughter must have been peerless.

"Now there's the look of someone quite Friday-faced."
A voice pulled Beau from his thoughts. He glanced at the
man who'd settled into the chair beside him.

"Evening, Sheridan," he said in greeting and turned
back to the fire. Cedric Sheridan was only a year older
than Beau; they'd gone to Cambridge together. The
viscount was also one of Ashton Lennox's close friends.
He was a cheery sort of man who loved horse races and
any outdoor sport a man could indulge in. It was difficult
not to be in a good mood when Sheridan was around.

"Ash said you planned to buy a shipping company
based out of New Orleans in the Americas?"

The talk of business was a welcome distraction. "Yes,
Lennox has quite a knack for buying and running such
things and I meant to join him in the endeavor. He's
offered a fifty percent partnership for three years and the
chance to buy him out at eighty percent of the market
value of the shares' cost. Rather a good deal, I would say."

"Indeed," Sheridan grinned. "He's wishing to be more
at home now that the children have come along. Crossing
the Atlantic isn't as easy once family becomes involved.
Lord knows Anne would kill me if I left her with the twins
for that long. Those little devils run the household." Sheridan's delighted smile told Beau those the *little devils* were
well loved.

Beau nodded, though he didn't agree. Having no wife or
children of his own made it difficult to imagine being bound

by relationships. In fact, the prospect of traveling to America seemed rather exciting to him. He longed for an adventure like that. Perhaps this was the change he'd been searching for.

"Ash takes too much on his shoulders as it is," Sheridan said as he played with a silver-knobbed cane. "The poor bloke hasn't left his house in three days."

"Because of his wife and children?" Beau shuddered at the thought that a man's daily activities could be so restricted by the domestic sphere.

"Lord, no. He's worried about his upstairs maid, you see."

"His maid? Sheridan, I'm not following you."

Sheridan chuckled but the laugh faded in the nearly empty drawing room.

"I'm being rather indirect, aren't I? I suppose the matter had been on my mind so long, I assumed everyone had heard. Someone attacked one of his upstairs maids. Nearly killed her."

"What?" Beau sat up, abandoning the remnants of his brandy when he set the glass on the table between them. "Who?"

"Lord Monmouth. Do you know him?" Sheridan leaned, speaking in a hushed tone.

"By reputation, but we've never been introduced. Though I am good friends with Lord Monmouth's father-in-law, the Duke of St. Albans."

"Nice fellow, St. Albans. Too bad Monmouth is anything but."

He shifted forward in his chair. "What did Monmouth do?"

Sheridan glanced around the room, then whispered, "He showed up for an appointment to talk business. Ash was in the evening room when he heard the sound of screams. He ran into the corridor and found Monmouth with both hands around a young woman's neck, trying to strangle her. Ash got in a good a punch and Monmouth let the maid go, but while Ash tended to her, Monmouth escaped. The poor girl was barely breathing."

"Good God," Beau muttered.

"Ash feels like it's his fault, only he can't figure out why Monmouth wanted to hurt the girl. The girl has no idea, either. So, until he solves the mystery he's been at home, a proverbial pistol at the ready in case Lord Monmouth returns."

"That doesn't seem likely, does it?"

Sheridan shrugged. "It depends what Monmouth's motives were. We've learned to assume the worst in such situations."

The door to the room opened and a man in Lennox's livery stood in the doorway, a letter in his gloved hands.

"Pardon for the interruption. I have a letter for Lord Sheridan from Lord Lennox."

Sheridan's brows rose. "Speak of the devil." He stood as the footman handed him the letter. Sheridan cracked open the seal but was interrupted when a commotion came downstairs in the club entryway.

"Help! A man's been hurt!" Someone shouted.

Sheridan shoved the letter into his waistcoat and rushed out of the room. Beau followed behind, and the two of them peered over the edge of the stair railing.

"What happened?" Beau demanded.

"The Lennox coach. A gang of ruffians set upon it. The driver was hurt."

"What?" Lennox's footman paled and bolted down the stairs, almost reckless in his desperation to reach the coach outside.

"Come on," Beau told Sheridan as they both rushed down after him. A small crowd had gathered outside the club, most of the gentlemen still holding cigars as they looked on in confusion.

"I say, what the devil's happened?" Freddy Poncenby demanded. The dandified gentleman looked ready to parade about in military fashion, which was ridiculous given his pink and white striped trousers and blush colored waistcoat.

"That's what we're trying to find out, Poncenby," said Sheridan.

The footman was on his knees on the sidewalk by the driver. "Mr. Lauder!" The middle-aged man was clutching his forehead. Blood trickled between his fingertips.

"They took her, Roger. Took her before I could stop 'em. One of the bastards hit me with a kosh. I couldn't even get a blow in."

"It's all right, Lauder." Roger replied, but the ashen look on the man's face worried Beau that something very grave and terrible had happened.

"Who did they take?" Beau stepped close, Sheridan shadowing him with a dark frown over his usual amiable face.

"Miss Wilson." The footman said. "Lord, we never should have let her leave the house." The young man's face was stricken with rage as he looked at the darkened streets. There was no sign of another coach or the young woman.

"Who is Miss Wilson?" Sheridan asked the footman.

"A maid in Lord Lennox's house."

"Wait, not *the* maid?" asked Beau. "The one Lord Monmouth attacked?"

Roger nodded. "It's my fault. I never should have let her leave the house." The young man tugged at his hair.

"Easy, lad." Beau clapped a hand on Roger's shoulder and looked to the driver. "Was Monmouth among the attackers?"

"T'weren't no Lord Monmouth." The driver muttered as he lifted his bloody face to Beau, Sheridan and Roger.

Are you sure, Mr. Lauder?" Roger asked.

"Quite sure. T'was a tall pale-faced man with a long scar on his brow and another one... Too pretty. I recognized that one. It was Lord Sommers."

"Sommers. You're sure?" Beau tensed at the mention of the dangerous young rogue's name, a name that scared half of London and enraged the other half. Whether it was a drunken duel or a forced seduction, he did as he pleased without care to the consequences. And it didn't help that he had the money and resources to avoid such outcomes with alarming regularity.

"It was him," Lauder confirmed. "I've seen that bloke before in the boxing rings."

"Christ." Beau growled. "What does he want her for?"

"Nothing good, that much is certain." Sheridan looked at Roger pensively. "Why was she even here?"

"Mr. Beaton decided she could come with me in the coach," the footman said. "She'd been feeling a bit down after being confined to the house the last three days, and Monmouth is said to be out of town."

Sheridan looked now to Beau. His expression was grim. "Convenient, isn't it? Sommers must have been watching the house. I need to go to Ash at once."

"But the girl," Beau said. "Someone has to go after her."

"We don't know where he could have taken her. We'll need to compile a list of Sommers's known haunts and spread out to search."

"There isn't time for that," Beau said. "I have a guess where he might go."

"Where?"

"An old property on the outskirts of London. The old Castleton Abbey. His family owns it." Beau had been there once, years ago, foolishly thinking it might be amusing to join the Devil's Own hellfire club. It hadn't at all been what he'd expected.

"You're sure he's there?"

"If I'm wrong, you and Lennox search his townhouse here in London. Bring the Bow Street runners." Normally a man couldn't simply search another man's house for evidence, especially if he was a peer, but with the help of Bow Street, Sheridan and Lennox might have luck getting inside.

Sheridan grabbed Beau's arm as he called for his coach. He handed him his cane. "You'll need a weapon. Twist it counterclockwise and pull."

Beau twisted the silver knob and pulled, revealing a silver blade.

"Thank you, Sheridan." Beau nodded at him and waited for his groom to bring his horse around.

He tried not to think about the head start that Lord Sommers had, or what he might do to the girl before Beau could reach them.

Beau gripped the cane tightly, wondering what Sommers wanted with Lennox's maid. The two men weren't enemies, nor were they friends. So what was the connection? Maybe it had nothing to do with Lennox. What if it was on behalf of Lord Monmouth, while he was out of town? Or perhaps he intended to ransom her, either to Monmouth or back to Lennox? No, that seemed unlikely. But if he had taken the woman to the Abbey as he feared, he might intend to use her for a Devil's Own ceremony.

Lord help the girl if that was the case. London had seen many hellfire clubs come and go over the centuries. Most only feigned at devil worship and were really excuses for drunken revelries with willing women there to entertain the members. But the Devil's Own was different.

The one and only time Beau had attended, Sommers had taken some poor girl and bound her on top of the old stone altar in the Abbey. His intent had been to take her in front of all the other men, but Beau had boasted that only a real man could take a woman when he was flat drunk. Sommers' ego had risen to the challenge. He and the other men got completely inebriated and during their drunken distractions, Beau had cut the girl loose from her bonds and taken her home.

But the most disturbing part had been just how sharp the ceremonial knife he'd freed her with had been. He'd never gone back, and for the longest time, Beau wondered if rape had been where Sommers had intended to stop that night or if he'd had far more sinister plans for the poor girl.

❧ 4 ❧

Philippa woke in a daze with a throbbing pain in her head. She marveled at the contrast of her pain with the comforting feel of something downy beneath her. She opened her eyes and realized she was lying in a bed. Her eyes slowly adjusted to the dim room. A fireplace on the opposing wall held a warm, healthy blaze; its heat reached her from across the room.

This was not a room at Lord Lennox's townhouse. Nothing looked familiar, not the large ornate bed made of mahogany with its massive four posts, nor the white marble fireplace, nor the ornate dresser and washstand. She reached up to touch the cap on her head, but she found only loose coiling hair. She winced. Her mouth hurt like the very devil. She shifted toward the edge of the bed, wrinkling the dark red velvet coverlet. She nearly fell off as she set her feet down on the floor. There was a small mirror on the dresser, and she crossed the room to reach it.

A gasp escaped her at the sight of herself in the looking glass. A bruise was forming on her jaw and the mark stood out in stark relief against her pale skin. She touched the sore spot, her head still feeling as though wool had been crammed inside it. Pieces of a memory came back, painfully flashing behind her eyes. A man had struck her. She'd been taken from the coach outside Berkeley's club. But the man who attacked her was not the Earl of Monmouth.

The bedchamber door opened, and she turned to face her intruder. Fear and rage roiled deep within her as she recognized the darkly handsome face of the man who'd hit her. The hairs on the back of her neck rose in warning.

"My God. He wasn't lying." The man's lips parted in awe. "You *are* exquisite. Even in that awful servant's dress, you look stunning." He stepped into the bedchamber. A filmy white peignoir was draped over one of his arms and he set it down on the bed.

Philippa stayed frozen near the dresser, her eyes darting between the bed and the man. He wore expensive looking trousers and a fine red silk waistcoat. He had to be a gentleman, at least in name, but there was an edge to him, an invisible shadow that seemed to surround him and made her body tense. Whoever he was, he was dangerous.

"Forgive me, I've been remiss." His voice was smooth, but not in a charming way. It was the kind of voice that warned a woman she was about to suffer if she stepped out of line. "I was too awestruck by your beauty. I am Alistair Sommers. You may call me Alistair, if you wish." He stared at her expectantly.

Philippa was rooted in place, but the man's strangely calm demeanor turned her fear into a deeper fury. She kept herself collected despite that the fact that she wanted nothing more than to grab the porcelain wash-basin next to her and hurl it at the man's head. That was not going to help her. She had to stay calm, play the part he wanted until she understood his intentions or found a means of escape. Her resolution gave her the strength to answer him, though her voice wavered more than she wished.

"I... I am Philippa Wilson."

"It is a pleasure to meet you, Miss Wilson. Please, change into this gown. You will join me tonight as my dinner guest."

"Thank you," she replied, barely above a whisper as she bowed her head. Alistair flashed a triumphant grin. He assumed he had cowed her into obedience, but he had another thing coming if he dared to think he would bed her tonight.

He gave her a long and overly familiar look before he stepped outside and closed the bedchamber door. Philippa waited until she heard his steps fade down the hall before she crept to the windows and tried to open them. The windowsill didn't budge and she growled in frustration. It was too dark to see much, but she learned she was at least one floor above the ground.

She checked all the walls next, hoping to find a hidden door or something that might provide an opportunity to escape. When she didn't find one, she looked to the bed where the expensive silk peignoir lay. She had no choice now, it seemed, but to change and go down to dinner with him.

With a heavy heart, she unbuttoned her gown and changed into the peignoir. She kept her stays on beneath the gown, but she still felt terribly exposed wearing such an intimate piece of clothing. She tried to think of how to escape, and whether she might be able to elude him if she had a better sense of where she was. She straightened her shoulders and brushed her hair back from her face. When she exited the room, Alistair was waiting for her at the far end of the corridor.

"Ahh," he said as he spotted her. "I was coming to fetch you."

Philippa combed her fingers through the tangled waves of her hair as he met her in the corridor. He stopped in front of her, his eyes wide and gleaming with open appreciation.

"You look..." He struggled for words, but she'd heard them all before: exquisite, stunning, remarkable, beautiful. Nothing he could say would sway her to like him.

"You mentioned dinner?" she prompted. Alistair's unwanted attention made her feel ill, and she had little appetite, but she needed to buy time, and she needed to see more of the house for an opportunity to escape.

"Of course, this way." He offered her his arm and she took it, though the last thing she wanted to do was touch a man who had struck her. A grand set of stained glass windows faced the ornate stairs they descended. There was a haunting beauty to this place, yet it was still a prison, all the same.

"Are you going to tell me why you struck me, Alistair?" she asked the question, caressing his name in a way she hoped he would find flattering.

"I am sorry about that," he replied, but she heard not one note of sincerity in his voice. "I was hired to fetch you away from Lord Lennox. You're far too lovely to be working as a mere maid for him. Knowing him, he pays no attention to you at all, does he?" Alistair cooed at her like she was a child who'd been ignored. He couldn't have been more wrong about her character.

"Lord Lennox is happily married and the father of two children."

Alistair snorted. "Brides and babes, is there no worse fate?"

His question didn't seem to require an answer, so she didn't respond.

He paused at the entrance to a large fancy wood paneled dining room. "Here we are."

"And where is here, exactly, Alistair?"

"Castleton Abbey. One of my many properties," Alistair said proudly. "A bit Gothic, I suppose, but that's what makes it so amusing."

"Amusing?" She sat down at the place he offered her and pushed her chair in. Then his fingers brushed down the fall of her dark hair and she heard him draw in a deep breath, as though his self-control was being tested. Philippa held her own breath deep within her chest until it burned her lungs.

"What do you know of Lord Monmouth?" Alistair asked quietly.

"Lord Monmouth?" So that was it. He and Monmouth were somehow connected.

"Yes. You see, he was the one who hired me to remove you from Lennox's care." Alistair waved one of the footmen over. The man poured two glasses of a dark red wine and held them out. She accepted her glass and waited until Alistair took a drink of his own. Only then did she take a small sip.

The weight of his silent focus made her stomach tighten. Her throat was still sore, but the bruises on her skin had started to yellow. She couldn't imagine how she appeared to this man, beaten and bruised as she was. Now she had a fresh bruise on her jaw. She touched the spot and did her best to look pitiful when she met his hawk-like stare.

"If you would have come quietly, I wouldn't have had to do that," he admonished as though what had happened was her fault.

Philippa kept a tight grip on her self-control. Shifting the blame onto her told her all she needed to know of the man's character. Do as you are told. Don't resist. Don't speak up. Obey. Be quiet. For as long as she could remember, Philippa had resisted the meekness that society forced upon her. Life within a cage, life for the convenience of someone else's pleasure... It was fundamentally wrong. Reprehensible. But she would not waste her breath explaining that to this man.

A second footman brought in a pair of shallow bowls full of leek soup. Philippa ate silently, her eyes slowly scanning over the room. The footmen stood in the corners. One had a long scar down his face. He had been one of the other men who abducted her from the carriage. When he saw her looking his way, he shot her a cold smile that made her skin crawl.

She tried to assess her current situation. She was at Castleton Abbey, which meant she was not in the city of London. Any escape would have to be clever and well timed. If she was able to get away only to find herself miles from food and shelter she could still face trouble. Until she had a better sense of where she was, she could not risk a break for freedom.

"So you are not acquainted with Lord Monmouth?" Alistair asked.

"No, I'm not." She finished her soup and a plate of quail with potatoes was placed in front of her. She took care to eat well now, lest he decide to deprive her of food later.

"Well, he seems to know you. He thinks you are a threat to his estate and his son's inheritance. Have you met his son, Roderick Selkirk?"

Again, Philippa shook her head. She'd never heard of Roderick before tonight.

"Interesting. All that he would tell me about you is that you looked like his late wife, who was rumored to be the most beautiful woman in England. That was twenty years ago. I admit, I found that claim to be dubious, though I never met her. I was a mere boy when she died, and portraits are always made to be flattering." Alistair didn't touch his food; he was too preoccupied with trying to puzzle out the intrigue of her connection to Monmouth.

"Who are your parents?"

"Mason and Beth Wilson."

"Their occupation?" Alistair asked.

"My father was a miller when he was younger but after I was born, they moved to London and opened a textile shop."

"You're their natural born child?"

"What? Of course, I am." She stared at him, What was the man getting at? "I've even met the midwife who delivered me."

"Did you now? How interesting. I wonder then why you would look like Lord Monmouth's wife?"

"Why would I look like Lord Monmouth's wife?" That made no sense. She had no connection to the earl or his deceased wife.

"That's what I don't know." Alistair twisted his wineglass by the stem, focusing on her—a brooding, fascinated tint to his expression that made her stomach tight with nerves. Being the focus of this man's attention was not a good thing.

"He wishes for me to kill you. When I'm satisfied with our time together, that is." He delivered this statement as though they were in the midst of delightful garden party.

Dread filled Philippa like heavy sand. It pressed on her lungs until she was dizzy. She steadied her hands on the table, lest she faint. He was supposed to finish what Lord Monmouth had started. But why? Because she resembled his late wife? What crime was there in that?

"But perhaps I'll let you live. You would prefer that, wouldn't you?"

She nodded faintly. The dinner she'd eaten rumbled ominously in her belly. The last thing she wanted was to toss her accounts in front of this man. It would make her seem even more vulnerable than she already was.

"Please Alistair, I have done nothing to Lord Monmouth. Or you. Please let me go. I won't tell a soul what happened—"

Alistair tisked. "It's far too late for that. Now that I've seen you, I believe the rumors about the Earl's late wife.

I'm sorry my dear, but I *must* have you." He pushed his chair and stood.

That was it. She had no more ways to delay him. As he came around the table, she stood from her chair and dropped her napkin over her knife. Her fingers slid around the handle when she leaned against the table.

"My lord, you do not need to do this. I'm sure every lady in London would desire a man as handsome as you."

"Most do, but I want to you, no one else." His handsome aristocratic features would have broken hearts all over England, yet they were tainted with a mean hunger that promised pain.

Philippa waited until he was just within reach before she struck. She lashed out with the knife, cutting his face across his cheek. Alistair bellowed in rage, snatching the knife from her but she didn't wait for his retaliation. She turned and fled toward the open doors that lead to the great hall. It was her only hope for freedom, and she was so close to—

One of the footmen tripped her as she passed. Her body hit the cold stone floor with a thud.

"Well done, Sampson." Alistair praised.

Philippa rolled over and scrambling back as Alistair headed for her with a handkerchief clutched against his cheek. Blood stained his white expensive neck cloth.

"Luckily for you, I like my women spirited," he growled.

Boom! The sound of a door crashing in front of them

made her and Alistair turn. Silhouetted against the moonlight at the front door not twenty feet away was a man.
His body heaved as if he had been running or ready for a
fight. Alistair raised the knife he'd taken from Philippa.

"Is that any way to greet an old friend, Sommers?" The
man's deep voice echoed in the dining hall.

"Who are you? Step into the light!" Alistair demanded.

The man moved inside where the gold lamps illuminated him. Philippa's heart stopped. The most handsome
man she'd ever seen stood before her with whiskey-
colored eyes and dark hair the color of chocolate. He was
taller than Alistair and had the hard muscled body of a
man in his prime, rather than the lithe body of Alistair
who was still in his twenties. Philippa was transfixed by
this stranger in a way she'd never been before in her life.

The man smiled, his arrogant expression strangely
charming. "Been a long time, Sommers."

"Boudreaux? What the devil are you doing here?"

The man called Boudreaux came deeper into the
entryway. "We don't have a meeting of the Devil's Own
tonight?"

"You were banished from the order, if you don't recall."
Alistair held the sharpened dinner knife threateningly.
"Leave now."

"Now now, don't be like that. I don't wish to miss
whatever entertainment you have procured for the
evening." Boudreaux shook his head, a wry smile upon his
lips.

Philippa stared at him, her hope for rescue fading away. If he was here to watch...

"You stole the last girl from me for your own amusement. You won't do that again."

Philippa swallowed hard. This man had stolen a woman from Alistair? Was he even more cruel?

"And I'm afraid I will again." Boudreaux slowly twisted the silver knob of his cane and pulled, revealing a slender but deadly blade.

"Miss Wilson, please stand if you can manage it and come to me." He waved an inviting hand. Philippa stared at him. How did he know her name? When she didn't move, Boudreaux gave a gentle smile.

"Your friend Roger sent me. Mr. Lauder is all right, but they are both worried about you."

"Roger sent you?" She started to stand, but one of the footmen behind her stepped forward in her direction.

"Steady on, my good man." Boudreaux warned the servant. "One more step and I shall reach for my pistol. I assure you, you will not like the outcome if I do."

The footman froze.

"Now, Miss Wilson, if you please." Again, Boudreaux waved a hand toward her. This time she rushed away from Alistair to duck behind Boudreaux. His muscled body felt like an impenetrable shield. She'd never thought of a man making her feel safe before, yet here she was, wanting very much to have this mysterious rescuer carry her away to safety.

"I wish I could say it has been a pleasure, Sommers, but I'm afraid that would be a lie. The lady and I will be leaving now."

The two of them began a careful retreat toward the door. Boudreaux kept his focus trained on Alistair and his two footmen.

"Can you ride a horse, Miss Wilson?" he asked her under his breath.

"Yes," she said only loud enough for him to hear. She'd only ridden once or twice in her life, but she would damned well figure out how to do so again if it meant escaping this nightmare.

"I have a horse waiting for us down the steps. When I say run, go to it and mount up. I'll be right behind you. Do you understand?"

Philippa was trembling, her nerves ragged as they passed the threshold of the old Abbey doorway. "Yes."

"*Go!*" Boudreaux hissed.

Philippa ran on trembling legs toward an imperious black horse. She grasped the reins and pulled herself up into the saddle. The beast danced uneasily at the unfamiliar rider. Philippa stroked his neck as she soothed it, glancing back to the doorway. Boudreaux now sprinted toward her with his cane tucked under one arm. He threw his foot into the stirrup and swung up behind her. His large body caged hers as he jerked the reins from her hands and kicked at the horse's sides.

"*Heya!*" he shouted, and the horse leapt into a gallop.

Philippa closed her eyes, hearing shouts of pursuit behind them.

Crack! She swallowed a scream as a pistol fired. She looked back and saw Alistair standing in the road behind them, a spent pistol still aimed at them.

"He's shooting at us!" she shouted over the horse's thunderous hooves.

"Yes, he is." Boudreaux growled. His deep voice held a resounding note of fury that frightened her.

Boudreaux kept the horse at a wild gallop for at least two miles before he slowed to a canter. His hold on her waist eased and she could feel the tension in his body slowly give way.

"We should be close to an inn. There's one not too far down the road," he said.

"But why would we stop? We need to get back to London."

"We need to stop because..." Boudreaux said, his voice growing breathless. "I've been shot."

5

Boudreaux closed his eyes, trying to think past the pain that was spreading out from his upper shoulder.

"You've been shot?" Miss Wilson gasped.

"Yes, Miss Wilson. Please remain calm. We shall reach..." He drew in a shallow breath. "The inn...and the innkeeper can summon...a doctor."

It was becoming harder and harder to ignore the pain. A slow numbness, thick as marmalade, creeped down his arms. Within minutes he was unable to hold the reins at all. The straps of leather began to slip through his loosening fingers.

"Take...the reins," he said to the girl a moment before he slumped against her. A sweet feminine scent filled his nose as he nearly collapsed on top of her.

"Mr. Boudreaux?" she whimpered, pushing back against him.

He wanted to apologize; she was such a fragile little thing. Too small to be carrying his weight.

"I can't hold the horse and you. Please try to stay awake." She pinched his thigh, but he wanted nothing more than to close his eyes and rest. The world around him spun wildly and he hit the grass on the side of the road. Fresh pain wracked his body, briefly reviving him.

"Mr. Boudreaux!" He felt his body being rolled onto his back and stared up at her face. Christ, her face. The woman was lovely... So lovely... And she was a ghost. A ghost that haunted him from an oil painting hung in the Duke of St. Albans's picture gallery.

"Albina..."

"Philippa," the girl said. "My name is Philippa. Please get up, Mr. Boudreaux."

"Philippa?" He liked the sound of that name upon his tongue, despite the fact that he was suddenly too tired to speak.

"Please..." the girl begged. Her dark hair, lit by the moonlight, fell like black water around her face. He tried and failed to lift his hand up to touch the undulating waves.

"Lovely ghost..." he said and promptly blacked out.

When he woke, he found himself lying in a bed. A fire crackling nearby and a man with spectacles peered down at him.

"Oh, good, you've come around." The older man smiled. "That bodes well. Mrs. Boudreaux, please come over. You may see him now."

"Mrs. Boudreaux?" he murmured, his tongue thick and swollen.

Philippa appeared beside him. Her face was full of concern. "Boudreaux, are you all right? The doctor removed the bullet and stitched your wound. It wasn't too deep in your shoulder."

"Thirsty," he murmured. "Water please."

Philippa vanished from view and he heard the sound of water being poured into a goblet.

"Well, Mrs. Boudreaux, your husband should be fine with plenty of rest. Best to hire a coach to take you home once he can arrange it. But he may need to rest on his back a day or two."

"Yes, Dr. Hensley. Thank you for all you've done." Philippa followed the doctor to the door and closed it behind him. Then she faced him, her gray eyes so full of worry that he felt ashamed he'd got shot.

"I'm so sorry, Mr. Boudreaux. I had to tell the innkeeper we were married. I was afraid he wouldn't have helped us otherwise." She sat on the edge of the bed beside his hip and he was suddenly aware of the fact that he was naked, at least from the chest up. Her eyes skated over him and a heavy blush bloomed in her fair skin. Had he been in better shape, he would've been tempted to seduce her, but at the moment he felt like death warmed over.

"Please calm yourself, Miss Wilson."

"Philippa," she corrected, meeting his gaze. "After everything you've done for me, you should at least use my given name."

"Philippa," he said. He felt weakness pulling him toward sleep again. "And you may call me Beau."

"Beau. Shortened from Beauregard?" she asked.

He hummed a weary note of agreement and closed his eyes.

"Would you still like the water?" He forced his eyes open again and managed a nod. She leaned over and pressed the goblet to his lips. He drank a few sips and laid his head back down.

"The doctor gave you a bit of laudanum," she said. "I'm sorry if you're tired. Best if you sleep. I'll help keep watch over you."

He wanted to stay awake, to talk to her, to figure out why she looked like a woman dead for twenty years, but the laudanum was a powerful master and he soon succumbed to it.

The last sensation he was aware of was the gentle press of hands on his brow, brushing a lock of hair out of his eyes. It felt wonderful to be touched like that, out of concern rather than a need to prove a physical devotion.

It was the touch of a friend...

PHILIPPA WATCHED HER MYSTERIOUS RESCUER LOSE HIS battle to sleep. She brushed her fingers over his brow, unable to resist touching him now. He was quite possibly the most beautiful man she'd ever seen. The fact he was partially naked hadn't gone unnoticed either. The doctor and the innkeeper Mr. Craddock had removed Beau's waistcoat and shirt so that the wound could be treated.

After Beau had fallen from the horse, she'd raced to the inn at the end of the road as Beau had told her. She'd informed the innkeeper that her husband had been shot by a highwayman. He'd taken a wagon and gone with her to collect Beau, then ridden for the doctor.

She'd looked on in frantic worry as the doctor dug the bullet out with a pair of pliers, then cleaned the wound with some alcohol and sewn it up with a dozen small stitches. The sight of it all had made her stomach roil but she kept hold of Beau's hand, hoping he could feel her comforting touch even while his senses were lost to laudanum. She hoped he would heal well from his injury.

"We've been lucky thus far," she said, still looking down at her hands and protector. It all seemed to happen so slowly, but now she realized how fast it had all really gone.

She was too tired to sleep. The fear that Alistair would search for them kept her wide awake. In case he found them, she had Beau's sword cane leaning against the bed within easy reach. She was not about to let that awful man hurt either of them. If that meant staying awake all night, so be it.

Of course, that proved easier said than done. Philippa was exhausted and her face still ached from where Alistair had struck her. The doctor had seen to her injuries and offered her some laudanum as well, she'd refused. When she'd offered to find a way to pay for his services, the doctor had patted her hand, smiled warmly, and replied, "You have reminded me that beauty still exists in the world."

She'd blinked in surprise and blushed, assuming he meant her looks as all men did, but then the doctor had said, "Beauty goes beyond one's skin. It comes from within. I have seen how brave you are, how strong and compassionate. It reminded me the world still has moments of light within it."

Now, as Philippa sat in the dark bedchamber, exhaustion dragged at her. Yet despite her weariness, her mind continued to replay this turn of events.

Monmouth's attack. Alistair's abduction. The hints at Lord Monmouth's involvement. All because of who she was... yet she still didn't know *who* she was to these men. Apparently, she looked like Monmouth's late wife, but what did that matter? She was just a maid, born to wonderful parents who owned a textile shop on Bond Street. She was not special, no matter whom she resembled.

She looked down at Beau where he lay sleeping in the bed. His face was lined with anxiety, as though the land of dreams he dwelt in were dark ones. The tragic thought of what his melancholy thoughts might be only enhanced his appeal.

She remembered the sardonic smile he'd flashed at Alistair when he'd stepped into the light. It was as though nothing could ruffle his confident demeanor. He'd moved with such grace, despite the danger he'd faced. She'd felt safe with him in a way she'd only ever felt with the footman, Roger, or her father.

Yet this was not brotherly or fatherly affection she felt for Beau. Indeed, she felt something else stirring to life within her. She'd worried that perhaps her heart and maybe even her body had been made of ice all these years. Yet being close to this man, seeing him hurt for saving her life... Something inside her was burning intensely.

"Papa..." Beau began to shift restlessly, speaking in a hushed whimper. "Papa, no please..." His movements were still lethargic from the laudanum.

"Please, papa... don't go." Beau's voice sounded young, as though he was a child pleading.

Philippa reached out to brush his hair from his forehead. His eyes shot open and he gripped her wrist suddenly.

"It's alright, Mr. Boudreaux. It's me, Philippa. You're safe." She hoped he could understand her and find some comfort in her words. The worry lines softened around his mouth and he relaxed, but he didn't release her wrist. After a moment, he brought her hand to his lips and placed a kiss to it. Something echoed deep within her, like she was calling out his name in a cavern. Somehow this stranger was finding his way into her soul, yet she only knew his name.

Finally, he let go of her wrist and his features relaxed as he once more settled into sleep. Philippa kept her vigil but rather than worry about the dangers hunting for them outside, she feared about the dangers right beside her. The life of this man, Beau Boudreaux, had become entwined with hers, and she knew not where this path might lead her.

BEAU TRIED TO BANISH THE NIGHTMARES OF THAT fateful night in Paris. How he had pleaded with his father not to leave, to stay with him and his mother. But his father, who had the same dark hair and whiskey colored eyes as Beau, had explained in a gentle tone that sometimes a person had to stand up for what was right, even in the face of those who would behead someone for simply voicing an opinion. His father had hugged him tight and his powerful body had held young Beau close as he whispered words of love before he let go, kissed his mother one last time, and rode off into the darkness.

They'd waited all night for him to return. When dawn

arrived, the deathly quiet in their country house was broken only by a rider who'd come bearing a letter written in his father's familiar hand.

My Beau, how I have loved you. But now I am gone. Take your mother to her family in England. Do not return here. This land has lost its soul. It bleeds each day with the blood of innocents from those who sit on the thrones of hypocrisy. It is a place for men of noble hearts no longer.

The last few words had been scrambled in apparent haste and ink droplets smeared the bottom of the page. Beau had looked up at the young man who'd delivered the message.

"Your father was shot by a firing squad. The gendarmes allowed this letter to be delivered to you." The man had said. "I am sorry for your loss." He gave young Beau a pat on the shoulder before he'd gotten back on his horse and ridden away into the growing sunlight.

As he pushed past the laudanum induced sleep, he slowly remembered what had happened and why he was in pain. He had rescued Miss Wilson, Philippa. He had been shot. He had passed out on the side of the road. There had been a doctor.

He tried to sit up, but his chest felt like lead. He saw a woman in a white peignoir, her dark hair spilling out across his bare chest. Philippa. She was asleep beside him, Lord Sheridan's sword unsheathed from the cane and held loosely in one of her hands.

Christ, she was as beautiful as the woman from St.

Albans's painting. She looked exactly like Albina. How was that possible?

After a few minutes, Beau moved out from under Philippa and slid off the bed. His back hurt like hell, but at least he could move. He pulled on his white shirt, wincing at the way it pulled at his stitches. Then he slipped on his boots and left the room. He headed down the stairs, smiling a little when he heard a woman singing.

"Ach! There you are, lad. You shouldna be out of bed." The rotund Scottish woman tried to shoo him back up the stairs.

"Please, can I have some food for my wife and myself?" He tried not to laugh at pretending to have a wife. Of course, he would be a lucky fellow to have a woman like Philippa waiting for him in his bed.

"Of course. You must be famished." The innkeeper's wife bustled about the kitchen. "My name is Mrs. Craddock, in case you don' remember, what with your injuries and all."

"Thank you so much for your help, Mrs. Craddock."

She beamed at Beau and pinched his cheek as though he were a boy and not a grown man of six and thirty.

"Well, we couldna very well leave you out there, not if those ruffians were to come back. Mrs. Boudreaux told us about your fight against those highwaymen, and how they stole all your belongings."

What other tales had had his sweet little "wife" spun

about their circumstances? And yet he had to admit it was better than trying to explain the truth.

"Er, yes. It was quite terrible, but I did have money stashed upon my person. I will be glad to pay you and Mr. Craddock for the rooms and food, as well as the doctor."

"There's no need to pay for the doctor, lad. He took one look at your wife and said he didna need any payment, except to see her beautiful face."

"Oh?" Beau wished he had been awake to hear that.

"Now dinna be getting jealous. The doctor's old enough to be her grandfather. He merely appreciated her sweet heart, he said."

"Hmm..." Beau didn't reply but gratefully accepted the tray of food from Mrs. Craddock. It hurt to carry the tray, but he was not the sort of man to show weakness if he could help it. When he returned to their bedchamber, he found Philippa spread out across the bed, reaching for all four corners of the feather tick mattress. She painted a delightful picture of feminine curves with riotous waves of dark hair. He set the tray down to stoke the dying fire and add a few more logs.

The sound woke Philippa. She bolted upright, welding the short sword from Sheridan's cane. She gasped when she saw him.

"Mr. Boudreaux, you need to be in bed." She abandoned the sword and rushed over to put the rest of the logs on the fire, then escorted him back to bed with her elegant hands curled around his bicep.

"I rather like it when you touch me. Perhaps I should keep escaping bed." He chuckled.

She shot him a furious look but there was no fire in her expression. "Please, rest. The doctor said—"

"Oh, hang the bloody doctor. Once dawn arrives, we need to hire a coach and get you back to Lennox's house. He'll be worried sick."

"I'm certain I shall not be welcome there." She said this so quietly he almost hadn't heard it.

"What do you mean?"

She pushed against his stomach. "Get in bed, and I'll tell you."

"Blackmail? You *are* a cunning wench." But he did as she asked and eased down onto the bed.

Philippa pulled the covers up to his chin, but he shoved them back to his waist, partly because he was warm enough, partly because he enjoyed seeing this woman blush. After having mistresses who knew how to pretend to be embarrassed by their arousal, he knew an act when he saw it, and Philippa was not acting. He liked that. She was open in so many ways, and that was not a thing he was accustomed to.

"Well, I'm in bed." He gestured toward the blankets, wanting to tease her again, but when she glanced up from fixing the tray of food and preparing him a plate, he saw her anguish.

"This is twice now that I've caused a scandal for Lord Lennox. He must cast me out. An upstairs maid is not worth this much trouble."

"I think you underestimate Lord Lennox's nature," said Beau.

"But he must think of his wife and children's safety. I cannot be in their house if men continue to try to kill me."

"Wait, *men*? Are you saying Lord Sommers also intended to kill you?"

"Yes." She suddenly realized what a revealing bit of clothing she wore at the moment and quickly pulled one of the blankets from the bed to wrap around her. "I thought he meant only to force himself on me, then he admitted that Monmouth hired him to kill me." She trembled and wrapped her arms tighter around herself. "Of course, he *wanted* to have me before."

The thought revolted Beau, but the second part also puzzled him further. "I wonder what drove Monmouth to hire a man. Why you?" He gestured for her to sit beside him, but she hesitated. "Come here and sit." He patted the bed beside him, which she eyed with worry. "I won't harm you, Philippa. Please, come."

He held up one hand, palm up. She placed her hand in his and he gave it a gentle squeeze as she sat next to him.

"Did Sommers say why Monmouth wanted you dead?"

Philippa bit her lip. "No, I was trying to get him to tell me, but from what he said, I think perhaps even he didn't know Lord Monmouth's reason for wishing me dead. He asked me questions about my parents, about my birth."

"Your birth? Something about that has caused a stir. We must get to the bottom of it."

Philippa stared at him in confusion. "We?"

"Of course. I cannot let you run about London without protection. No, we need to discover what this is about."

"How will we do that?" she asked.

"We must first talk to Lennox. But we shall worry about that in a few hours."

She left the bed and returned with his food. He paused after a few spoonfuls of stew when he realized she hadn't prepared her own plate, but was merely standing by the bed, watching him eat.

"Why aren't you eating?" he asked.

"Oh, I couldn't. It wouldn't be proper." This time when she blushed, he hated himself.

"Philippa, please, eat. While I am assisting you, I shall treat you as I treat *all* women. As a lady. Being in service does not mean you deserve less respect."

"Most don't seem to think so." But she collected a plate of food herself with no further argument.

Once they'd both eaten, he patted the bed again. "You need rest, like I do. There's plenty of room. I promise your virtue is safe here. I could barely carry that tray up the stairs."

He settled back into the pillows and closed his eyes. A few minutes later, he felt the bed dip as she lay next to him. He waited another minute before he cautiously pulled the covers up higher over them.

But he didn't drift back to sleep at once. He was too worried. How did one exquisitely beautiful servant woman earn Lord Monmouth's fatal interest, so much so that he was willing to engage another to finish what he'd started?

ALISTAIR SOMMERS CLIMBED OUT OF HIS COACH AND walked up the front steps of Lord Monmouth's town-house. He reached reflexively to touch the plasters applied to the cut on his face and winced. It was an hour until dawn, but what he had to say could not wait.

An exhausted butler answered the door. "May I help you?"

"Tell Lord Monmouth that Lord Sommers is here. It's a matter of great urgency."

"I'm sorry, my lord. His lordship and his son have left for their estate in the country."

Alistair cursed. He hadn't a clue where Monmouth's country estate was. "Could you write down the address for me?"

"Just a moment." The butler disappeared back into the dark house. A few minutes later he returned and pressed a piece of paper into Alistair's hands.

Alistair returned to his coach, his thoughts racing wildly. He needed to pay a call to Monmouth in person, but not today. He had to visit a doctor and have his face taken care of.

The pretty bitch had ruined his face and she would suffer dearly for it. But first he would make Lord Monmouth admit to the girl's true importance. He'd paid far more than he bargained for in this affair as it was.

As for the girl, his man Lewis would be engaging with his usual contacts right now while trying to find her in London. If he saw the opportunity, he would take her and hold her until Alistair returned.

He wasn't done with the girl, oh no. He *wanted* her and he would have her, one way or another. That thought brought a cold smile to his face.

❦ 6 ❦

By midmorning Philippa had eaten and borrowed an ill-fitting dress from the sweet Mrs. Craddock. Mr. Boudreaux had borrowed one of Mr. Craddock's shirts and had hired a coach to take them back to London.

She followed him to the waiting coach but jolted when he offered his hand to help her inside. Her cheeks warmed and her heart lurched; it felt so inappropriate to be treated this way. She shook her head, muttering a thank you as she gently but firmly pushed past him and pulled herself into the coach.

They sat on opposite sides of the coach, a strange tension growing between them. She'd spent the night in his bed and while nothing happened, she felt changed.

She'd woken with her body coiled around his, their limbs tangled in a quiet intimacy that she'd never known before. Ever since she'd left home, she'd always felt so alone, and yet as she stirred just an hour after dawn, she hadn't felt that way at all. She'd had some wild, unexplainable connection to this man. It both excited and frightened her.

"Mr. Boudreaux..." she began uncertainly. The woolen gown she'd borrowed hung limply on her and she felt very self-conscious of that fact. It was unladylike to pry into his life, not to mention unprofessional, but she desperately wanted to better understand this stranger who had saved her life.

"Just Beau, if you please." His deep voice made her think of distant thunder and the promise of summer lightning. She loved how his baritone made her feel, even when he spoke only a handful of words.

"Beau, when you were asleep last night, I thought you were dreaming."

His face shuttered, closing her out of whatever she'd hoped he might have shown her. "People dream at night. It's nothing unusual." His tone wasn't biting but she still felt stung by it anyway.

"Yes, but you were calling for your father. What happened to him?"

The playful, sardonic side of Beau was gone now. His lips pressed into a hard line and she thought for a moment he wouldn't say anything. Even darkly disapproving, the man was still far too handsome for her to be comfortable.

She was about to apologize for her imprudence when he answered.

"He died a long time ago." That single sentence warned her that she'd crossed some unseen line and should not ask him anything further on the matter.

She busied herself rehearsing what she would say to Lord and Lady Lennox when she returned home, assuming it was still her home. Kind as they were, it was hard for her not to see herself as more trouble than she was worth right now.

If they cast her out, she would have to return to her parents' shop until she could find new employment. Her parents could employ her at the shop, but she wanted to get out and see what she could of the world. Being an upstairs maid, while hardly her dream, was as close as she could come to seeing a bigger life, even if it was just short glimpses of handsome men and beautiful women in glittering gowns swirling by the half-closed ballroom doors.

"Philippa, I'm sorry. I was unkind to you earlier," Boudreaux said. She looked at him and saw only sincerity in his gaze.

"You need not apologize, sir."

"I do. A gentleman should never speak to a lady as I did." He looked at his hands in his lap where they twisted one of his gloves. "Losing my father was painful. I was only a boy when the French gendarmes had him shot."

She hated seeing the pain laid bare in his eyes, but she had to know more. "Why did they shoot him?"

Beau's eyes lifted and for a moment, he was that vulnerable boy, the one who'd spoken during his dreams. Her heart filled with sorrow.

"He spoke out against the violence in Paris just three years after the Terror when the streets ran red with blood. And he was an aristocrat. They saw his wealth and privilege as evils, and they killed him to take his home and his money. My mother and I fled to her relatives in England before they came for us too."

"I'm so sorry, Beau." Without thinking, she reached across the coach to take his hands.

His lips curved. "It's all right. I'm a grown man and it's all in the past."

She wanted to agree with him, but if she was honest, the past never seemed that far away. She wasn't sure why, but she sometimes dreamed of a darkened room and a woman whispering her name, a sob catching in the woman's throat and an angry deep voice growling words she could not remember. It always seemed just out of reach. A singular, dark, yet defining memory of a memory.

The coach rolled to a stop. The footman met them as Beau opened the door. It was then that she recognized the footman as one of her friends, Clement.

"Pippa!" he exclaimed, but went silent and rigid as he caught sight of Beau and assisted them both down before closing the coach door.

Clement leaned over to whisper as she walked past him. "Are you all right?"

"Yes, I'll tell you all later," she whispered back as she followed Beau up the townhouse stairs and into the Lennox's entryway. Mr. Beaton was there to greet them.

"Please come in, Mr. Boudreaux. We're so relieved to see you." His eyes drifted to Philippa. He looked as though he wished to say something more but kept his composure and merely nodded once at her.

"Is Lord Lennox at home? As you can see, I had success in locating Miss Wilson."

Mr. Beaton looked to the stairs. "I believe word has already reached him."

"Boudreaux, thank God!" Ashton Lennox strode down the stairs to meet them.

Philippa ducked her head, waiting to be chastised for all the trouble she'd caused. The Lord Lennox's boots appeared in her line of vision and a hand lifted her chin, so she was forced to look up at her employer. What she saw left her stunned. There was no fury, no disappointment, only relief and joy.

"Philippa, we've all been so worried about you. We're glad you're home. Please go to the kitchens and have some hot tea while I speak to Mr. Boudreaux."

"You don't wish me to pack my things, my lord?"

"Pack?" Lennox asked. "I'm afraid I don't understand."

"She's afraid you will terminate her position here," Beau said, humor in his tone. "I told her you wouldn't."

"Lord no, Philippa. Why would you think that? Your position here remains yours."

Tears blurred Philippa's eyes. She'd been so afraid she would lose her friends and the people she'd come to view as a family, but she was safe. Lord Lennox wasn't sending her away. Even though the Lennox family had only ever been kind to her, she knew that causing a scandal would be bad enough to make even the nicest families send a servant away.

"Now, you've been through a lot, I'm sure," said Lord Lennox. "Why don't you get something to eat as well. You can settle back into your duties tomorrow."

"Thank you, my lord." She rushed away to the kitchens where she bumped into Ruth.

"Pippa!" Her friend squealed and hugged her. "I heard you were found! What happened? Are you all right? Roger's been terribly upset. Come and sit. Mrs. Murphy will put the kettle on."

They moved into the kitchens, where Mrs. Murphy was busy cooking up a luncheon for the household. The kitchens were warm, and the air was full of delicious scents that reminded Philippa how hungry she was.

"Pippa, dear. Thank heavens you're back." The stout, merry-faced cook, abandoned the stew for a moment and to hug Philippa. When she cupped Philippa's face, she stared deeply at her.

"Are you all right, love? You're bruised all over. Roger said a man grabbed you. In broad daylight, no less! We feared...well..." She didn't finish.

She was quick to reassure all her friends she was fine.

"Mr. Boudreaux, a friend of his lordship, helped me escape from my captors."

"What? Oh dear, we had better hear the whole tale."

BEAU FOLLOWED ASHTON INTO HIS STUDY WHERE Cedric Sheridan sat waiting. Beau handed the viscount his cane.

"Thank you, Sheridan. This proved quite useful."

Sheridan accepted the cane. "Glad to hear it. How's the maid?"

"Shaken." Beau settled into the seat beside Sheridan. "Sommers took her to the Abbey, as I suspected. I got there just in time; he was about to force himself on her."

"Christ," Sheridan muttered.

"Bastard," Ashton said in a dark and deadly tone. "I'm constantly amazed that man is still alive."

"Sadly, the man's name does carry weight, and I thought given the difference of our social standings, I ought not to murder a peer, no matter how much I was tempted to."

"I doubt I would have had your self-control," Ashton said.

"Believe me, my control was tested. Sommers is fortunate that I only learned of his full plans after I'd escaped with the girl."

"His full plans?" Sheridan's brown eyes widened.

"He intended to kill her. Lord Monmouth instructed him to abduct her and dispose of her." It made Beau's blood boil all over again.

"Monmouth again? What the bloody hell is going on?" Sheridan demanded.

"Where is Sommers now?" Ashton asked.

"Not sure. He shot me in the bloody back as we rode away from the Abbey."

"Good God, man," Ashton gasped. "Are you all right?"

"Well enough, though I won't be lifting anything heavier than Sheridan's cane for some time. It's why we couldn't return last night. Philippa is to be commended. She ran to a nearby inn and fetched help. A local doctor removed the bullet and stitched me up. The laudanum left me unable to ride until late this morning, so we rested at the inn for the night."

Sheridan whistled softly. "Well done, Boudreaux. The girl was lucky to have you."

"I was lucky to have her." He was silent a moment, a dozen thoughts about Philippa plaguing him. "Lennox, where did you find this girl?"

"Find her?" Ashton repeated.

"As a maid to employ. How did you find her?"

"The usual way. A posting in the paper. Rosalind interviewed her. She didn't have any references, as I recall, but her parents have a textile shop on Bond Street. Rosalind knew the shop and decided to take a chance on the girl.

Once I saw her, I believe I understood why she hadn't found employment elsewhere."

Beau nodded. "She's stunning. A true diamond of the first water. I'm sure most ladies would be far too concerned about the wandering eyes of their husbands to hire her."

"Exactly. That's why we took her on. Rosalind will always have my sole love and attention, and I never take advantage of my staff."

Lennox narrowed his eyes on Beau slightly. "You spent an entire night alone with my maid. Should we have a discussion, Boudreaux?" It wasn't a threat, not exactly.

"I will admit she is the most beautiful woman I've ever seen, but I did not act upon my desires. I'm not a bastard. Besides, I was too preoccupied with laudanum and a bullet in my back."

Lennox cracked a smile. "Fair enough. But well and healed, would you have?"

Beau shrugged. "If the lady wished me to take her to bed, I would, but she would have to be quite clear about her intentions. Women in service often feel compelled to accept a gentlemen's advances." Then he added with a smile, "Besides, I prefer women to come to me." All of his mistresses had pursued him first, even the opera singers or ballet dancers. Though he was tempted to break his rule for Philippa.

"You might be one of the few men in London I can trust to send her to."

"I beg your pardon?" Beau didn't like the contemplative gleam in Lennox's eyes.

"Clearly Monmouth has an interest in her, and if we are to protect her, we need to know why. I won't have an innocent woman murdered." Lennox declared this with a low and dangerous tone.

"So you wish to send the maid to a notorious bachelor's residence?" Sheridan chuckled. "Only you, Ash. *Only* you."

"I'm not certain sending her to me is wise," Beau replied. "Besides, I have no need of another upstairs maid. What would I do with her?"

Lennox leaned back against the edge of his large rosewood desk and crossed his arms. "She won't be your maid. She shall be your ward. The daughter of an old friend from the country that has passed away. Now she has come to live with you, as per his dying wish. You shall take her to balls, dinners, the opera. Be as open and public with her as possible."

Beau blinked. "You wish to use her as *bait?*" He'd heard Lennox could be ruthless, but to use an innocent woman as bait was more than he could have imagined from him.

"You've done an excellent job protecting her so far. You could do the same for a few more weeks. By keeping her in the public eye, you reduce the chances of another attack. You will also need to avoid any sense of routine. Do not take her to the same opera house twice or visit the same friends for dinner if you can help it."

The wound in Beau's back began to throb and make his shoulder ache, as if to remind him how dangerous it was to protect Philippa. "Might I remind you she was snatched in full public view on her first day leaving your house?"

"You'll have to trust me," said Lennox. "There is subtle mind work at play here. It's for the very reasons you mention that Monmouth will think twice about another attack. He will suspect it's a trap and will spend his time wondering as to your motives. Why expose her so easily? Why change her name? If it is a trap, why take such precautions against routine? It will keep him unbalanced, and unaware of what Sheridan and I are doing behind his back."

It sounded reasonable, but Beau remained unconvinced. It seemed reckless.

"Please, Boudreaux," Lennox said more softly. "I wouldn't trust her safety with anyone else."

Beau felt the weight of Lennox and Sheridan's hopeful gazes. "Bloody hell, you want me to play guardian to the most beautiful woman in London?"

Both of them chuckled. "I think we would beg to differ on the most beautiful. Have you seen our wives?" Sheridan smirked.

"The most beautiful unmarried woman, then." Beau amended with a laugh. "You honestly think London would approve of me as a chaperone? If I'm not careful, I could end up leg-shackled."

"Nonsense, man. We'll be there to support you in society, confirm your story, and act approving of your guardianship. We need only play this masquerade for just long enough to draw Monmouth, or whoever he has contracted, out." Ashton waited for Beau's answer expectantly.

Beau finally conceded. "Very well. But it's been too long since I played nursemaid. My poor staff haven't had a woman in residence. They'll be in an uproar." He also needed to decide how he would handle St. Albans seeing the girl and noting the resemblance to his deceased daughter.

Lennox merely laughed again. "Your staff will be fine, Boudreaux. *You* will be fine. Do not let a pretty woman make you nervous. They are easier to share a house with than you realize."

Beau highly doubted that. There was a reason he always kept his mistresses at quaint little love nests away from his own residence. He liked having room to breathe.

"One week," Beau warned. "I cannot promise much beyond that."

"So says the confirmed bachelor," Sheridan joked.

Beau shot him a glare. "*One* week."

"One week," Lennox agreed. "Any longer and I fear Monmouth will strike again. If we haven't learned the truth by then, I will find another way to protect her."

"Has anyone asked if Miss Wilson will be accepting of such an arrangement?" asked Sheridan.

"She might take some convincing," Lennox admitted. "But I believe she will. However, I would prefer not to frighten her too much. We mustn't let her know the danger, not yet."

"But you *must* warn her. I won't shelter her innocent of the risks. She must be told at least some of it," Beau insisted.

"Cedric, have Mr. Beaton bring Philippa here."

Sheridan left the room, leaving Beau alone with Ashton.

"I will provide money for her care. She will need clothes and jewels, a horse for riding."

Beau held up a hand. "If she is to be my ward, real or feigned, I shall pay for her. I will need to be publicly seen providing for her."

"Very well but let me reimburse you."

"If you insist, but I assure you it's not necessary." Beau strangely couldn't stomach the thought of being paid back for assuming protective duty and caring for a lady.

The study door opened, and Sheridan ushered Philippa in. She still wore the ill-fitting dress from the innkeeper Mrs. Craddock and her face was lined with anxiety.

"My lord?" She looked to Lennox, who gestured to the seat next to Beau.

"Please sit, Pippa. I would like to propose a plan to you."

Philippa obediently sat down beside Beau.

"Pippa, would you be willing to help me stop Lord Monmouth?"

Philippa looked between Beau, Lennox and Sheridan in confusion. "Stop him? How? He's an earl."

"No man is above the law," said Beau. "But yes, the sad reality is that there are those among the peerage who require unassailable evidence to be brought against them to see justice done."

"Lord Monmouth is one such man," Lennox added. "No doubt he feels safe from repercussion so long as he distances himself from any direct actions. We need to understand why he wishes to hurt you so that we can expose him."

Beau leaned closer to her. "But in order to do so, we need your cooperation."

Philippa's full focus was on was him now and it made his blood hum sweetly in his veins.

"My cooperation? In what way?" She kept her gaze on him, as though her trust was stronger in him than the others, which was to be expected, given how they'd met.

"We need you to become a public figure. Someone that Monmouth will see, a woman invited to balls, dinners and such."

Philippa tensed, her hands fisting in her skirts. "But won't he try to attack me again?"

"Not directly, no," said Lennox. "His first attack was in the heat of the moment. He now knows it was a mistake.

Had he killed you, there would have been consequences. Even for him."

"Which is why he later engaged Sommers," Beau added. "But it is Lord Lennox's belief that the very fact that you are exposing yourself as a target might protect you for a time."

Philippa frowned. "Because he will believe it's a trap?"

"Precisely," said Ashton. "And regardless, we shall be there to protect you."

Philippa looked at Beau. "Will you be there?"

He nodded. "We believe you should come to live with me at my townhouse. We will tell everyone you are my ward, the daughter of an older friend of mine from the country. I've been charged with your care for a year until you turn twenty-one."

Her lightning gray eyes studied him. "Live with you? Alone?" The hesitation was there as he expected, but she wasn't protesting so far.

"Philippa," he said softly. "You can trust me, can you not?"

She considered a moment and then gave a nod.

"I promised your safety. At the risk of my own, if necessary."

She released her viselike grip on her skirts. "When is this to happen?"

"Now, today." Beau glanced at Ashton for confirmation.

"Take any of your belongings you wish. We will have my coach take you to Boudreaux's home in Mayfair. We will conceive of a deeper story for you, but for now, you may be called Miss Wilson and go by your own given name."

"And afterwards... I'm allowed to come back and continue in service to you?" Philippa asked.

"Of course," he promised.

The last bit of tension in Philippa seemed to ease.

"Go on. Pack your things and come back down when you're ready," Lennox said.

Philippa left the room.

"Well, that went better than expected," Sheridan said. "I would think that most ladies would hesitate to live with a bachelor under such circumstances."

"Philippa isn't most ladies," Beau said. "She's braver than anyone I've ever known."

Lennox and Sheridan shared a knowing look before Sheridan clapped a hand on Beau's shoulder. "That my friend, is how it begins."

"How what begins?" Beau asked.

Sheridan's brown eyes glinted with mischief. "Why spoil the surprise?"

Beau simply stared at his two friends. What the devil did they mean?

7

"Pippa?" Roger asked as Philippa entered her room after meeting with Lord Lennox. Both he and Ruth waited anxiously by her bed, their eyes round and mouths tight. "Pippa, are you allowed to stay?"

"Yes... But his lordship needs me to help him first."

"Help him how?" Ruth asked.

"They want to expose Lord Monmouth. They think I can help them draw him out in public."

"How?" Roger's face was tight with worry.

"They wish for me to go live with Mr. Boudreaux and pose as his ward, the daughter of an old friend from the country."

"Boudreaux? The tall dark haired man who rescued you?"

"Yes, the one with dark, intense eyes." Lord, she loved

those whiskey-colored eyes, the way they always made her feel warm and safe, even as his lips promised dark, dangerous and sinful pleasures.

"Do you feel safe to be with him?" Ruth asked. Her fingers played with the hem of her white apron. "I've heard he's a bit of a rake."

"He could've taken advantage of me after he rescued me, but he didn't. Lord Lennox trusts him." She retrieved a small cloth bag from next to her bed, large enough to hold a few undergarments and one of her better dresses. She also collected her pouch with her necklace given to her by her mother. Everything else could be left here until she returned.

Ruth hugged her tight. "Oh, do be careful." When she let her go, Roger took her place.

"Remember, a knee to his groin if he tries anything," he said, miming the action to demonstrate.

"Roger!" Ruth exclaimed in a scandalized tone.

"What? It's good advice," he replied, not at all embarrassed.

"Thank you. I will send word once I'm settled."

"Good." Ruth hugged her once more, and they followed her back down to the main floor.

Philippa froze at the sight of Lord Lennox, Lord Sheridan, Lady Lennox and the two Lennox children waiting for her at the foot of the grand staircase. Beau was there too, lingering at the edge of the small crowd.

"Be safe, Pippa," Lady Lennox said.

"Yes, be safe," Malcolm, their oldest, replied solemnly. He was only four but he, like his younger sister Rose, liked Philippa immensely.

Rose waved a chubby hand before burying her face in her mother's blue velvet skirts. "Bye, bye."

"Goodbye, my dear little ones," Philippa said to the two children before facing Lennox and Sheridan. "I hope I won't be gone for long."

"As do I. We'll be watching over you," Lennox promised; Sheridan echoed the sentiment with a nod.

"Thank you, my lords." She passed by them to stand in front of Beau Boudreaux. Those warm eyes of his seared her as he looked her over.

"You have all that you need?" The question was soft, full of tenderness and concern.

"Yes, I believe so." She wanted to tell him she was afraid, afraid to leave her protected and predictable world behind, but the words caught on her tongue. She followed him down to the black and tan painted coach that bore the Lennox family crest. Beau offered her a hand inside. She hesitated at first, then accepted his hand and stepped in. He settled across from her.

"Mr. Boudreaux," she said.

"Beau," he corrected.

"Beau, what is expected of me while we are trying to expose Lord Monmouth?"

"You shall dress and act like a lady of good breeding, someone from an aristocratic family. We want him to see you in as many public settings as possible. If he sees you as a threat to his son's inheritance, then we shall give him every reason to think so. Once he realizes what's happening, he will feel compelled to act. And yet, according to Lennox, the very nature of our public display will stay his hand and fill him with doubt. With his attention focused on you, we may be able to find out what his motives truly are.

"What if... What if he simply does not like me, or like servants? It could be that I simply upset him somehow."

Beau pushed back one of the coach curtains, illuminating his face, which was trying to hide a smirk. "I don't know what stories you've heard, but earls or other members of the peerage do not go about strangling young women for no reason."

"But they can," she replied quietly, her nerves coming back. "I've read about such murders in the Morning Post."

"Those are the acts of mad men. Monmouth, as far as I'm aware, is not a mad man."

"How can you be certain??"

The smirk on his face faded. "I guess I cannot. Sometimes such madness is temporary or comes out in a fit of passion. The fact you resemble his late wife... I wonder if perhaps he killed her and thought you were haunting him, reminding him of his guilt."

Philippa's gaze fell. "I still find it hard to believe I resemble her."

"Believe it. I have seen it with my own eyes. She was the daughter of the Duke of St. Albans, a man that I look upon as my surrogate father. She died in childbirth giving Monmouth a son. A few days before you and I met, my friend showed me her portrait. You look like the living ghost of Albina." He leaned forward, their breaths mingling in the quiet coach. "There is a reason that matters to Monmouth and we must learn why or you will never be safe."

Philippa suddenly felt very small and afraid. "But I don't matter. I'm no one..."

Beau turned to look at her in bewilderment. "What an odd thing to say. No one is no one, Philippa."

"Even upstairs maids?" She was trying to be playful, but her heart was still quivering with fresh fear, knowing that a man wanted her dead for reasons she couldn't fathom.

"*Especially* upstairs maids," Beau said with that lazy smile of self-assurance. "Men like Monmouth hold far less esteem in my eye. Character defines worth, not status." Beau had a relaxed confidence that put her at ease and made her feel protected, though he was a seasoned rake sixteen years her senior. The gap between them felt like a lifetime in some ways. He was worldly; she'd lived a sheltered life with her parents and now a life of service.

"Philippa, if you aren't too tired, we should go shopping. As my ward, you'll need new clothes." He waved at the baggy gown from Mrs. Craddock hanging on her smaller frame.

Philippa held up her small cloth bag so he might see. "I packed my best Sunday gown."

"Have you now? Well, let me see." Beau leaned forward as she removed part of the dark blue muslin gown from her bag.

"Ahh, Yes. That is a lovely gown. But I'm afraid you need two dozen more, at least."

"*At least?*"

"Dinner gowns, opera gowns, certainly a riding habit. Several ball gowns. Day gowns, evening gowns, promenade dresses..." He trailed off.

Her mind reeled with the thought of so many wonderful gowns but then the truth of her situation poured over in a dreadful icy reality. She didn't have the funds for such clothing. Swallowing hard, she confessed to Beau her problem with his plan.

"I haven't the money for that, Mr. Boudreaux."

"Beau," he corrected yet again. "During this charade, you will be my guest. Lennox and I have agreed it was only fair that we cover your necessary expenses. Playing the part of a woman in the *ton*, you will have great demands when it comes to your wardrobe. I shall be more than happy to provide you with the items you need."

Philippa fell back against the coach's cushioned seat. "Heavens..."

"So, what do you think? Are you up to the task of spending my money on fine gowns, maybe even a few jewels?"

"Oh, but I have a necklace." She dug into her bag once more and found a small velvet pouch. She emptied the contents onto her palm. The sapphire necklace gleamed in her hand.

"Are those glass?" he asked.

"No... they are real sapphires. It was a gift from my parents when I turned sixteen."

"A fine gift. Lennox said your parents run a textile shop, is that correct?"

She tucked the necklace back into its pouch and returned the pouch to her cloth bag. "Yes, on Bond Street."

"Well, let's keep that necklace safe. I'd hate for you to lose something so personal. I will buy you other jewels to wear."

Philippa still couldn't believe what he was saying. It was like some fantastical dream.

"Shopping then? Or would you prefer to go home to rest?"

"I suppose I could do a little shopping," she conceded. Although in truth she wanted to curl up in bed and sleep for two days straight. Beau opened the door of the coach and told the driver to head to Oxford Street.

Philippa had been to Oxford Street before, usually on errands for Lady Lennox. Now she was here on her own with a handsome gentleman. As Beau escorted her out of the coach, she felt the eyes of a dozen men and women upon her. The oversized woolen dress she wore was suddenly too large and stiff. She ducked her head in mortification.

"I must look like a beggar to these people."

Beau slipped her arm in the crook of his. "Eyes up, Philippa. You have nothing to be ashamed of." She could smell that warm, dark, enticing sent of his that had soothed and aroused her last night was she'd fallen asleep in his arms.

She did as he commanded and raised her head, gazing down the street. Dozens of windows displayed the wares of silk merchants, milliners, corsetiers, line-drapers and haberdasheries.

He nodded at a nearby modiste's shop that had a black and gold painted sign that said Harper, Howell and Co. "Shall we start here?"

She recognized the name. It was one of the finest dressmakers in London. "If that is what you believe is best." She had no idea where to start. She had perused Lady Lennox's fashion magazines when her ladyship was done with them, but Philippa didn't know much about current fashions at all.

Beau escorted her into the brightly lit shop. The

sunlight poured in the bay windows, illuminating the roles of expensive silks and velvets. A glass display case held elaborately embroidered or bejeweled reticules. Kid gloves in various colors were displayed on a circular table and at the center were a trio of delicately woven poke bonnets.

Philippa touched her hair reflexively, the hastily fashioned chignon felt messy and only caused her further embarrassment.

"May I help you?" A young woman in a dark blue brocade gown approached them. Her eyes swept quickly over Philippa before alighting on Beau.

"Mr. Boudreaux! What a lovely surprise." The woman's smile was warm and open to Beau. Philippa wondered if the woman fancied herself in love with him.

"Jessica," he greeted. "How are you?"

"Wonderful. What brings you here?" She looked curiously at Philippa. Philippa glanced away, still self-conscious of her looks.

"I have charge of a new ward. This is Miss Philippa Wilson. She is the daughter of an old friend of mine who recently passed. As I am to be in charge of Miss Wilson until she is of age next year, we have need of a new wardrobe including the full array to prepare her for the usual rounds of balls and parties."

"Yes, of course. Come this way, my dear. I hope you're not too attached to this." Jessica plucked at one of the loose folds of the skirt of Mrs. Craddock's gown.

"No, but I do need to keep it so I may return it to a friend."

"Not a problem, Miss Wilson. Let's look at some of the ready-made gowns. Once you have something more suitable to wear immediately, I should like to create a full wardrobe for you."

Philippa's head was spinning as she followed the young dressmaker into a small changing room. Jessica assisted her in disrobing. It was so awkward for her to be on the opposite side of this treatment.

"You'll need corsets. I can recommend a shop just a few doors away." Jessica pursed her lips and brushed a stray wisp of blonde hair out of her face as she examined Philippa.

"What is it?" Philippa asked.

"Nothing... You're very lovely." Jessica sounded wistful. "We won't even have to bother with cosmetics. Your complexion is clear, your features quite perfect." She tapped her chin. "Remarkable, really. Most colors will work well on you, except perhaps yellow. Hardly anyone looks good in that." She tilted Philippa's chin up. "Gray eyes... Like diamonds beneath a still lake. I know just the thing." She exited the changing room.

Philippa stood still, shivering slightly after being so bundled up for so long in the woolen gown. When the dressmaker returned, she had several gowns tossed over her shoulder. "Let's try a few of these on and see if one fits."

It turned out they all fit. There was a riding habit in bishop's blue with white frogging on the jacket, an evening gown of Capuchin dark orange that seemed to change color in light and shadow. Two day gowns, one of dark Spanish green and the other a delicate willow green. There was an opera gown of carmine red that made Philippa blush. The last gown, though, was one that made the dressmaker gasp.

"This evening gown is a special piece. I designed it a few weeks ago but the client changed her mind, so I put it in the ready-made stack."

With Jessica's assistance, she tried on the gown. It was a silvery color called Nakara which Jessica explained was close to a pearl or the inside of a shell.

"There..." The dressmaker turned Philippa so she faced the mirror in the dressing room.

Philippa gasped, stunned to see a stranger in the glass. The pearlescent gown made her eyes glow, as though they channeled moonlight. Her curves were accentuated but not flaunted. For the first time in her life, she didn't feel ashamed of her beauty.

What would Beau think when he saw her like this? A hint of longing passed through her and she briefly closed her eyes, imagining what he might do... That he might hold her, whisper sweet words in her ear. That a woman dressed like this might deserve the attention of a man like him. Warmth gathered low in her belly and she placed a hand to her stomach, her face heating as she looked away from her reflection.

"Mr. Boudreaux will see this fine gown and he will see that the wearer is even finer," Jessica said with a satisfied smile. "But we won't let him see just yet. Let's put you back in that dark green gown while we complete your wardrobe."

Fifteen minutes later, Philippa left the changing room. Beau was leaning back against the wall, a trio of young ladies in the corner opposite him whispering and giggling. Beau watched them with an amused smile on his lips, but he made no move to speak with them.

Jealousy prickled at her and she shot the three woman a glare before walking to Beau. His focus shifted to her and the lazy amusement vanished. His mouth parted and he pushed away from the wall, his mouth wide open. Beau met her halfway in the center of the shop.

"Well now, Jess has done a fantastic job." He raised her chin, examining her face. Then his eyes swept down her body and Philippa's womb clenched as she recognized his clear interest as he studied her. "*Fantastic* job," he repeated.

You are safe with him, she reminded herself. But she couldn't help but wonder if perhaps she didn't want to be safe with him. Some risks might be worth it.

"We had quite a bit of success with our ready-made gowns," Jessica said. "I have her measurements and would be happy to compile a wardrobe now if you would like to peruse some of the fashion plates?"

Beau finally released Philippa's chin. "Yes, thank you."

Jessica shooed the trio of giggling girls the way one might scatter pigeons in the park. They fluttered off with renewed giggles and whispers, only to regroup near the display of kid gloves. Jessica opened several books on the table for Beau and Philippa to examine.

"Word will be out across London about Miss Wilson before dinner," Jessica warned Beau, casting a glower at the young ladies.

"I expect so." He seemed unbothered by it, which calmed Philippa a little. After all, it was the plan, wasn't it? Beau pulled a magazine of fashion plates over to her. "Philippa, look over these gowns."

"I honestly don't know what I need," she admitted. "I trust you to order the necessary things."

Beau frowned. "You should try to enjoy this. Most ladies do." His brown eyes, so rich in color, like honeyed ochre, distracted her from replying right away.

"Mr. Boudreaux... May I purchase a new gown for Mrs. Craddock? I will reimburse you for the cost." That mattered more to her, returning the innkeeper's wife's gown and sending a gift along with it since the innkeeper and his wife had been so helpful. Beau's expression softened and he smiled again, the fine lines around his eyes showing her he smiled often.

"That is an excellent idea. Jess, please use the

measurements from the gown Philippa brought in to make a new gown. A lovely day gown will do. Have it sent to this address with the old gown." Beau took a sheet of paper and pencil and scribbled down the Craddocks' address.

"I'll see it done. Miss Wilson, why don't you look at some gloves and boots? Mr. Boudreaux and I shall see to your wardrobe."

Relieved, Philippa abandoned the stacks of magazines. All the colors, fabrics and cuts made a painful pulse beat behind her eyes. She wandered about the shop, examining the fine feathered fans, running her fingers over the silky gray ostrich feathers.

After a moment she realized the three girls had come closer, creeping toward her as she looked about the shop.

"Excuse me," one of the girls asked. She was taller than the others with pale blonde hair and blue eyes. A fair beauty. Her two companions were just as pretty.

"Yes?" Philippa replied.

"Are you Mr. Boudreaux's mistress?"

"Pardon?" Philippa gasped. "I most certainly am not." Philippa could not believe the girl had asked her that. It was beyond the bounds of propriety to ask such a thing.

"I meant no offense!" The girl's guileless eyes were far too wide and innocent to be genuine.

"But, if you aren't his mistress..." One girl asked in a hushed whisper. "Then why are you here alone with him while he buys you a wardrobe?"

Philippa frowned at the girl as she remembered the details of her story.

"I am his new ward. My father recently passed, and I had no other living relatives, so I was sent to live with Mr. Boudreaux for a year."

"You must be too old to debut," the third girl said. "Between Mr. Boudreaux as your chaperone and your age, I'm afraid you don't stand a chance."

"Chance of what?" Philippa demanded.

"Finding a husband, of course." The first girl laughed. "What else can we mean?"

"Oh, I have no desire to marry," Philippa replied much to the horror of the other ladies.

"But... That's..." One of the girls stammered. She looked so baffled that Philippa almost laughed.

"What else is there? Marriage is essential," another of the girls replied. All three of them seemed quite mystified.

"She must be coming into a great inheritance," one whispered to the others.

"No, I am not, but marriage is far from the only option for a lady," Philippa said with an unexpected burst of confidence. "There's quite a bit out there for women, if one knows where to look. I think I might travel to the Americas, or perhaps to the West Indies. Maybe I shall join a pirate crew." By the looks of the astonishment on their faces she knew she'd gone too far in her teasing.

"Ladies, we should leave. It isn't suitable to be associating with someone so..." The girl in charge didn't bother to finish. The three of them paraded past her, noses in the air as if they couldn't bear the sight of her.

Beau and Jessica saw them leave and rejoined her.

"Chase the chits away, eh?" Beau teased.

"I suppose I did." She was a little embarrassed now. That was not how she should have conversed with them. It might reflect badly upon Beau.

"What on earth did you say to them? I should like to know if or when I wished to be free of their giggling nonsense."

"I..." Philippa didn't want to repeat what she had said.

"Come now, you can tell me." Beau's warm honey brown eyes tempted her.

"Oh, if you must know I told them I never wish to marry and that I wanted to run away to the Caribbean and join a pirate crew. I don't think they liked that idea at all."

Beau laughed and the smile that crinkled the corners of his eyes made her body hum with feminine awareness.

"A pirate crew? Heavens, you are a delight," he murmured before he turned to Jessica. "Please have everything packed and delivered to my townhouse in a few hours."

"Of course, Mr. Boudreaux." Jessica gave her a friendly wink. Philippa wasn't sure what to make of the modiste's friendliness. She'd expected the woman to be displeased at fitting gowns for a mere maid, but then, Jessica didn't know she was a maid. Perhaps that was it.

"Well, we've done enough for today." Beau put his top hat on. "Wouldn't you agree?"

Philippa nodded, eager to leave the street all the shops.

"Let me take you home then."

He escorted her to the coach and helped her inside. She wondered what danger still lay in store for them. The charade had only just begun, and as much as she trusted Lord Lennox, she'd been hurt twice now. Frankly, she saw no way any man could keep her safe.

8

Beau escorted his exhausted charge up the steps of his townhouse on Pall Mall. He glanced about casually as he did so, checking for any coaches lingering nearby or men watching from the corners of mews, but it was too early for that. He suspected it would take at least a day for word to spread, and for Monmouth's suspicions to be raised.

Pall Mall was composed of stately aristocratic dwellings, but if one journeyed east they would soon stumble into the slums of London. The impoverished were an ever present specter haunting the edges of the privileged sections of the city. Most of the ton pretended not to notice, but Beau did, and when possible, he offered coin to the hungry families he came across.

"Welcome back, sir." His butler, Rees Stoddard, shared a warm smile as he accepted Beau's hat.

"Thank you, Stoddard. Is Mrs. Gronow here? I must speak with you both."

Stoddard, a tall thin man in his forties, nodded. "I will bring her to your study."

"Yes, that would be good. Oh, and Stoddard, this is Miss Wilson."

"Miss." Stoddard bowed and then disappeared in the direction of the servants' stairs.

"What should I do?" Philippa asked. Every syllable she spoke was tinged with weariness.

"Stay with me for now. Once I've spoken to the staff, I'll have you shown to your chambers." He offered her his arm and she leaned a little more heavily on it as he escorted her up to his study.

She pointed at the dark blue velvet settee in one corner of the room. "May I sit?"

"Of course. Remember, you are a lady as long as you are here. You need never ask such things. You may send to the kitchens for food and drink at any time and you may have a bath prepared at your leisure."

"Thank you, Beau." She yawned and nearly collapsed into the small couch.

He sat at his desk and reviewed a few letters Stoddard had laid out for him. There was a soft knock on the door and his butler and housekeeper entered.

"Sir," Stoddard greeted. Beside him, Mrs. Gronow, a woman in her fifties, stood waiting for his orders. The pair had been running Beau's household since he was of age.

He knew he could trust them. He nodded for Stoddard to close the door to give them privacy.

"You know that I have no care for silly cloak and dagger nonsense, but it seems we have found ourselves in the midst of such a situation anyway."

"Oh?" Stoddard's eyes never left Beau's face, but he clearly knew their new guest was central to what he was talking about.

Beau gestured to Philippa. "This is Miss Philippa Wilson. Her parents own a textile shop on Bond Street and she's an upstairs maid to Lord Lennox."

"It's a pleasure to meet you," Philippa bowed her head respectfully. It was a measure of his butler and housekeeper's respect that they waited for him to continue his explanation without exchanging glances of concern.

"For reasons unknown, Miss Wilson was accosted at Lennox's home. A few days later, she was abducted by another man outside of Berkeley's Club. I was there at the time and was able to rescue her. But the reason behind these attacks remain a mystery. Lord Lennox and I decided it was in Miss Wilson's best interest for her to come home with me. She will pose as my ward, Philippa Wilson, a young woman from the country. We will say her father died, and she was sent to me to be looked after for the next year until she turns twenty-one."

"I see." Mrs. Gronow smoothed her hair back primly as she looked at Philippa more closely, though not unkindly. "She'll need a new wardrobe if she doesn't have one already."

"Already taken care of. Most of the dresses will arrive this afternoon."

"Louisa will suit you as a lady's maid, I think." Mrs. Gronow added to Philippa.

"Good, good," Beau replied. "Now, only you two will be entrusted with who she really is. Tell the rest of the staff only that she is my ward. I must ask you both to be cautious. Share nothing with the others in the house unless you know that they can be trusted. Ms. Wilson's life will be in danger until we discover why she's being targeted."

"Sir, if I may ask, who were the men who perpetuated the earlier attacks?" Stoddard asked.

"The Earl of Monmouth and Viscount Sommers. From what I've learned, Sommers was engaged by Monmouth to abduct and murder her after Monmouth's attempt failed."

"Good heavens!" Mrs. Gronow covered her mouth as she looked at Philippa. "Poor child. You must be in quite a state!"

"Thank you. I'm fine though," Philippa whispered, her face red with mortification. The bruising on her neck was still visible in faint, haunting, yellow strips and her jaw still had a reddish mark from where Sommers had struck her.

"She's quite tired," Beau added. "She saved my life after Sommers shot me in the back."

"My word!" Stoddard exclaimed.

"He saved me first!" Philippa added hastily over their gasps, as if her brave act was some sort of faux pas that had to be explained.

"You've been shot?" Mrs. Gronow clutched her bosom. "We must send for a doctor."

Beau almost laughed but that would only have upset his housekeeper. "Now, now be at ease Mrs. Gronow. I have already been seen to. As I'm sure you can surmise, the wound was minor. You didn't even notice when I returned."

Stoddard's eyes sharpened. "Your shoulder?"

"Yes. In the back, more precisely." He shrugged out of his coat, wincing a little, though in truth he wanted to roar like a wounded bear. "See?" He moved the injured arm and his servants watched him with worry.

"So..." Mrs. Gronow continued. "Miss Wilson is to remain here as your ward?"

"Yes. I plan to introduce her to society. We need her visible and public, so that Monmouth and Sommers will have all their attention focused on her."

"Isn't that dangerous, sir?" Stoddard inquired.

"It is, but Lennox believes that being so public with her will in fact put them on guard. They will suspect it's a trap, and yet have no choice but to keep an eye on her at all times. Still, the longer we play this game, the more likely they will risk taking action. If we have not learned Monmouth's motives within a week, we may need to relocate her again for safety. Miss Wilson is never to be unaccompanied when she leaves this house."

"Of course, sir," Stoddard replied and squared his shoulders.

"Now, Miss Gronow, I think we should take Miss Wilson up to her new chambers."

"I would be happy to take her up myself, should you wish to rest yourself," Mrs. Gronow replied.

"No, that's all right. I don't mind. She is my guest, after all."

"Your ward, sir," Stoddard reminded.

"Quite right." He came out from behind his desk and Philippa followed. As they climbed the stairs, he watched the way Philippa's eyes widened as she saw Boudreaux Hall in all its glory. Many well-to-do young men had bachelor residences that served as quaint little places to sleep at night while they were out carousing in the town. But Beau was in his mid-thirties, well-settled and his taste in art and architecture were clearly defined.

The admiration he saw upon Philippa's face was gratifying. His architecture was Palladian with Corinthian columns of warm sand-colored Italian marble. Rather than tapestries, he had large paintings of ancient landscapes or scenes from Roman mythology in ornate gilded frames. Every piece here had meaning to him. Philippa looked his way, unspoken questions in her eyes. There would be time for that later.

"Miss Wilson, this is your room. The master calls it

the Leda room." Mrs. Gronow opened the door and left them alone after Beau gave her a small nod.

Philippa walked ahead of them into the feminine bedchamber. "The Leda room?"

He had a rule never to bring mistresses here, but he couldn't seem to live in a townhouse that did not have at least one feminine bed chamber prepared, in case he ever changed his mind.

The bed was a four poster with lion paws at the feet of the four posts. The two chairs by the fireplace and the chaise at the foot of the bed all had distinctive lyre shapes in their chair backs and supports. All of the pieces were made of rosewood which blended elegantly with the heavy gilt on each piece of furniture. Above the headboard hung a large painting of a beautiful woman wearing a sheer pale blue tunic. A white swan was nestled against her, its head rested on her breasts, the bird's eyes half closed as the woman stroked it snowy feathers.

"Leda and the Swan." Philippa spun to face him, her cheeks reddening. "That's Zeus, yes?"

"Yes." Zeus was far from an admirable character, in Beau's opinion, but had to admit that the story of a god taking on such a vulnerable mortal form to be with the woman he craved was intriguing. No one ever thought about stories where gods made a sacrifice or took a risk for a mortal. There was a part of Beau that always wondered what it meant to be in love with a person so much that you would risk everything for them. The idea terrified him as much as it captivated him.

"The painting is very pretty," Philippa said.

"You are familiar with the story?"

"Yes. My mother read me mythology when I was a young girl. She insisted I should be schooled far above what she had been. She even had a tutor for some of the sciences and mathematics. I can't imagine how she managed to afford those lessons."

"Parents can achieve amazing things when it's done for their children," he said.

His mother had done everything in her power to see him raised happy and healthy, but she'd died when he was eighteen. If it hadn't been for her and the Duke of St. Albans, he never would have become the man he was today.

Philippa bit her bottom lip. Her dark hair was a loose tumble of waves down her shoulders. Beau reached up to brush the locks with the backs of his fingers. She shivered as she drew in a quick breath.

He withdrew his hand. "I'm sorry." But her eyes had met his and he saw no fear there, only desire. After everything that had happened to her, he hadn't expected to her to respond to him that way. Yet the look in those lightning-silver colored eyes told him she was not like other women he'd known. She was fierce in her own way. Like a brave lioness.

"No... It's only that..." Philippa reached to touch her hair where his hand had been moments before.

"Only what?" He pressed closer, wanting to know what this dark-maned lioness would say.

"*You*. You make me feel so strange. Half dizzy, half excited. No man has ever made me feel that way. I confess I do not know what to do."

"You need not do anything. You are safe in this house and I have no expectations. You need only to"

He promptly forgot whatever he meant to say because she grabbed his neck cloth and pulled his head to hers to cover his lips with her own.

Beau was startled by the rush of desire that swept through him like an inferno. He wanted to hold her and never let go, to drink of her lips forever. But he couldn't move. Some last sensible bit of him dug its invisible hands into his frayed self-control. Her lips were soft, and he groaned as his hand spanned her waist. She felt so small in his hold, so delicate, and he felt a protectiveness build within him, a desire to shield her from the world and all that might harm her. Their breath mixed in the half-darkened room and he was overcome by the quiet intimacy of the fire crackling in the hearth and the feel of her trembling body against his as the heat of their shared passion grew.

Her gentle lips released him, and she spun away, offering a dozen silly apologies. And all he could do was stand there and dream foolishly of where that kiss could have led and the potent magic that seemed trapped within Philippa. The magic he feared to pursue, let alone believe in.

"I am terribly sorry, Mr. Boudreaux... I... I have no excuse. I was not myself... I... thought... I don't know what I thought..."

He caught her arm and spun her back into his embrace. She gasped as she collided with him. Her palms settled on his chest as he held her close.

"One should never apologize for a kiss as sweet as that," he said as gently as he could.

"Never?"

"Never." He lowered his head to whisper.

"But it's inappropriate of me to..."

"Inappropriate? Perhaps. But these are trying times for you, and such stresses find odd ways of coming out. Kept bottled up, it no doubt would be harmful."

"But I am just a maid and you..."

"Nonsense. A release is healthy, and I am more than willing to oblige, within reason." Then he added in a seductive purr. "But be warned, each time you steal one from me, I will steal one in return. Unless you wish for me to let you go?"

"One stolen kiss," she whispered back in agreement. That was all he needed. He held her tight in his arms, one hand exploring the hollow of her back, the green satin gown was smooth beneath his wandering fingers. Philippa relaxed into him and her arms draped around his neck as he claimed her mouth with an urgency that stunned her.

It was as though he'd never kissed a woman before, as if this taste of exquisite passion was his very first. He worried he would be drunk upon it. He licked the seam of her lips and they parted for him. When he flicked his tongue against hers, she became almost boneless in his arms. It seemed as if the kiss had the same effect on her and a gloriously uncontrollable force was sweeping through them both. He felt that the mere touch of her would make him catch fire, that the sight or scent of her would make him mindless with need.

I should leave this room... but I can't. The thought was soon buried by others infinitely more wonderful. He softened his kiss, letting his mouth dance over hers in a whisper and it made him shiver straight down to his soul. His mind filled with dreams of her, carrying her to the bed, stripping her down to her skin and covering every inch with kisses.

She was all that he could think about, all he could focus on. There was nothing outside this room. Nothing beyond this kiss. He surrendered to her, to the feel of her hands in his hair. Her mouth nibbled at his lips as she taught herself to kiss him in a dozen different ways.

I have died... He thought. *I have died and this is some secret place in heaven that she is sharing with me.*

"*Love is an ever burning fire, a glimpse of heaven. To lose it is to die...*" His father's words came back to him across the decades, a haunting reminder of the devastating power of love.

And just like that... His father's face intruded upon the sweetness. The solemn look of heartbreak as his father left to meet his fate. His mother's sobs as she read his final letter. The agony in St. Albans eyes as he spoke of his deceased daughter.

To lose it is to die...

All those lives were lost or destroyed by love.

Beau jerked back from Philippa. Her arms fell to her sides as she panted, her eyes over bright.

"That...that should be sufficient. Don't you think?" He tried to act casual, as if he'd simply been helping relieve her of the fears she carried. "I...should go."

He all but fled the room, but it was too late. He would never forget Philippa's taste, or the way she responded to his kiss. He could almost hear the bells ringing out his doom. Each heavy *bong* screamed "run...run..." But he feared he wouldn't escape whatever fate held in store for him, and that terrified him most of all.

Philippa raised her fingertips to her lips and fought off tears. What had she done? She'd been a fool. A foolish girl. Needing to be comforted, she'd thrown herself at Beau, just to feel his arms around her and then she'd kissed him.

But when he kissed her back, she'd realized her grave mistake in judgment. What he'd done, what he'd *shown* her in that second kiss, was like nothing she'd ever dreamed. It was not the kiss of a man trying to take what she didn't wish to give. Nor was it a dry chaste kiss of a father or friend. She had felt *him*, his heart and soul in those few moments, and she sensed he'd meant to let her see that part of him.

As he fled the room, she tried to regain her breath and coiled her loose hair over one shoulder as the tremors inside her finally subsided.

It was clear kissing her had upset him. He might be one of those men who preferred not to romance servants. If that was the case, she wished she hadn't just thrown herself at him like some ninny. She could have no expectations from him. He was a gentleman, the son of a French Marquis.

And I am only the upstairs maid he rescued as a favor to my master.

The was first time she'd tasted something more, something she never thought she wanted, and now she would never get it, at least not in an honorable way.

Philippa moved to the bed and brushed her fingers over the fine sapphire blue coverlet. When she looked up at the painting of Leda and the swan, she saw something of herself in the woman holding a transformed God close to her heart. One could only hold onto that irresistible mythical being for so long before they had to let go. Gods and mortals could never be together, just as gentleman and servants could not.

She lay back on the bed and closed her eyes. That night she was plagued with dreams. Dreams of a woman whispering her name and the furious threatening voice of a stranger... A stranger that seemed all too familiar now.

Lord Monmouth was haunting her, even in her sleep.

❧ 9 ❧

Beau stood in the center of his bedchamber down the hall from Philippa. He held his breath held as he replayed the kisses that never should have happened, yet he could not bring himself to regret.

His young valet, Freddie, was muttering about the quality of the borrowed shirt that belong to Mr. Craddock. But the valet's mutterings went ignored as Beau stared bare chested out the windows facing the gardens behind his home. He couldn't seem to shake the vision of kissing Philippa back out of his head. He'd encouraged the kiss, and the sweetness of it all had left him in a wonderful daze. It was as though he'd glimpsed an endless garden and the sweet smell of an eternal spring had filled him until he became almost drunk upon her kisses.

Had kissing any of his mistresses ever been like that? No. Why was this woman so different? Perhaps it was those gray eyes of hers which seemed to be as pure as silver or as mercurial as winter storms. It was one more part of the mystery of her. Yet he feared she would pull him deeper and deeper with every kiss as he tried to uncover those mysteries. The magic she wove around them would not fade over time. The more he came to know Philippa, the more he wanted her. It would never be enough.

"Sir?" Freddie cut in.

"Yes?" He turned to face his valet, who held up his waistcoat and pushed his finger through the bullet hole.

"I don't think I can salvage this, sir." the valet confessed.

"That's all right, Freddie. Just fetch me a new one"

"Of course, sir." Freddie folded the up destroyed waistcoat and set it aside before he laid out a fresh pair of buckskin trousers, shirt and pale blue satin waistcoat.

Once he'd dressed and pulled his coat and top-boots on, Freddie helped him tie his simple yet elegant cravat.

"Taking a bullet..." Freddie muttered. "Ruining clothes, bringing home strange young ladies... What the devil will be next?"

The young man pursed his lips as he ran a brush over Beau's coat and then nodded to himself, finally satisfied with Beau's appearance. Freddie's father had been Beau's valet for nearly ten years and had only recently retired. Poor Freddie, while just as dedicated to his job as his father had been, was not quite so used to the unpre-dictability of a bachelor's existence.

"I take it you do not approve of my adventures, Fred-die?" He couldn't resist teasing the young man.

"Certainly not at the cost of one's wardrobe," the valet said flatly. "Am I to be cleaning blood out of your waist-coats from duels next?" This last was muttered but Beau still heard it.

"Not to worry, Freddie, I have not dueled in at least six months."

The young valet's eyes flashed, and Beau chuckled as the young man continued to fuss with his coat.

"What's the talk downstairs?" Beau asked.

"The talk?"

"Yes, about my ward." He was curious to see if the rest of his staff had heard Stoddard and Gronow's story.

The valet did not answer. He turned away and focused on sorting Beau's collection of snuff boxes inside a large wooden box with a glass lid. Beau walked over and gently pressed the lid down, removing the distraction from his valet.

"Freddie..."

"It's not for me to... I don't think you would wish to hear, sir."

"That bad, eh?" Beau chuckled. "Well, out with it."

"They believe she's a mistress, a new one. Some say you've run through all the opera singers and ballet dancers and now you've gone searching for women in the country."

"Goodness...that does sound bad." Beau was torn between laughing and shaking his head.

"I don't agree," Freddie continued quickly. "With what they are saying, I mean."

"I wouldn't hold it against you if you did." Beau patted the young man's shoulder. "Now fetch my hat. I have a call to pay this afternoon."

Freddie presented Beau's top hat to him as he left his bedchamber. He went to Philippa's room and eased the door open. It was quiet and dark, except for the fire in the hearth. Louisa, the maid Mrs. Gronow had assigned, must have added in fresh logs.

Beau searched the room and found Philippa in bed, asleep. He set his hat down outside the door, then quickly tiptoed into the room and retrieved a spare blanket from a tall wardrobe. He unfolded the blanket and covered her with it.

"I made a promise to keep you safe, even from me," he said, too softly to wake her. He left the room and retrieved his hat, then told Stoddard his destination.

In a matter of minutes, he stood at the threshold of St. Albans's home with his hand poised over the door's knocker. He drew a deep breath and lifted the brass ring. The duke's butler, Mr. Jarvis, answered.

"Is His Grace in?"

The butler smiled. "For you, sir? Always." Jarvis stepped back and allowed Beau inside the palatial home. Beau passed his hat to the nearest footman.

"His Grace is in the library," the butler informed him.

"Thank you, Jarvis."

Beau went up the white marble stairs and down a long quarter until he reached the expansive library of the Duke of St. Albans. The duke was seated at a reading table with a quizzing glass held up to one eye as he peered at the text. He cursed to himself and reached for a pair of spectacles, tucking the quizzing glass back into his pocket. Then he nested the spectacles over his nose and examined the book more closely.

"Your Grace," Beau said softly. The duke glanced up and his concentrating frown dissipated.

"Ah, my boy, what brings you by?"

"I wished to ask you something."

"Ask away, my boy. I was only reading. Or trying to."

"Anything worth recommending?" Beau asked as he examined the reading table.

"Keats. You know how much I love the fellow."

Beau did indeed. As a younger man, he'd had trouble dealing with the death of his mother. St. Albans had sat with him out by the lake and recited Keats's "Ode on Melancholy" and it had given him a new perspective on the world around him.

"But when the melancholy fit shall fall
Sudden from heaven like a weeping cloud,
That fosters the droop-headed flowers all,
And hides the green hill in an April shroud;
Then glut thy sorrow on a morning rose,

Or on the rainbow of the salt sand-wave,
Or on the wealth of globed peonies."

Those words had given him some peace in the second set of dark days that Beau had faced. He owed so much to St. Albans, and here he was about to cause more pain.

"I've been thinking about Albina," Beau said.

The duke closed his book and removed his reading spectacles. "Albina? Why?"

"May I see her portrait again?" Beau had to be sure the resemblance between her and Philippa Wilson was not something he'd imagined.

The duke, clearly curious, led him to the portrait gallery. They stood silently before it. Beau's heart raced as he took in the details of the woman trapped within the oils and compared them to Philippa. She could have been an identical twin to the woman in the portrait. Any differences between them were so minute they were not worth mentioning.

"Why are you here?" The duke asked.

"To see you," Beau replied.

The duke touched his shoulder, pulling Beau's focus away from the painting.

"No, why are you *here?*" St. Albans emphasized with a nod toward Albina's portrait.

Beau could feel the eyes of the dead woman on him. Her gaze from the past was frozen in time upon the canvas, yet no less powerful than when the portrait artist had painted her.

"Best if I do not talk about it. The last thing I wish to do is cause you pain, Your Grace," Beau said. "And I believe my reason for coming here would do so."

His old friend glanced between him and the painting. "It has something to do with Albina?"

"Not directly, but yes." The resemblance was beyond uncanny. No wonder Lord Monmouth had reacted so violently to seeing Philippa. She was a mirror for Albina.

The duke met his gaze with a serenity Beau hadn't expected. "My boy, I doubt there is much anyone can do to add to my pain."

"Then I shall tell you a story," Beau began, still uncertain this was the right thing to do.

"I'm the one who usually tells the stories," St. Albans joked, but Beau had no humor left in him

"It begins with an upstairs maid who had an unexpected and dangerous meeting with an earl..."

After he had told St. Albans the details of Philippa's misadventures, the duke stroked his chin. "So, my son-in-law tried to strangle this poor girl?"

"Yes." Beau forced his gaze to stay away from Albina's portrait.

"But you have no idea why?"

"Theories only, with no facts to support them. Is it a possibility that Albina's death might not have been an accident? I think perhaps the maid reminded Monmouth of your daughter."

"Possible? I suppose...I didn't arrive in time to see her

except to attend the funeral. Monmouth allowed only a quick ceremony, and no one examined the body that I was aware of. I heard only from him that she'd bled out during childbirth." St. Albans frowned. "You think he might have killed my daughter and somehow this girl brought up memories from the past?"

Beau nodded. "It could explain Monmouth's unexpected attack as a crime of passion. Then once he realized his mistake, he let rational planning prevail and hired Sommers to obtain the girl. But I stopped Sommers from fulfilling his plans. Sommers must be equally as desperate to kill her because he shot me in the bloody back to stop our departure."

"What?" St. Albans stared at him in horror. "You were shot?" His eyes darted over Beau, seeking evidence of any injury. It amused Beau that everyone reacted so wildly to that announcement.

"'Tis only a scratch. A doctor patched me up."

"Bullets don't leave *scratches*, my boy." St. Albans muttered. "I took a bloody bullet in my leg at Waterloo. Luckily, it was easily removed, but I limped on a cane for nearly five years until I managed to push myself to walk unaided."

"I had no idea, Your Grace."

"There's much about my past you do not know, but those are discussions for another day. Now, what are your theories about the girl?"

Beau steadied himself but perhaps if he dealt the blow

quickly that would be best. "We know only that the lady is a threat to Monmouth."

"But how? I cannot see how a maid Cornelius doesn't know would upset him to the point of attempted murder."

"Of that I have no idea, but the maid looks exactly like your daughter."

"But Albina is..."

"Yes, gone." Beau dragged a hand through his hair. "Did your late wife have any relatives? Perhaps the lady has some blood relation?"

"No. My wife had no other relations still living. No distant cousins even. I'm still confused. Beau, this girl, she cannot really look like Albina, can she?"

"That's why I came here. I needed to see the portrait again. I was hoping I'd imagined the physical resemblance, but I haven't."

St. Albans stroked his chin. "Cornelius has a guilty conscience, perhaps?"

"I'd wondered something similar. Their resemblance may be a coincidence, yet Monmouth might have thought it was Albina's spirit come back to haunt him."

"Fear would explain such a thoughtless lashing out... yet I find it hard to imagine that man has any conscience to torture. I want to see this girl at once," St. Albans announced.

Beau had expected this reaction. "Tonight, dinner at my home. She's resting this afternoon."

"Is it proper to have this woman at your home? You are a bachelor, after all..."

"Lennox and I have concocted a story to protect her. As far as anyone knows, she is my ward."

The duke turned pensive. "Why didn't Lennox keep her?"

"Given the danger, it was best for her to stay with me. I have no wife or young children to endanger should Monmouth make a play for her again."

"You could always send her here. I can look after her." The hope in St. Albans tone made Beau's chest tighten.

"Your Grace, I didn't wish to burden you with this. Albina is gone, taking in this young lady would not bring her back."

The duke flashed him a frown. "I am old, Beau. I have no granddaughters. Perhaps this woman is my chance to spoil someone. I adore Roddy—thank God that boy doesn't take after his father—but it's far less amusing to spoil a boy than a girl."

"Even if you wish to, I cannot give her up," Beau said.

St. Albans eyes narrowed. "You are interested in her. What of your mistress? The opera singer?"

"Please, Your Grace. This is not the time to talk about such things. This girl is still in danger. I must keep her under my watch until Lennox and I can expose Monmouth. In the meanwhile, I will not let the girl endanger anyone but me."

The duke clapped a hand on Beau's shoulder. "All the

same, I would love to meet her tonight. In fact, bring her here."

"Dinner with a duke, that might terrify the poor creature," Beau mused.

"Nonsense. Your plan requires her to socialize, does it not? You might as well start with a private affair with someone you consider a friend rather than a large party of complete strangers. Besides, women are the braver sex. It's no wonder you haven't married if you haven't realized that." The duke shook his head with a wry smile. "Now, no more protests. Bring her here at eight tonight and let me look this child."

"Very well. But remember, I wished to keep this pain away from you."

"And I appreciate that, but pain is a part of life. Without pain, a man never appreciates pleasure."

Beau looked upon Albina's portrait once more. But this time he saw not a dead woman, but Philippa, alive and smiling. Happy, safe. Fear swept through him, raking his soul. Keats's poem about melancholy returned to him and he murmured the stanza aloud.

"She dwells with Beauty—Beauty that must die;
And Joy, whose hand is ever at his lips
Bidding adieu; and aching Pleasure nigh,
Turning to poison while the bee-mouth sips:
Ay, in the very temple of Delight
Veil'd Melancholy has her sovran shrine,
Though seen of none save him whose strenuous tongue

Can burst Joy's grape against his palate fine;
His soul shalt taste the sadness of her might,
And be among her cloudy trophies hung."

The duke's eyes went bright. "Keats understood. Pain, pleasure, hate, love, sorrow, joy, they are all part of the same ineffable equation. Whenever I feel weary and my heart cold, I read Keats and am reminded that we all have our journeys, some long, other short, and it's up to us to brave the rise and falls that come with this glorious thing called life."

Beau's throat constricted as he looked at the older man, so much unsaid resting upon his lips. "You're a good man, Your Grace." That was all he could say. Pain from the past, love from the past, all threatened to choke him from further speech.

"As are you, *my boy.*" He emphasized the last two words, and this time in them he heard a father's love. It made his heart ache in a way it hadn't in years.

"Now, off you go. And bring that girl to dinner this evening."

Beau left St. Albans's home, feeling more lost than ever, yet he didn't feel alone. He was torn between an older man's fatherly affection and a young woman's budding passion and trust. Love would come and he could not escape it or the pain it would cause him and everyone around him. The very pain he had tried to avoid from the day his father died.

❦ 10 ❧

Philippa stirred at the sound of someone moving about in the room. She opened her eyes and saw a curvy maid bent over the hearth, adding a few logs. Even though it was October, the weather had been warm until the last few weeks. Now Philippa welcomed the heat of a fire. She sat up and a blanket fell off her body. She stared at it, puzzled. She hadn't remembered going to sleep with that over her. The maid must have done it.

"Hello," Philippa greeted.

The maid spun, her curly red hair escaping her cap. "Oh! Pardon me, miss. I didn't mean to wake you."

"It's fine. Thank you for the blanket." She removed the blanket and folded it.

"Oh, that wasn't me, miss."

"Oh." Philippa frowned slightly. She wondered who had. "I'm Philippa, by the way."

"Louisa, miss."

"It's nice to meet you, Louisa. Please, I insist you call me Philippa." She knew only too well how ingrained it was in the service to use the correct forms of address, and Louisa had been told she was a lady from the country. But Philippa desperately needed a friend if she was to endure this, so she would insist the maid learn to say her given name.

"Philippa," Louisa's freckled face deepened with a blush.

"What time is it?"

"A little after six in the evening."

"Heavens! I've slept the day away!" Philippa struggled out of the warm confines of the ornate bed.

"The master told me to let you sleep. He's been worried about you." Louisa opened a tall Rosewood armoire and began unpacking the dress boxes on the floor.

Philippa recognized the ready-made gowns from the modiste. She had truly overslept if the clothing had arrived. She had only meant to take a brief nap.

"Do you wish to bathe before dinner with the duke?" Louisa asked calmly as she worked.

"The duke?" Philippa's voice came out an octave higher than usual.

The maid turned to face her. "The Duke of St. Albans. He and the master are very close. He's like a second father to Mr. Boudreaux. Practically raised the master as young man, or so I've heard."

The Duke of St. Albans. She had heard of him. The duke was a good and kind man and the Lennox family liked him immensely.

"Is there a reason we are to dine with him?" Philippa asked as Louisa pulled a bell cord to summon the footmen.

"None that I know of. The master dines with him at least once a week, when he isn't with his..." Louisa didn't finish her sentence.

"With who?" Philippa asked.

"Oh, I shouldn't tell. It isn't my place." The maid hedged.

"Please, Louisa," Philippa begged.

"His... mistress. Although..." The maid's face reddened. "Mrs. Gronow was saying to Mr. Stoddard that the master has gone his separate way from his latest mistress a few days ago."

Was that when he pulled away from her? Was he still pining for his former mistress?

"I don't know if it's true. He's been with so many over the years. He's likely looking for his next lady if that's the case." Louisa opened the bedchamber door for a pair of footmen carrying buckets. One of them tripped when he caught sight of Philippa. He was young, perhaps her age, and his face turned a deep ruddy red.

"My apologies, miss. Please forgive me." He recovered and poured the remaining water into the tub in the adjoining room before rushing back to mop up the spilled water with a cloth.

"Don't mind Tobias. He's shy around pretty ladies." Louisa smirked and Philippa couldn't help but laugh a little as she smiled at Toby, which only made him stumble again as he tried to leave.

Louisa gave an amused sigh. "Oh dear, it's going to take them ages at this rate to fill your tub."

But in truth, it only took fifteen minutes until she was sinking into a hot bath. The large copper tub had a tall back which went above her head by several inches. She'd never really bathed like this before. She and Ruth shared a shallow tub and they managed lukewarm baths at best. It was simply too difficult to get hot water when the footmen had no time to assist them. Now she leaned back and almost groaned in delight as the water heated her tired, aching limbs.

"Soaps and perfumes?" Louisa offered.

Philippa accepted it all, feeling a measure of guilt as she knew she shouldn't be indulging herself like this. She felt like a fraud. But it was so nice to be cared for after all this time as a servant caring for others.

Once she was washed and feeling fresh, she dried off and watched Louisa sort through her gowns.

"How about this one? It would look stunning with your eyes and coloring." She displayed the silver evening gown that Jessica had sold her.

"Yes, if you think so," she replied.

"I do. You should wear these with it." Louisa displayed a pair of silver slippers that were embroidered with bolts of lightning. Another clever choice that Jessica had offered.

"These would be perfect," Philippa agreed.

When it was nearly a quarter to eight, Philippa was fully dressed in the silk satin gown and the silver slippers. Her hair had been pulled back in a loose Grecian style and while ringlets around one's face were more in fashion, Louisa had said such a style would spoil Philippa's natural beauty.

When Philippa had seen herself in the mirror, a lady she didn't recognize stood before her. A strange pulse of excitement and dread shot through her. It felt as though someone had trod across her grave. The eerie feeling only dissipated as she turned away from the mirror and focused on Louisa's instructions about being in the presence of a duke.

"Remember, it's *Your Grace*."

"Yes," she echoed, remembering from years ago when she'd learned the proper modes of address. She was relieved, however, that Louisa had guessed she lacked the knowledge that most ladies would have about things like seating arrangements and conversation topics. Apparently, very little was acceptable for women to discuss with men. The weather and social gossip—such dull choices!

When she felt ready, she walked down the corridor and paused at the top of the stairs. Was this truly happening?

Was she really going to attend a dinner at the duke's home masquerading as a lady?

Beau and Mr. Stoddard stood in the foyer below her. She watched them unobserved for a moment. The butler was listening intently to Beau. They spoke in low tones but suddenly Stoddard said something, and Beau burst into laughter. It lit up his face and for a moment Philippa forgot to breathe.

She remembered his lips on hers, felt them conquer her body and soul. She was entranced by the sight of him, but it also sent fear skittering through her. Because of her looks, she lived her life in dread of what men wanted from her and what they might do to get it. She'd never once considered how she would feel about a man like Beau in return.

Stoddard noticed her and cleared his throat. To Beau, he gave a little jerk of his head in her direction. When Beau looked upon her, his face quickly paled.

"Ghost..." The word seemed to echo as she descended the stairs toward him. He quickly recovered and reached for his neck cloth, tugging at it slightly.

"You look..." But he was unable to finish his thought.

"Exquisite?" Stoddard offered just behind Beau.

"Yes... Exquisite seems to be the only word one could think of, but it somehow doesn't seem to be enough." He twirled a finger. "Turn around, let me see."

She picked up her skirts in one hand and spun in a slow circle.

Beau nodded. "Yes... Yes, Jessica did well... You look..." He caught himself and whatever he'd been about to say. "Well, let's fetch a cloak for you and we'll be off. You don't mind walking, I assume? It's only at the other end of the street."

"Not at all," she assured him. Honestly, she would have walked across town if he'd asked. She loved to be outdoors and move about. She'd just had so few opportunities while in service.

Stoddard had a footman fetch her new cloak, a lovely dark blue velvet with a white ermine trim. She put it on and left her hood down as she followed Beau to the door.

The night was cold but not unbearable. It was the perfect temperature to make one wish to move more briskly. She held her hands in her ermine muff as she kept pace with Beau who, despite his long lean legs, made his strides considerably short while still appearing natural. He must have walked often with women to have perfected such a skill. Louisa's comments about his mistresses came back and she frowned.

"What's bothering you?" Beau asked, intruding upon her thoughts.

"Oh, 'tis nothing."

"You need not always close the door to me, Philippa. I hope you remember that."

"Close the door? What do you mean?"

He exhaled a weary side. "To your thoughts. You shut me out, but you need not."

"Oh…" She hadn't meant to do that, but since she'd gone into service, she'd gotten used to keeping her own counsel. Not everyone liked a pretty girl. In the past, other servants had hurt her feelings when should she'd dared to share her thoughts. It was simply safer not to open her mouth unless necessary. Lord Lennox's home had been different. She'd been welcomed there far more than she ever could have expected.

"I'm not certain you would wish to hear my thoughts," she finally replied.

"I won't be upset if you're honest with me. We are to be together for a time, and I wish for you to feel comfortable being yourself around me."

Philippa doubted that, but she took the chance anyway. "I was thinking about your mistresses. You keep pace with me so effortlessly. You must have learned that while walking with them."

"Ahh," Beau chuckled. "So, you've heard about my sterling character?"

"Oh! I didn't mean any offense." Panic shortened her breath.

"I'm teasing. I have had mistresses, a number of them over the years. But I do not have one now. Does that make you feel more at ease?"

Philippa didn't look at him. "I never said I was ill at ease." She kept her gaze on the moonlit houses.

"Then what worries you?"

"*Nothing,*" she said firmly, letting him know she had no intention of speaking anymore on the subject.

"Very well. Here we are." They reached one of the larger houses on Pall Mall Street and walked up the steps. The door opened for them as they arrived.

"Evening Jarvis," Beau greeted the man who faced them.

"Please come in, Mr. Boudreaux. Miss Wilson." It was clear that even the duke's butler adored Beau. The man was beaming as if he was an old friend.

"His Grace is excited about dinner. He's talked of little else since you left this afternoon," Jarvis said.

Beau's solemn expression brightened. "That's good to hear. I was worried I left him in rather poor spirits."

Philippa surrendered her cloak and muff and before accepting Beau's offered arm as he escorted her deeper into the beautiful house. Where Beau's home was warm with hints of Italy and Greece, this palatial house was more reserved with white marble and old English tapestries. There was a more mysterious feel to this place compared to Beau's home, which beckoned one in with its promised wealth of exotic adventures. Philippa wondered what the duke was like. Would he reflect his home in style and manner the way Beau so clearly did his?

"His Grace is in the drawing room," said Jarvis.

"Thank you." Beau led her down a corridor lined with portraits. She felt his body tense, but he said nothing until they had passed through into another corridor. She kept her gaze on the floor, an unexpected tension building within her as well.

"The duke is a kind man. Do not be afraid of him."

Philippa nodded, but she was still nervous. Beau ushered her into the drawing room, where she saw a figure standing facing the fireplace with one hand resting upon the tall marble hearth.

"Your Grace," Beau said, announcing the two of them.

The Duke of St. Albans looked their way and Philippa's breath stopped somewhere between her lungs and her lips. The man before her...she was certain they'd never met, and yet it was as if she knew him. The duke's silver gray eyes mirrored hers and there was something about the way he stared at her that made her lips tremble. How could a total stranger affect her so?

"Your Grace, allow me to present Miss Philippa Wilson to you." Beau had to tug her to get her feet to uproot themselves from the floor.

She dipped into a curtsy, her hands shaking. "Your Grace."

The duke beckoned her closer. "Come here, Miss Wilson. Come closer to the light. My eyes aren't what they used to be."

She released Beau's arm and moved toward St. Albans until she was next to the warm, crackling fire. The duke's silver eyes moved slowly over her face, his expression solemn, perhaps even perplexed. He seemed to be seeking something within her features, but she didn't know what.

"My God, Beau, she's..." He faltered and his voice roughened with unexplained emotions. Was he responding to her beauty as other men did? No. There was no lust in his eyes. There was desire, but not of an amorous kind. It was more like *wonderment*. A need to understand what his eyes were taking in.

"I told you, Your Grace." Beau offered Philippa a small smile of encouragement.

"You did, but I didn't believe you."

"Pardon me, but what are you talking about?" Philippa broke into the conversation.

The duke looked at her. His eyes were gentle in a way that made her heart still.

"You look exactly like my daughter."

"Your daughter? You mean...?" She looked to Beau. "Monmouth's wife?"

Beau nodded.

"Yes," St. Albans said with venom in his voice. "That cad took the best part of my life from me. She deserved better"

Shock left her speechless. She shot her gaze to Beau, searching silently for answers.

"Perhaps we ought to show her," Beau volunteered.

"Indeed." The duke held out his arm to her and she accepted it, still completely astonished.

They took her to the portrait gallery. Both men stopped in a darkened corner.

"Bring the light," the duke called out. A footman soon

brought them a candelabra. The duke held the candle aloft and gestured to a painting.

Philippa barely controlled her gasp of surprise as she glimpsed the figure reclined on a settee in the portrait— none other than herself. Yet she knew she'd never posed for such a portrait in her life. The woman in the painting wore a silver gown and she had laughing gray eyes and a mischievous smile. She was an ageless beauty that went beyond her features. It was clear, whoever this woman was, she was full of fire and life in a way Philippa had never felt. So this was Lord Monmouth's wife...St. Albans's daughter.

"The ghost..." She remembered Beau's pain-induced whisper from when he lay on the ground after being shot.

How is this possible?

"She was your daughter?"

"Her name was Albina." The duke patted Philippa's arm gently. "She died twenty years ago this month."

Albina, her mirrored reflection caught in oil in and canvas had been dead for as long as she'd been alive. Goosebumps prickled over her skin and the fine hairs rose on the back of her neck.

"Did... Did you know her, Beau?" Philippa wondered if perhaps that's why her kisses had left him distressed. Had he known and loved this vibrant woman? Was she some painful reminder that rubbed salt in his old wounds?

"No, she died a year before I met Lord St. Albans."

Philippa stared at the reflection of herself, spellbound. Then she saw the duke's eyes were upon her.

"She died in childbirth as she brought my grandson into this world."

"Philippa, this is why I believe Monmouth is trying to hurt you. You remind him of his late wife." Beau was watching her with worried eyes.

She struggled past the ringing in her ears. "But... I am not his wife. Why would he lash out at me when I have no connection to her?"

"We feel there must be some connection. It's possible her death was not so innocent, and that perhaps Monmouth carries the guilt of her death upon his shoulders. Seeing you might have driven him mad with that guilt," Beau replied as he put a hand on the small of her back, offering more than physical support. His touch sent wild flutters of excitement through her. Yet she also felt calmed by it, knowing he was there beside her.

"We are all invested in this matter, Miss Wilson," the duke said. "I have love for my grandson, but none for his father. It would give me some peace to see him punished for what he did to you, since there was no justice served when he stole away my only beloved child."

"I wish he'd never seen me, that I'd stayed to my duties and followed Ruth to the servants' quarters that night." Philippa felt the dizziness sweep through her. She'd never been prone to fainting and here she was swooning, a headache pounding behind her eyes. It was all so overwhelming now, so real. The evidence of what she'd been told but never truly believed staring back at her across time.

Beau's hold on her back became firm as he banded an arm around her waist. "Philippa?"

"I believe I need to sit down," she managed to say.

"Yes, of course." Beau and the duke took her to the dining room where she almost collapsed into the chair St. Albans pulled out for her.

"Let me fetch you some water."

"Would you feel better if you ate? You haven't had anything all day," Beau reminded her. The duke poured her a glass, then waved to the footmen attending them to bring in dinner.

Philippa ate with relief. St. Albans took this opportunity to provide some advice on how to maintain her façade at future engagements, and Beau told St. Albans more about her past.

"Your parents are named the Wilsons?"

She nodded. "Yes, they own a textile shop on Bond Street."

"Yet you work in service? Not in their shop?" The duke seemed intrigued by that. No one else had ever really questioned her decision.

"I love my parents very much, but I felt it was important to earn my place and to learn about myself while being on my own. I wanted a place in a shop, but no one would hire me."

"Why on earth not, my child?" The duke's brows rose he leaned forward in his chair.

"My looks, Your Grace. I was too pretty. Too much of a distract distraction bound to catch attention of men in the wrong sort of way."

"What?" Beau laughed. "That's ridiculous."

"It isn't." She fixed Beau with a look. "Imagine you take your wife shopping and she sees a shop girl far lovelier than her. You might be tempted to show her attention and your wife would be upset. Shopkeepers are not fools. Pleasing the customer is their paramount concern."

"Oh..." Beau reddened a little. "I hadn't thought of it that way."

Philippa stared at her empty dinner plate as footmen collected it. She reached for a loose lock of her hair that had slipped from the hairstyle Louisa had done for her. She twined it about one finger and pulled, tightening the coil. If she did enough it would leave a loose curl to bounce against her cheek. It was a habit her mother had tried to break her of but never been fully successful. She glanced up and found the duke watching her, an unfathomable look in his eyes.

"I wish you could have met my daughter, Miss Wilson. I believe she would have been delighted in seeing the striking similarities you bear."

"I wish I could have met her as well," Philippa agreed. Other women might have been threatened by the idea of looking so much like a countess, but Philippa found it intriguing. Were there others with a mirror double running about England? Would she see another Beau as she walked down Pall Mall Street?

"Well then, what are your plans, my boy?" St. Albans asked. "How do you plan to draw his attention, short of issuing a formal invitation?"

"Lady Essex is throwing the ball tomorrow evening. I know Her Grace well and I believe I have no doubt I will be able to secure an invitation for my new ward."

"I shall attend as well. Essex and his wife are lovely, and it would be good to see them. It will also allow me to keep a watchful eye over your new charge."

The duke smiled at Philippa and the tenderness in his eyes made her heart clench. If Beau had been taught the ways of a gentleman by this wonderful and kind man, it was no wonder he was so charming.

After dinner, Beau and Philippa bid the duke good night, but as she turned to leave the duke's home, she broke with propriety to throw her arms around the older man and hugged him fiercely. He was startled a moment before he hugged her in return.

"Rest well tonight, my dear," the duke said and let her go.

She bit her lip and joined Beau on the sidewalk.

"I take it you liked him?" Beau asked.

"Very much. He's a wonderfully kind man. I can see why you adore him."

Beau grinned boyishly. "He's like a father to me. I owe him much."

They walked in companionable silence in the darkness, stepping through pools of light every dozen or so feet as they passed beneath the tall oil lamps lighting Pall Mall.

"Are we truly attending a ball tomorrow?"

"Yes. I'm afraid so. You must suffer pretty gowns, jewels, and the attention of the richest men in London."

"Sounds dreadful," she muttered.

Beau laughed. The sound echoed down the nearly empty street.

A flash of embarrassment made her hot all over. "What?"

"You never cease to surprise me, that's all. Most women would be thrilled to be in your position."

She huffed. "To have men so desperate for you they make you feel unsafe? To have other women scorn your presence because they believe you will seduce their husbands?"

"Hmm," Beau hummed softly. "I'm sorry, Philippa. That does indeed sound dreadful. Once we ferret out Monmouth plans, you may return to anonymity if you wish."

Philippa didn't wish that, but she did wish that she could do something different, something *more* with her life. Being with Beau had awakened other desires within her, ones she was afraid of. But she would be strong and survive all of this. Even Beau.

❄

ALISTAIR SOMMERS STARED UP AT THE EDIFICE OF THE old country estate of the Earl of Monmouth. He told his coachmen to wait for him as he knocked on the door. Given the lateness of the hour it took a few minutes before someone answered the door. He was shown into a drawing room where he paced the floor by the fire. When Cornelius entered the room some time later, Sommers's temper was fraying.

"What are you doing here?" Cornelius demanded in a low growl.

"I'm here to tell you that the little chit escaped. I had her in my hands, only to have her stolen from me."

Cornelius' color drained. "What? Who?"

"A fool by the name of Beauregard Boudreaux."

It seemed Monmouth knew the name. "Boudreaux? But he and St. Albans are close. If he has the girl, he might..." Cornelius stopped speaking, as if he knew he'd revealed too much.

"You owe me answers, Monmouth." Alistair stared at Cornelius. "Who is this woman to you? Your wife's illegitimate child? A woman can't inherit. Why would she matter?"

"Albina was never with another man. Neither she nor I have any base-born children." Cornelius snapped.

Alistair spun on him. Cornelius tried to step back, but Alistair grabbed him by the throat and squeezed hard.

"Talk or I'll kill you where you stand!" Alistair was done with the man's games. He preferred to be in charge, to know all the players and the rules in order to cheat and win. If that meant threatening to kill an earl, well that was far less than many sins he'd happily committed before.

"All right!" Cornelius gasped. Alistair released him. He stumbled and cursed, massaging his throat.

"Well?" Alistair's tone was icy.

"That girl is my daughter," Cornelius said.

"Your daughter?" Alistair stared at him. "What does that matter? And why did you not claim her if she wasn't illegitimate?"

"Albina bore twins, a boy and a girl. The boy was stillborn. He never even drew a breath upon this earth. Philippa is my only living true heir and as such, she cannot inherit my estate or my title."

"But your son, Roderick..."

"Is not mine. Not by blood." Cornelius wiped a hand from his face.

Alistair was not following him at all. "Then how...?"

"The local miller and his wife bore a son a few days before Albina. I gave them my daughter and took their son in exchange."

"All to keep your title and lands?" Alistair was amused. Such a silly charade.

"I've worked my whole life to build my fortune. I'm not dying only to pass it onto some oafish cousin. Better to have a boy I raised, a boy I love."

"Why kill the girl now after all these years?" Alistair asked.

"You saw her... She's looks just like her mother. I never imagined she would grow up to mirror Albina. Once I saw her, I knew that if the Duke of St. Albans or anyone else who knew my late wife saw the girl, they would know she was mine and Roddy's inheritance would be challenged."

"They wouldn't assume your wife took a lover?"

"No, everyone who knew Albina knew she loved me and would never have strayed from my bed. The pretty little fool truly cared about me."

"Why let the girl live then? Why not kill her that night she was born?"

"I thought about it," Cornelius said quietly, dark shadows flitting across his face. "But I thought if I sent her away, I'd never see her again. I didn't expect her to grow up into a beauty, or to take after Albina so thoroughly. Such a foolish assumption has cost me. Thanks to your inability to do the task I assigned you, the girl's in the midst of some of the most influential men and women in London." Cornelius turned dark, loathing eyes upon him. "We have to go back to London and finish this."

"This is more trouble than it's worth already," Alistair warned. "I'm doubling what you owe me."

Cornelius's face hardened. "Money is not my problem. You may stay here tonight; I'll have a room prepared. Tomorrow you and I shall return to London after we see to a few loose ends."

Alistair followed Cornelius out of the drawing room, but his mind was miles away. He was imagining Philippa in his bed and Beau Boudreaux dying on the floor, watching helplessly as Alistair took her. The thought brought a cruel smile to his face.

Beau stared at the array of jewels before him. Mr.
Preston, one of the most prestigious jewelers on
Oxford Street, waited expectantly as Beau
considered the pieces.

"We have the most exquisite sapphires and the darkest
garnets." Preston retrieved a tray from beneath the glass
counter and set it out for Beau's inspection.

Beau waved the tray away. "Pearls, show me pearls. A
double strand perhaps, and earrings that match.
Teardrops, if you have them."

The jeweler scrambled to collect some new items per
Beau's request. While he was in his storeroom, Beau
looked out the shop window. Oxford Street was full of
shoppers, despite the cold late-fall wind rushing down the
streets; it was strong enough that it tugged at the cloaks
and skirts of passersby.

Beau lost himself in a pleasant daydream about Philippa, wondering whether she would be a good dancer and what they would talk about at dinner. His thoughts were interrupted when he noticed a red-haired man staring at him through the window.

"Boudreaux!" The man laughed warmly and came inside the shop, offering his hand in greeting.

"Rochester, how are you?" He grinned back at Lucian Russell, the Marquess of Rochester. "It's been too long."

"That it has. I heard from Ashton and Cedric that you found yourself in charge of a little beauty. A ward?" The rakish marquess winked at Beau as though they were in some sort of secret club.

So, word was already spreading. "Not by choice, but yes."

"Never complain about having to care for a lovely woman."

"Noted," Beau replied with a smile. "What brings you to Oxford Street?"

"My wife. I'm shopping for our anniversary. It's still a few months away, but I thought it was wise to start early. And you?"

"I'm purchasing some jewels for my new charge. Something to be seen in at social gatherings."

"Ahh." Rochester nodded in understanding.

Preston reemerged from the back rooms with a velvet-lined tray covered with pearl jewelry. Beau and Rochester examined the necklaces he presented. Beau settled on a double strand that held a quiet elegance and a pair of small pearl drop earrings. They would suit Philippa perfectly. She didn't need an abundance of jewels, she already sparkled more than any gem, but he did have a strange longing to spoil her. With past mistresses, these sorts of purchases had been obligatory, but right now he wanted to buy these for Philippa simply because she was Philippa.

"Lovely choice, Mr. Boudreaux." Preston packaged the items up, leaving Beau to talk with Rochester.

"Are you and your wife attending the Essex ball tonight?"

"We are."

"If it's not an imposition, would you inquire of your wife whether she could take my ward under her wing a bit? I assume has Lennox shared the details of the situation?"

"He did, and I'm sure Horatia would be delighted."

Beau wasn't surprised Rochester knew about Philippa. For as long as Beau could remember, the lords Sheridan, Rochester, Essex, and Lonsdale were close friends of Lennox. The London papers often called them the League of Rogues. While many saw that moniker as either scandalous or charming, Beau knew better. The League were dangerous men to their enemies, but they had good hearts and could be trusted.

Rochester pointed at an expensive but elegant pair of garnet studded earrings. "Preston, let me see those earrings."

"Yes, my lord." His business with Beau now complete, the jeweler turned his attention to Rochester.

"I shall see you this evening." Beau nodded at his friend and collected his purchases. He had a few more stops to make. Jessica had placed orders for hats, boots and corsets, all of which he'd planned to collect for Philippa before returning home. He waved at his young footman, who followed behind as he headed toward his next stop.

Two hours later, he was home, packages in tow. They had a few hours until they needed to leave for the ball, and he thought he should rest his sore shoulder. He could feel the stitches pulling in his skin. He'd have to have them removed sooner rather than later.

"Sir?" Stoddard met him at the door. "Is it your shoulder?"

"Yes, rather it's my back," Beau muttered. "The bloody stitches are pulling."

"Why don't I have a look? My father was a surgeon."

"That's probably for the best. I don't want to bother a doctor just yet." He headed to his room, Stoddard on his heels. Beau stripped out of his shirt and tossed it on his bed so his butler could examine his back.

"The area is a bit red, sir. But it doesn't seem to hold any inflammation. I believe you're healing well, and the stitches are tight as your skin connects back together."

"It itches and aches." He felt like a child for complaining.

"I could fetch some laudanum," Stoddard offered.

"No, no more of that for a while. It gives me bad dreams." He also didn't like the way it made his brain feel, as though someone had stuffed it full of thick wool.

"Sir!" Philippa's anxious tone startled him and Stoddard. They turned to the open doorway where she stood dressed in a pale green gown like frost covered jade. "I'm so sorry. I heard your voice and came to tell you..." Her eyes roamed the length of his body and settled on his bare chest.

"Leave us for a moment, Stoddard." He nodded at his butler, who raised his brows but did not question Beau's orders.

"I...should leave." Philippa tried to go but he moved quickly, reaching her at the door and catching her arm.

"Stay. I have a present for you." He pulled her into his chambers, knowing how tempting she was at that moment. Her gray eyes seemed green now, reflecting her gown, and her hair was pulled loosely back. He could imagine how good it would feel to sink his fingers into those silken strands.

"Beau, I..." But she didn't pull away. He handed her the two black boxes from the jewelers. Her gaze became fixed on the boxes, and the memory of their earlier kiss seemed to shimmer in the air between them, taunting them both. More than anything, he wanted her to open the boxes and give him a sunny grin of innocent delight before she wrapped her arms around his neck and begged him to take her to bed. But she wasn't that woman, the one who conducted a relationship with him based on transactions. Instead, she was the woman who appreciated a gift and her response was born of true affection for him. And that confused him and delighted him in such a way that he didn't know what to do or say. He'd made a promise to hold his desires at bay, but at this moment, he wanted to forget he'd ever made those foolish vows.

"Open them," he encouraged.

She pulled at the red ribbons tying the boxes together. The smaller box opened, revealing the gleaming opalescent pearl earrings. She stared in awe.

"Now the other one." His heart was racing. Why did this feel so different from the other women? Why was *she* different? Why did he need to see her joy, need to feel it like the sun upon his face after a long winter?

Philippa opened the box with the double strand pearl necklace and gasped.

"Oh no, sir, I can't. These are far too precious." She tried to give the boxes back, but he shook his head.

"Please. Consider them a gift for saving my life."

"But you saved mine first," she reminded him.

He smiled and sighed. "Bloody Christ, woman, just let me give you something beautiful. I saw them and I thought they reflected your beauty."

Her embarrassment turned to open discomfort and he realized his mistake. "Your *inner* beauty, darling." He cupped her chin; remembering he was only half-clothed. Her face was bright red, like a ripened strawberry.

"You don't know me," she said quietly.

"No, but I am learning. Learning that you are sweet, thoughtful, amusing, and brave. You are all of those things, Philippa, and I felt these pearls reflected that."

Her blush deepened as she clutched the pearls to her bosom and a heartfelt sincerity filled her eyes as she looked at him. It made his chest tighten. She seemed so grateful, so thankful and appreciative. It humbled him and in that moment, he felt completely unworthy of her.

"Thank you, Beau." She stood up on tiptoe and brushed her lips on his. It sent wild bolts of desire through him, and when she tried to step back, he curled an arm around her waist.

"I warned you about stealing kisses," he said.

Long dark lashes fanned down as she softened in his arms. "I remember. One for one." Then she flipped those lashes up, and he saw an impish look in her lovely eyes that invited him to kiss her again.

"Good," he murmured before he captured her mouth with his. He wasn't gentle. He had fantasized too much about how he wanted his next kiss with her to be to allow tenderness. He wanted her wild with excitement, to be aroused and unafraid of his ferocious passion.

He lifted her up by the waist and set her on the bed. He raised her skirts and pushed her legs wide as he stepped in between them. Her thighs were smooth, and he brushed his fingertips on the outside of her knees. She delighted his mouth with the sound of giggles against his lips. It was like drinking champagne. His little ward was ticklish. He rather liked that.

"That was more than one kiss," she teased.

"I fear it takes several of mine to equate one of yours," said Beau. "I hope you don't mind."

She dropped her jewels on the bed and curled her arms around his neck as he trailed kisses down her lips to her throat. He could feel the erratic beat of her pulse under his tongue as he kissed and licked, hunting for new erogenous zones. Philippa squirmed a little and he moved closer, their bodies pressed tightly to one another.

"Beau..." She spoke his name in a tone that made him painfully hard. "I want..." She ducked her head as he returned to kissing her lips. He tilted her chin up.

"What do you want, darling?"

"I..." She licked her lips. "I don't know."

Beau wanted to keep kissing her, but his senses came back to him in that moment.

"We should get ready for the Essex ball." He stepped back and pulled her skirts down. She could get off the bed on her own, but he wanted to continue touching her, so he set her down gently before he handed her the pearl necklace and earrings.

"You will look lovely tonight, inside and out." He brushed a loose lock of hair back from her face and she smiled at him hesitantly.

"I never wanted that to matter," she said.

"It doesn't, at least on the outside. But you've been blessed with both. Don't be ashamed of that." He winked at her. "And any man who comes to close I shall beat him off with a stick."

She laughed at that. "I shall hold you to that." Then she left him alone to change for the ball.

Three hours later, Beau wanted to do just that: beat every man away from her with a stick.

Sheridan joined Beau by the refreshment table in the Duke and Duchess of Essex's ballroom. A footman was pouring punch.

Sheridan collected two glasses and handed one to Beau. "How are you faring?"

"Is it normal to want to challenge every man in the room to a duel?"

Sheridan laughed, the hearty sound disrupting a group of young ladies gossiping nearby. They all fluttered their feathered fans in warning, but Cedric paid them no heed.

"It's quite normal when you're enamored with a woman."

"I'm not," Beau replied too quickly.

"You are." Cedric sobered. "Every man in the room knows it. You practically growl when a man gets too close to Miss Wilson."

"I merely want to protect her." His eyes sought her out on the dance floor. "Any man here would take advantage of her if they could."

"Or they might simply ask her for a dance."

"That's how it starts, as you well know."

"Everything has to start from somewhere," Sheridan said. "But sometimes a dance is just a dance."

Beau's eyes narrowed as he focused on one young buck clearly hoping to make his way towards Philippa. He caught Beau staring at him, and Beau slowly shook his head. The man wisely changed direction.

But dancing was inevitable, of course, and soon Philippa was involved in a cotillion dance, her energetic movements so flawless one would never have guessed she spent the morning and early afternoon with Mrs. Gronow and a few maids learning the very same movements. The Capuchin brown gown she wore tonight made her glow like an autumnal pagan goddess as she laughed and twirled beneath the gilded lamplight.

"Don't challenge *me* to a duel Boudreaux, but may I ask why you don't marry her?" Cedric then took a drink of his punch and frowned, muttering about it needing a bit of brandy.

"Don't be daft. I'm not the marrying kind." Beau's eyes still followed Philippa, drinking in the way her smile illuminated her from within.

"Plenty of men have married servants," Sheridan added. "It's not unheard of."

"It isn't that," Beau replied. "I don't want to be in love. I don't need that sort of weakness."

Sheridan smirked. "Perhaps I will have to challenge *you* to a duel instead."

"I did not mean to offend."

Sheridan's brown eyes deepened with understanding. "No, I understand. No one wants to be weak, old boy, but avoiding love doesn't make you strong. It's rather the opposite. Take it from one with experience in such matters." He left Beau to brood and stare daggers at any man who engaged Philippa in conversation now that the dance had ended.

A petite auburn-haired woman with violet eyes materialized next to him, like a fae queen summoned by his innermost thoughts. It was the Duchess of Essex, Emily St. Laurent.

"Good evening, Beau," she said, beaming at him.

"Your Grace," he bowed, momentarily distracted from his vigil.

"Are you enjoying the evening?" She nodded to the couples queuing up to the next dance. A minuet, Beau judged correctly by the dancers' positions.

"I am. Please have my thanks for extending your invitation to my ward."

Emily nodded. "My pleasure. She's quite lovely to talk to, once one coaxes her out of her shell. She reminds me of myself when I was young and coming out."

Beau chuckled. "You are still young, Your Grace."

"I suppose so, but after marriage and children one can feel very old. I hope I'm wise at the age of four and twenty." She drifted closer, her pale blue gown glimmering as she moved. They watched the dancers in silence for a time before Emily spoke again.

"She's been waiting for you all night."

Beau looked at the young duchess. "I beg your pardon?"

"Philippa. She's been looking at you at the end of every dance...waiting to be asked."

"Asked?"

Emily rolled her eyes. "*To dance*. She wants you to ask her to dance."

"No. I don't think I should," he hedged. "It wouldn't be appropriate."

"Why not?" Emily asked.

"She is supposed to be my ward."

"Oh, what rot and nonsense. A dance is simply a dance." Emily waved a hand. "You aren't a blood relation and she is twenty years old. She's not a silly child. She's a woman. A woman who wishes more than anything for you to ask her to dance."

It was such a dangerous request to dance with the most beautiful woman he'd ever seen. It couldn't end well, yet he started moving toward Philippa anyway as the minuet came to an end. A group of ladies, mostly the wives of Lord and Lady Lennox's friends, were ringed around Philippa. She smiled gaily and laughed as she talked. It was the most relaxed he'd ever seen her in their short acquaintance.

"Oh hush now, ladies. A gentleman approaches," Anne Sheridan, Cedric's wife, warned playfully and they all ceased their laughter at some private amusement once Beau reached them.

"Good evening." Beau bowed to the intimidating group of beautiful women.

"Evening, Mr. Boudreaux," they replied together as though they'd rehearsed it. How the devil women were able to do that, he would never know. Perhaps they practiced such things whilst the men were smoking cigars after dinner. That seemed a likely possibility.

"Miss Wilson." He cleared his throat nervously. "Would you do me the honor of the next dance?"

Philippa lifted the tiny card tied to her wrist, examining the list of upcoming dances. "That's a waltz?" she asked.

Lord, he thought, *a bloody waltz*. That meant he would be holding her in his arms, inhaling her sweet scent until he was half mad with longing. He considered asking her for the next one instead.

Instead he said, "Yes."

"I would be delighted to accept." She moved to take his arm, and he stole her away from her protective harem.

The musicians in the corner of the ballroom changed the sheet music in a soft fluttering sound. All the couples engaged in the next dance took their places. Beau found himself suddenly unsure of his decision as they moved onto the dance floor.

"Beau, I think you must touch me during the waltz." Philippa's tone was playful, but he saw her uncertainty.

"Right, touching," he murmured as he slid a hand around her waist. His other hand clasped one of hers.

A waltz was unlike other dances. There was no set formations or participation with other couples. A man and a woman turned toward one another, keeping away from other couples and had no obligation to keep pattern with the other dancers but could spin inward in their own private universe. There was no need to converse with other dancers either. It was, as one of his mistresses had described it, the most personal and romantic of all dances. The music began, slow and gentle, and straight away Beau nearly trod on Philippa's toes when he accidentally tried to move forward rather than back.

"Sorry," he muttered, his face turning hot.

"You're making me nervous," Philippa said softly, but there was a teasing glint in her eyes.

Why did this moment feel so significant? He'd never cared about dancing, he performed them when necessary, but this felt like so much more. The feel of Philippa's body in his arms, the hint of her scent drifting in the air between them, and the eyes of everyone not dancing upon them.

He took deep breaths, trying to calm himself as his dancing memories came to the fore and he began to do the damn thing properly.

"When one truly dances, the steps are effortless, the partner

perfect, the music endless." His old mistress, the dancer had once said when she told him tales of lavish balls in Europe. She had once danced with a Russian Czar as snow fell on a terrace outside the winter palace. The way she talked of dancing had fascinated him, and yet until this moment, he never truly understood what she'd been trying to tell him.

Dancing like this is a way for one's soul to sing.

He'd thought his soul had no songs left, that his soul had been silenced after he'd been orphaned. He gazed at Philippa, taking in every detail about her—her ivory skin, to the delicate arched brows over emotional silver eyes that lit with lightning and silent delight as she moved with him in perfect step. Everything about the moment was right, down to the wayward curl that had escaped her coiffure to bounce against her neck. Beau pulled her closer, fearing that if he let her go it would break something inside him.

"Philippa..."

"Yes?" Her serene expression transformed into one of hope.

"You're a lovely dancer." It was not what he wished to say. He honestly didn't know *what* he wanted to tell her.

"Thank you. You are as well." She looked away then and it cut his heart.

Christ, the woman was doing something to him, something he never wanted to happen.

As the dance came to an end, he kept her close for longer than he should, until he heard the murmur of whispers traveling about the ballroom like a flock of starlings taking flight. When he finally let go, his hands were shaking. He rubbed them together as casually as possible to try and hide it.

"Would you like some punch?" he offered, needing to take any chance now to get as far away from her as possible, if only for a moment to collect himself.

"That would be lovely, thank you." She stood there, looking forlorn. The snowdrop flowers tucked in her hair and sewn into her bodice made her look like a doomed princess facing a century of solitude tucked away in a tower. The tower he'd left her in because he was afraid of being her white knight.

THOMAS WINTHROP, THE DUKE OF ST. ALBANS, HELD his breath as he watched Beau and the maid twirl in a waltz. It was abundantly clear they were in love with each other, yet it was equally clear that neither of them could admit that fact. The maid was far too innocent and the gentleman far too jaded. Yet love had blossomed this night, taking root with every perfect spin as the couple danced.

"You are done for, my boy. And it's about time." Thomas's heart soared at the thought that he finally had a way to see his boy married and happily in love.

Philippa stood alone now, her face a mask of pleasantness as Beau abandoned her to fetch punch. Such a silly thing to do. It would leave the girl open for other men less frightened of love. Yet not one man came. They had all seen what he had. The seasoned rake, Beauregard Boudreaux, had fallen in love and no one would dare stand in his way.

The maid began to play with a loose curl of her hair, twining it over and over around her finger, spooling the lustrous dark hair tight. Then she released it. Thomas's heart stopped. Albina used to do that when she was nervous. He had never seen another woman do it quite the same way, but the maid had.

"Papa... Be happy for me." His child's words drifted back to him across two decades as she begged him to forgive her for running away to Gretna Green.

How was this woman before him now such a ghost of his lost daughter? Albina couldn't have had another child, could she?

Thomas remembered Albina, six months pregnant, explaining how she hired a midwife. What was her name? Lucy? Yes, that was it. Lucy was to be present for the birth. If there were any truths to be revealed, Lucy would have the answers. Thomas didn't wait another minute, he left Philippa and Beau in the safety of their friends' ballroom as he rushed out into the night. He would not rest until he knew the truth about the night Albina died.

12

Philippa stared into a pair of dark fathomless eyes. Her heart pounded with excitement but a twinge of fear shadowed it too.

"You're positive he won't bite?" she asked.

The massive horse directly in front of her said nothing, which was somehow worse than any response. The interior of the rented stables near Hyde Park were dim despite the sunlight outside.

"Easy, darling. Just relax around him. Animals respond to fear. If you're not afraid, he will have no reason to be." Beau wound an arm around her from behind. Feeling his hard body against her back and bottom made her shiver and her womb clench.

"He's just so large... I'm not certain I should do this."

"You are quite capable of this, I promise you. Remember, you rode with me as we escaped Lord Sommers." Beau gave her waist a little squeeze.

"On that particular occasion, I was acting entirely on the instinct to survive. I honestly don't know how I managed to mount that horse on my own."

Beau brushed his hand on her waist, momentarily distracting her from her fears.

"Your instincts are sound. Now stop stalling. Reach up and brush your fingers down the length of his nose. Don't hesitate. Horses cannot stand hesitant people." He spoke of the animal in such a fond way that Philippa had to smile.

She did her best to quell her nerves and stroked the horse's nose. It was a black gelding with a white star on its forehead right between its eyes. She brushed back its mane to better see the white painted star. The horse huffed softly and bumped its nose against her arm.

"See? He's formed an attachment to you already."

She continued to stroke him as Beau moved around her to the side of the horse. Philippa felt quite unsure of herself, even though she looked every bit the equestrian in her Bishop's blue-colored riding habit. She even wore a jaunty hat that was pinned to her hair. Louisa had said she looked very smart that morning before she and Beau had set out.

It had only been a week since the ball, yet between dinners, parties, paying calls and afternoon teas, she'd felt like she'd lived a lifetime as a lady already. It was the oddest feeling, and it left her strangely unsettled.

Philippa listened to Beau speak to the horse in gentle tones while he fit a blanket and saddle on its back. She couldn't help but notice with trepidation that he had prepared a sidesaddle.

"Must I write a sidesaddle? The few times I have ridden a horse it has always been astride."

"A lady astride would be too much of the wrong kind of attention for town. In the country, of course you may ride as you wish." He offered her an apologetic look. "For today, we will walk slowly, and I shall be by your side."

Philippa bit her lip as Beau tightened the girth and patted the horse's neck. "He's ready for you."

She looked at the horse's solemn eyes again as he chewed on his bit. "Does he have a name?"

Beau touched the horse's nose and then checked the bridle again. "Albus."

"Albus?" Philippa wrinkled her nose. "For a horse?"

"Absolutely. A noble creature deserves a noble name. Albus was the name of my maternal grandfather. I never had the chance to meet him, but my mother said he was a kind soul who loved fiercely."

"Oh..." Philippa's face heated. "That is a lovely name indeed."

Beau gave her an amused look. "You're stalling again. Come here."

He grabbed her by the waist and before she could

protest he'd set her upon Albus's back. He showed her how to arrange her legs to sit properly, then handed her the reins. Beau mounted a dappled gray horse named Lady, one that would have made most men look feminine, but not Beau. Riding the lovely gray mare only made him look more attractive and confident. He and Lady rode well, like two halves of a split heart reunited.

She tried not to think about her fear of riding and instead focused on Beau. "Why do you ride a mare? Most men prefer geldings or stallions, do they not?"

He clicked his teeth and Lady trotted out into the sunlight with Philippa and Albus right behind them. "I rescued Lady from a man who took pleasure in beating his animals. I caught him trying to whip her after he'd ridden her to exhaustion." He stroked a hand down the mare's neck where faint scars striped her fine gray coat. She touched her own neck, her heart going out to the horse. They had both been ill-used by cruel men.

"How did you do that? A man's property usually isn't something he would surrender willingly."

"Indeed not," he agreed. "The man wouldn't let me buy her, either. So, I challenged him to a duel. I told him that he'd offended me by refusing my offer. When I told him my name, he threw the reins at me and stormed off."

"You didn't fight him then?"

"Sadly no. Though I would have liked to fire a shot at his black heart."

Philippa couldn't contain her gasp. Why was it that a

healthy man always seemed to look for trouble and throw themselves into danger with such reckless ease? At least that's how Roger put it when he shared stories with her of Lord Lennox and his friends and they danger they got into before they were married.

"Have you fought many duels?" Philippa asked, dreading to hear his answer.

"A fair few. I've won all of them, but I've never killed a man. I suspect Lady's previous owner knew of my record once I divulged my name."

Philippa didn't know what to say. She was puzzled by Beau. He was dangerous, protective, fierce, yet there was vulnerability and a gentleness to him that came out when she least expected it. It seemed he had a passion for rescuing unfortunate creatures, whether they were horses or upstairs maids. Either way, she was forever in his debt.

"Well I am glad you rescued her. It seems to be a particular habit of yours."

"What? Dueling?" Beau asked.

"Rescuing ladies."

His rich laugh made her grin and he leaned over to whisper in her ear. "I suppose I ought to make a career out of it. The benefits are quite worthwhile." He winked at her and she felt her spirits buoyed.

They rode their horses through Hyde Park and Philippa found herself relaxing as Albus stayed close to Lady's side without much coaxing. He was as gentle as Beau had assured her he would be.

"Feeling more confident?" Beau asked as they entered a part of Hyde Park which had more riders. Philippa did her best to act the part of the lady she was masquerading as. Two gentleman rode opposite them with open interest as they looked between her and Beau.

"People are staring at us," she said when she and Beau were out of earshot.

"It's me," Beau said. "It must be quite a shock to see me riding with a lady. Everyone knows I never ride with innocent creatures like you." He was teasing her, but Philippa felt embarrassed by the moniker, nonetheless.

"I'm not that innocent," she grumbled.

"You are, darling. More than you know." His stare met hers for a moment too long and her heart fluttered in response, but she didn't wish to look away as this connection between them grew. As he spoke again, his voice deepened, a slight huskiness to it making her dizzy with excitement.

"There is nothing one should apologize for when it comes to being innocent. I hope you stay that way as long as you can. Life finds a way of robbing one of that glorious innocence far too soon."

He looked away then, a note of melancholy to his tone that stirred her heart and forced an exhalation of breath from her lungs. He must have been speaking of losing his parents.

"Oh, Beau, I'm"

"Mr. Boudreaux!" A woman called out, interrupted

Philippa. The woman rode up alongside them, smiling broadly at Beau. She had no chaperone, but a trio of other ladies awaited her at a distance, clearly members of her riding party.

He nodded in polite greeting. "Miss Monroe."

Philippa studied the woman. She had dark hair and black eyes, and her face, while pretty, held a subtle meanness that Philippa recognized instinctively. She'd seen it cast her way far too often in the past. She didn't keep her eyes on the woman long in case she drew her attention. It was best to stay away from women like this.

"Miss Monroe, please allow me to introduce you to my ward, Miss Wilson. Philippa, this is Miss Courtney Monroe."

"Pleasure," Courtney purred, but there was a subtle threat in the sound.

"It's lovely to meet you," Philippa replied.

"However did you become burdened with a ward? It must be a dreadful thing to be responsible for some poor creature." Courtney pretended that Philippa was not even present.

"A friend from the country passed away and he sent his daughter to me in hopes that I would watch over her until she turns twenty-one next year."

"Dreadful, simply dreadful. What must I do to rescue you, my sweet Beau?"

Beau laughed at that and the sound knifed Philippa's

heart. Did he actually agree with this woman? That helping her and saving her life was a burden?

"It's not as bad as all that," Beau replied. "I rather enjoyed myself at the ball last evening."

"At the Duchess of Essex's home? Yes, I heard you did a fair amount of dancing for a man who usually avoids it. You are a wonderful dancer. I always love it when we waltz." Courtney shot Philippa a triumphant smile while Beau was looking down at his horse for a brief moment.

"And what of you, Miss Monroe? I didn't see you last night." Beau said.

"Oh..." Courtney's face pinkened with a delicate blush, but her eyes were dark with rage. "Lady Essex no longer seems to care for me. She dared to give me the cut direct the other day."

"That doesn't sound like Emily," Beau said, his eyes wide in surprise.

"Well, she did. To be perfectly honest, I've always thought her far too presumptuous. It's as though she's forgotten that she wasn't always a duchess. I'm the daughter of an earl. My pedigree makes me far more important than her. She forgets that breeding matters. Doesn't it, Miss Wilson?"

The look Courtney gave her had a distinctively sinister nature that only cruel women gave to those they wished to grind beneath their expensive riding boots.

Philippa was furious. No one should speak of Lady Essex that way. She was a genuinely lovely person, and no doubt if Miss Monroe had been given the cut, it had been for good reason. "Actually, Miss Monroe, I must respectfully disagree. Breeding is not what defines someone's character. Lady Essex is one of the finest women I know."

Courtney's eyes narrowed. "Well, I'm sure you're right." But her tone said she didn't agree at all.

"I do hope you and Emily will resolve your issues," Beau said.

"I'm sure she'll come around." Courtney turned a bright smile upon Beau and once again dismissed Philippa's existence entirely. "Are you riding all morning?" Courtney asked him.

"No, this is Philippa's first ride. We are only riding for a short time."

"You don't know how to ride? Poor thing. How unfortunate." Courtney's smile looked far more like a sneer.

Philippa gripped her reins tight and tried not to scowl at her.

"She's doing rather well," Beau said with pride, which soothed Philippa's temper bit.

"Oh, look Beau!" Courtney pointed out a pair of riders heading their way. Beau waved at the men, who glanced at Philippa with open curiosity.

"I'll only be a moment, Philippa." He maneuvered his horse across the dirt path to speak with the two gentlemen.

"Beau, wait!" she gasped, tugging on her reins. Albus gave a disgruntled snort, wanting to stay close to Lady.

"You'll be fine. You're doing well," Beau assured her before he steered Lady away and abandoned Philippa to with the viper.

"So, you are living with Beau?" Courtney asked, a hint of an edge to her tone.

"Yes, per my father's request."

"And where did you say you were from?" A cunning light in her eyes made Philippa's nerves tighten.

"Sussex, a small town, just outside of Arundel." She prayed this woman didn't know anyone from Arundel.

"Ahh... The Duke of Norfolk's home, Arundel. Are you acquainted with him?"

Philippa knew better than to fall for that trap. "No."

"Shall we ride on for a bit? I'm certain Beau can catch up."

"I really think rather we should wait"

Whack! Courtney brought the edge of a riding crop down on Albus' flank and the horse reared up on its hind legs, screeching with pain.

Philippa screamed and nearly fell off as the horse planted its front legs back on the ground with a thud. She had only a fraction of a second to control herself as Albus tore off down the dirt lane, scattering the other riders with shouts of panic.

The next few moments were a wild blur, yet Philippa seemed to experience it vividly, raw, and so full of terror she would never forget what happened.

Albus left the safety of the path and tore through the

bushes, ripping through brambles and sharp branches. But the pain, while sharp, was brief. Her sole focus was staying on the horse's back. When he approached a low hedge at full speed, Philippa lowered her body over his neck and tried to move with him.

Albus leapt over the hedge and somehow she stayed on top of him...until another rider cut across the horse's path and he veered. The sharp turn sent them both to the ground. Philippa didn't even have the breath to scream before the horse came down on top of her.

She must have passed out, Philippa mused as she looked at the ring of trees above her. The red and gold leaves whispered like fine ladies in a ball, the gossip beyond her hearing as she lay far beneath them... Her body ached with pain.

Suddenly a large black face with a white star peered down at her. Albus nudged her cheek, huffing softly with what she took for an equine apology.

"It wasn't your fault," she whispered, though the words made her chest twinge with pain.

"Philippa!" Beau's terror stricken shouts reached her but she was still too shaken to move. Beau soon appeared in her line of vision as he knelt down beside her. "Christ! Where does it hurt?"

"Everywhere..." She blinked back tears as he cupped her face and stared down into her eyes. He looked so frightened that it scared her even more. How badly hurt was she?

"Beau? Is the poor creature all right?" Courtney's voice intruded upon the relief Philippa felt at being alone with Beau.

A cold fury gathered inside Philippa like a black cloud as she struggled past her pain and discomfort to sit up. Courtney rode closer, her face a mock expression of concern.

"Oh dear. She should have taken care to learn to ride before coming to London."

"Philippa, perhaps you should lay back down," Beau suggested.

It was far too late for that. Philippa stood on violently shaking legs and as Courtney slid off her horse and came over to them. Philippa snatched the woman's riding crop from her grasp and swung it hard, smacking Courtney across her backside.

"*How do you like it?*" Philippa snarled. She hit the woman again, and raised her arm for a third strike, but Beau snatched the crop and threw it to the ground.

"Philippa, stop that at once, do you hear me?" he bellowed.

Philippa shrank away from him, not from fear, but shame. She stumbled back to Albus, seeking comfort in the horse's tall, solid presence and buried her face in his neck.

Beau spoke to Courtney a moment, extending his deepest apologies.

"She's a nasty little hoyden, Beau. Send that brat back

to the country where she belongs," Courtney cried out far too loudly.

Philippa closed her eyes, fresh tears making the tip of her nose sting. She heard Courtney leave, but didn't dare look at her again. After a moment she sensed Beau standing beside her.

"That was badly done, Philippa, badly done indeed. You *struck* another lady." Beau's disapproval and disappointment were layered with anger. "I think we'd better go straight home."

Philippa wanted to go home to her parents. To hide from the humiliation of this moment. Beau assisted her back onto her horse. It only deepened her shame as she was forced to ride past dozens of spectators to her disastrous adventure.

Beau remained tall and proud in his saddle, but Philippa slumped, curling in on herself as they rode in silence back to the stables by the park. Beau saw to Lady's care first and then assisted her down from Albus.

"He's hurt," she whispered, pointing to the scratches on his legs.

Beau said not a word as he retrieved a pot of salve from a box in Albus's stall and applied it liberally to the scrapes.

"She hit him, Beau. Hit him with her crop so hard he screamed," she added, still in that quiet voice which made Beau pause.

"She did *what*?"

"She waited for you and Lady to be far enough away that you wouldn't see."

Beau still didn't look at her as he ran his palms over Albus's body.

"Sorry, old boy. I didn't know. Forgive me?" He stroked the horse's long face and Albus half-closed his eyes and shifted his stance so one back leg bent in as he relaxed. Then Beau blanketed him and secured him in his stall.

Philippa followed Beau to the door of the stables where he waved down a passing hackney to take them home. They rode home in silence, the air filled with tension. She'd never felt so alone and...cold now that Beau was angry with her. She wanted desperately to run back to the safety of her parents' home, or the Lennox House and her downstairs family. She bit her lip hard as she shot glances at Beau. He stared straight ahead at some spot on the wall of the coach. His eyes were vacant, as though his thoughts were miles away.

When they entered Boudreaux Hall, Philippa rushed straight to her room and closed the door.

She had acted no different than Beau had with the man abusing Lady, yet she was drowning in shame. Each second of that encounter in the park latched itself around her, pulling her down into its murky depths. She lay on the bed, her body still hurting from the fall, every bone and bit of sinew felt bruised and stretched beyond normal. But none of that compared to the look of disappointment she saw in Beau's eyes.

That pain would never go away.

BEAU SAT ALONE IN THE DINING ROOM, HIS GAZE darting to the grandfather clock in the corner. He'd been alone with his thoughts for five hours now. Stoddard entered the room and looked at the footman and then at Beau.

"Shall I have the first course brought in, sir?" the butler asked politely.

Beau pulled himself from his ruminations. "What?"

"The first course, sir. It doesn't appear that Miss Wilson will be joining you. Mrs. Gronow just informed me that the young lady has refused dinner, claiming she doesn't feel well."

Guilt gnawed at him from the inside. Had he been too harsh on her today at the park? Probably... Yes. *Definitely*. He'd seen Albus roll over onto her and if she hadn't stood up and hit Miss Monroe, he would have feared she'd been terribly hurt. Those feelings had made him react more strongly to her actions than he'd intended. And when he'd learned of her reasons...

I was too harsh with her.

"I believe I will go up and check on her. Have two trays prepared and sent to her room." Beau pushed back from the table and headed up the stairs. He tried to rehearse an apology speech. He was so unaccustomed to these sorts of conversations. With a mistress, an apology always came in the form of diamonds. But he knew diamonds wouldn't matter to Philippa.

When he reached her chambers, he knocked and pressed his ear to the door. When he heard no footsteps approaching, he tried the door latch. It turned and he eased the door open. Was she asleep? The last thing Beau wanted to do was disturb her if she was.

The bedchamber was dark except for the fire. He could only just make out Philippa's form curled up on a chair facing the flames. He stepped into the room and closed the door behind him. His heart beat hard against his ribs as he prepared to apologize, but he hesitated a moment before joining her by the fire.

"Philippa... We should speak about what happened today." He looked down and saw her cheeks shimmering with the tracks of tears. She wiped her eyes as she met his gaze.

"You scolded me like a child. I'm not a child, Beau," she said softly, her voice husky with emotion, painfully reminding him she was a grown woman. One with a pure heart that he'd treated poorly.

"You're right. I scolded you for your temper and I shouldn't have. Lord knows I would've done the same thing if I'd been in your place, had it been a man who'd done it."

"You excuse Miss Monroe's actions because she's a woman?"

"Certainly not. But I won't raise a hand to a woman, even a terrible one." He looked at the vacant chair beside her. "May I sit?"

"It is your home. You may do as you please." Her sullen reply made him smile for reasons he couldn't explain.

"It is. But this is your room while you remain here." He sat down and started to reach for her hand on the armrest but stopped himself. It was too soon.

Philippa resumed her vigil staring at the flames. "Do you care about her? Miss Monroe?"

"Miss Monroe? Christ, no," he answered with a bemused chuckled. "That woman is a gossip monger and has only her own interests at heart, assuming she does have a heart, which I've often wondered about."

"But you were so polite to her. She called you Beau and"

Beau raised a hand, silencing her. "I am civil to a great many people that I do not like. It makes life easier. And she, like many women who have longed to snare me in a Parson's mousetrap, use my given name at their leisure. I could be cold and correct them, but it's rather amusing to watch a dozen ladies in a room all call me Beau and then realize the other ladies also have that privilege. It sows seeds of discord amongst the little gossips." He cracked a smile as he saw a flicker of mirth in Philippa's eyes.

"But you let me call you Beau. You even insist upon it."

He waited until their gazes locked and, stunned by the

openness between them, he felt compelled to be honest. "Because I *like* you, darling."

Philippa was quiet another long moment. "I am sorry I caused you embarrassment."

"Don't be. She deserved that punishment. I only wished the majority of the *ton* hadn't seen you do it."

"Because of the scandal?"

He chuckled. "On the contrary. You will likely become a hero to half the people in London. Miss Monroe does not have friends, only enemies and future enemies. I imagine as word spreads, we will have dozens of calling cards for poor Mr. Stoddard to sort through. You and I shall have to start accepting house calls. But it leaves me to wonder how Monmouth will interpret this, and whether such attention will encourage him to act instead of observing as we'd hoped."

"So, you aren't angry with me?"

He scrubbed a hand on his jaw. "I was afraid. When I saw Albus fall, taking you down beneath him... Philippa... I never want to feel that terror I felt then ever again." He leaned forward, and this time he was brave enough to clasp her hand. "Now, let me have a look at you. Did you get hurt? I can send for a doctor. I should have done so hours ago." But he hadn't because he'd been brooding. What a pointless exercise that had been.

"I have only a few scratches. I'm fine."

"Scratches?" He tugged on her hand to urge her to her feet. "Where?" He searched her face and arms but saw no rips in the cloth. She gestured with a blush toward her blue velvet skirts. Only then did he see the tears in the voluminous fabric that she'd been hiding from him.

"Would you let me look?"

Her eyes searched his, for what he did know, but then she finally nodded.

Beau led her to the bed where she sat on the edge. He then lit a candle and set it nearby on the table to cast some light for him to better see her injuries. He lifted her skirts and the riding habit pooled around her knees as he glimpsed the scratches. She had removed her boots and stockings. The poor white silk streaked with blood was draped over the changing room screen, but he'd not noticed that until now.

"Does it hurt?" he asked.

"They sting a little," she admitted and flinched as he stroked the skin above the cuts, exploring them.

His blood began to pound as he tried to remind himself that she needed looking after, not seduction. "Would you let me tend to them?"

She answered with a small nod.

He left and retrieved a jar of salve he kept in his own room. Whenever he nicked himself shaving the salve came into good use. When he returned to the room, he found her waiting for him. She had pulled her skirts up past her mid-thighs, but she glanced away shyly as he approached. It stopped him in his tracks for an instant as he had to push back his instant desire for her.

Get it together, man, he growled inwardly.

"This will help ease the sting." He held up the salve. "Part your legs a little wider."

He drew close, unscrewing the jar and dipping an index finger into the heavy substance. She drew in a sharp breath as he stroked his finger over one of the deeper scratches.

She'd been through so much and he'd rewarded her by yelling at her for it. Now he would do what he could to make up for that error. He applied the salve on every cut and scrape he could find and then wiped his hand on a towel by the wash basin before he returned to her.

"Philippa..." The words he wanted to say stuck on his tongue, but he dragged them out. "I'm sorry."

She blinked slowly, her long lashes fanning down and then up. She raised her hands to curl her fingers around his wrists. "Please never yell at me like that again."

"I won't." He bent his head, so their noses brushed and his forehead touched hers. He cupped her face and searched her fathomless mercurial eyes, for what he wasn't quite certain. "I swear it." The vow was carved in his heart. He would never hurt her like that again, not even if he was afraid for her. They held each other in silence until she shifted closer to him.

"Why do you make me ache?" she asked the question so innocently that it nearly killed him.

"What kind of ache?"

She pressed one hand to her lower belly. "Here. A deep, powerful ache. Is that...?"

"Desire?"

"Is it?" She stared up at him in wonder. "I didn't know what it meant to feel like this. I've stayed away from gentleman and passion. I've seen what others call desire in their eyes, but to me it looks like possessiveness. Like I am something to be owned. But when you touch me...the way it makes me feel? I want more. Please, teach me?"

The sweet beseeching of her tone broke him. How could he deny her? He was hers to command.

"Yes, I'll teach you."

With the kiss that followed, he feared he would be forever lost.

❧ 13 ❧

Philippa couldn't believe this was happening. The most handsome man she'd ever seen was in her bedchamber kissing her in a way that made her body ache and her toes curl with waves of desire. His sexual confidence had lured her into his arms as easily as a moth to a flame and she didn't care if she got burned.

It had been foolish to ask him for this. There was no possible way this could end well. But she was tired of fighting her own desires. He broke the kiss and gave her body a raking gaze causing a flare of heat to emanate from his focused look.

"Do you trust me?" he asked, his voice husky with need.

She nodded without hesitation. She didn't trust *herself* but given that her body had won the battle tonight against her mind, it no longer mattered.

He helped her slide off the bed, then unbuttoned the front of her riding habit and peeled the coat off her shoulders. Her pulse quickened as he unhooked the skirt and it fell to her feet in a puddle of blue velvet.

He twirled his fingers and she turned, offering him her back. A playful spark skittered under her skin as his fingers plucked at the cords of hers stays. Even the touch of his fingers against her bare back as he removed the stays, gave a wild yet quiet sort of intimacy to this moment. She reached up to cover her bare breasts with sudden embarrassment, but he didn't stop her. He continued his gentle touches and movements of slow, sweet seduction as he pulled the pins from her hair. It tumbled down in wild waves and he leaned into her, burying his face against the crown of her hair.

"Why do you remind me of a garden every time I'm near you?" he murmured. His warm breath whispered over her scalp and each word was a searing breath that shot waves of pleasure down her body. "You're more dream than woman."

He brushed her hair back from her shoulder and pressed soft kisses against her neck. Beau's breath was warm. As tingles slid down her spine, she slowly released her hands and let them fall to her sides. He gripped her waist from behind before he moved his palms to cup her breasts.

Philippa moaned as he kneaded the soft, aching flesh and lightly pinched her nipples. She'd never known how sensitive her body could be until he touched her. It was as though every caress lit some flame within her, making her feel like a beacon of intense light. She hadn't imagined she could feel so glorious and so alive.

His hard body behind her blurred with the sensation of his mouth on her neck. His erection gently nudged her lower back, and she was overwhelmed by curiosity about his body. Beau made her feel...brave in a way she'd never felt before, brave enough to make sensual demands of him.

"I want to touch you," she gasped.

He chuckled and turned her around to face him. He unbuttoned his waistcoat while she watched, eager and breathless. Slowly he removed his shirt and let her drink her fill of his body. She never could have imagined that seeing a man undress would be such a powerful and exciting experience. He unfastened the front of his trousers and lowered them off his hips.

There was a pause, where he stood with his breeches low on his hips, his body so clearly wanting hers, while they stared at one another. Philippa saw the question in his eyes. Was he allowed to continue? Did she want him to keep going? It was her decision, but from the moment she first saw him there had never been a choice, only desire. This quicksilver passion that flashed and burned between them had, in some ways, been inevitable. She bit her bottom lip as he bent to shuck his pants and boots off.

Philippa's eyes strayed south down his chest to the trail of dark hair that started below his navel and led to his shaft. He was hard and the sight fascinated her. She reached for him, but hesitated.

He seemed to know what she wanted and gently grasped her hand, entwining their fingers briefly before he brought her palm to his chest. He was smooth except for a tiny patch of dark hair that started below his naval. Fascinated, she trailed her hand down his chest, feeling each corded rope of muscle that adorned his abdomen before she dared to touch his erection. When she finally did, she curled her fingers around his thickness. His eyes closed as she stroked him. His obvious pleasure and the feel of his soft, hot, velvety skin was so enticing to her. Philippa drew a deep breath to settle herself as she leaned towards him.

He opened his eyes as he thrust his hips toward her while she continued to stroke him. But the balance of power was turning now as he cupped one of her breasts and flicked his thumb over her nipple until she clenched her thighs together. There was something magical about touching each other like this. He was teaching her how to open up to her desires and she adored him for it.

Beau raised her up, and she gasped as she released him. He carried her back to the bed and lay her down on it. For a moment, they simply stared at one another, both knowing that this was no longer a game, no longer an exploration or even a lesson, but a journey they would take together.

"You need only say the word and I will stop," he said, but that was the last thing she wanted. She tilted her head back and let go of the last vestiges of propriety and embarrassment to give in to her own desires.

"Never stop," she commanded. "Please, never stop touching me."

His rakish smile could have given her wings to fly.

"Yes, my lady," he replied, and she knew she was lost to him, now and forever.

He stroked a fingertip from her neck down to her mound. She trembled as his finger parted her folds. She blushed at the wetness she felt pool there. Beau stroked her, teasing patterns in her hot flesh until her legs were shaking and a need too strong to ignore had built inside her.

Philippa expected him to enter her, to take her the way she was told men were supposed to. But he didn't. He bent over her, kissing her breasts, flicking his tongue over her nipples and sucking on the tender peaks. She hissed in shocked pleasure.

"You like that?" he murmured against her, his voice deepening with desire.

"Yes!"

He took his time kissing his way down her body, exploring her valleys and peaks and curves. She took note of a dozen places on her body she'd never thought to be special. Yet with each flick of his tongue, or press of his lips, she'd come alive with fresh pleasure and anticipation.

He continued to toy with her nipples while his mouth moved to her folds. His tongue played with her until her entire body was hot and she felt like she almost couldn't breathe. She was sweating and suffocating with pleasure.

"Please... I need..." She didn't know what she needed but *he* had to know. When she looked down the length of her body, she saw that carnal knowledge in his gaze.

He spread her legs wide, fit himself at her entrance, and leaned over her as he entered. He thrust hard and pain pinched deep within her. She cried out, startled by the invasion.

"Breathe, darling, breathe," he encouraged gently.

When he did move inside her, she calmed as her short breaths evened out.

"Better?" he asked.

"Yes, much." She gazed into his whiskey colored eyes, marveling at how they'd become a deep tawny gold as they reflected the firelight.

Then Beau began to move, withdrawing and surging back in. Slowly at first, then harder. Each thrust made her slide on the bed forcing him to grip her hips to take full control of her in a way that made her dizzy. She couldn't deny that she relished the feeling of safety with him, even as he made love to her so fiercely.

As her need grew and the peak of pleasure she sensed came so close, she had a realization: he was tearing apart her soul. A sudden ache burned deep inside her heart. He had tied her to him, yet she feared this moment for him was merely satisfying a physical need.

He was a rake. And French nobility. Such men didn't fall in love with servants.

"Stay with me, darling." His words broke through her sad thought and she met his intense stare. Just like that, the sensations of him filling her were too much to resist. The pleasure which followed was pure, hard, and overwhelming, like a cascading waterfall crashing down upon overly dark moss-covered stones.

She sucked in a breath as her heart swelled. A dozen emotions flooded her eyes with tears. It was as though everything around her was glowing and glorious. Beau leaned over her, whispering sweet words of comfort. A few moments later, when she'd calmed, his expression changed. The sweetness was replaced by intensity as he began to thrust back inside her again. Sensitive nerve endings rippled to life again and she cried out in exquisite torture as he pumped into her over and over. His hands held her hips possessively in a way that sent her senses spinning.

Beau gasped her name as his body turned rigid and he emptied himself into her. She'd never felt incomplete before, yet coming together with him, feeling the tenderness of his touch when he claimed her mouth with a kiss left her feeling full-hearted. She was overwhelmed, and for a long while, neither of them spoke or moved, except to kiss.

"So, this is what everyone fusses about in such hushed tones?" she asked when their mouths finally broke apart.

"Rather nice, isn't it?" Beau replied, his rakish grin making her giggle.

"It rather it is." She curled her arms around him. Would he leave now or would he stay? She didn't dare ask. He ran his palms along her back as he nuzzled her neck.

"Thank you for the gift," he said as she closed her eyes. "Gift?"

"Your first time with a man. It was a wonderful gift and I am honored by your trust." He finally pulled back enough to stare at her. "You must be tired. I came here to see you were well after your fall, not to take advantage of you."

"You didn't." She assured him. "You could never do that. I'll always want you."

His eyes met hers as she said that, and she wondered if she had made a mistake in her confession.

"You should get into bed. We have a long day of social calls, followed by dinner tomorrow evening." He stepped back, their bodies separating, and she instantly felt the loss of their intimate connection.

"Would you...stay?" she asked, biting her bottom lip.

He averted his gaze from her. "I don't think that is wise."

"Please," she pleaded. "I won't ask again. Just tonight." She caught his hand in hers and he looked down at their linked palms.

"I cannot deny you," he muttered with a small smile.

She scrambled to the other side of the bed as he pulled

back the covers for them. She curled up against him once he joined her and rested her head on his chest.

As she started to fall asleep, she wondered about how everything that felt right to her always turned out to be wrong. How could this not be the same? But that would be tomorrow's problem.

THOMAS WINTHROP ALIGHTED FROM HIS COACH outside of the small village of Islington just before midnight. A chill wind dragged its claws along the back of his great coat, and he moved restlessly, looking about.

The stone cottages were dark and the moon above was waning, allowing only a faint milking glow to illuminate the tops of the trees and the houses on the lane. Wisps of night clouds stretched thin over the distant stars. It was the sort of night to make a man feel very alone in the world. Thomas shuddered and drew his coat tighter about him.

Lord Lennox, after much searching had discovered the whereabouts of the midwife who'd delivered Roderick. He'd informed Thomas that the woman, Lucy, lived in a cottage with a bright blue painted door in Islington. The cottage in front of him now fit the description. He instructed his driver to wait before he crossed the cobblestone road and unlatched the white, painted gate. A small garden graced the yard in front of the residence, but all the plants were now dormant from the approaching winter.

He saw no lights save one in the cottage window. He walked up the short path to the door and knocked. No one answered. He rapped the knocker again, but still no one came.

"Excuse me," he called inside the half open window. Still nothing. He'd hoped the woman wouldn't mind as he tried the door latch. It turned and opened with a long creak. A cold pit of dread filled his chest as he stepped into the darkened cottage. A single candle set upon a modest roughhewn table flickered.

And there, half shrouded in shadows, lay a body. The skirts of a blue muslin dress identifying them as a woman.

"Christ!" Thomas rushed to the body and knelt. He turned the woman over and held the candlelight to her face. Blood splattered her dress. Two distinct wounds, one in her chest and one in her abdomen, clearly showed where she'd been attacked.

"Ahh..." She gasped softly. Thomas almost fell backward in shock.

"Lucy?"

A flash of recognition crossed her face as her eyes opened. "St. Albans?" she said in a rasp.

"You know me?"

"Albina... looked like you. I knew you would come. It's the only explanation why..." He could only assume she meant the reason for this attack.

"Who did this to you?"

"A man. Handsome...cruel." Her eyes started to close, but Thomas gently shook her shoulder.

"Wait, please. I need to know. Did Albina Monmouth have another child? Other than Roderick?"

Lucy's eyes were barely open. "Twins...but the little boy...poor child...the Wilsons took her...because of...the twins..."

Her body stilled, the rasp of her struggling breaths finally at a merciful end. The words she'd spoke were a chaotic jumble, but one thing was clear: Albina hadn't one child, but two.

Thomas held the midwife in his arms as he collapsed onto the floor. He wasn't sure how long he sat like that before the cottage door opened. When the driver saw him, the man went running into the night calling for help. But it was too late, far too late for so many things.

Only one thing mattered now: the truth. And that truth was he had a granddaughter. One whose life was in grave danger.

Monmouth knows. But so do I now and I will stop him.

❧ 14 ❧

There was nothing more wonderful and terrifying than waking up in a bed beside Philippa. They had slept clear through the night and dawn was peeking through the curtains by the window overlooking the gardens in the back of Boudreaux Hall.

Beau lay flat on his back, replaying the night's stunning turn of events. Bedding Philippa had been the best moment of his life. There was no doubt of that. She had erased all of the memories of other women in his mind. He half-smiled as he looked down at her. She lay tucked beside him, deeply asleep, hair spilling across his chest, her arm curled tight around him as though she feared he would try to slip away.

He sighed at feeling her breath against his skin and watching her lashes twitch as she dreamed, hopefully of him. It was enchanting. He could have watched her forever, memorizing the smallest features in his mind until he could never forget them.

He knew he should slip away before she woke, but he couldn't. If he was being honest, he didn't *ever* want to leave this bed as long as she was here with him. His fingers trailed down her back and she stirred but didn't fully wake. He repeated the action and she sighed softly before she murmured something.

"What's that, darling?" he asked, holding in a chuckle.

Her nose wrinkled. "Five more minutes, Ruth," she grumbled and burrowed deeper into him.

Lord, what a lovely disaster this situation was. He shifted a few inches and pulled the bell cord to summon the maid. His stomach grumbled and he realized with an inward chuckle he and Philippa had been too distracted by what had happened between them that they likely hadn't heard the footman knock with their dinner trays. The poor man had likely heard the sounds of their lovemaking and gone back down to the kitchens.

So, by now the entire household would well be aware of this new development. He couldn't prevent the spread of gossip inside his house, but he knew his staff would keep quiet to anyone else.

The door opened a few minutes later and Louisa appeared around the door. Her eyes were wide as she saw him in bed with Philippa.

"Breakfast, please," he whispered.

She nodded hastily and ducked back out of sight. A few minutes later, a footman entered and set a tray of food on the bed near Beau's hip. He added more logs to the fireplace before discreetly leaving them again.

The smells roused his sleepy lover and she rolled away from him, her eyes blinking slowly as she stretched and yawned before she saw him watching her. She gasped. Clutching the covers up to her neck, her face reddened, and she shut her eyes tight.

"Please tell me we didn't... Did we?"

"We did, darling."

"Not a dream..." she said to herself, opening one eye to peep at him. "And was it...good or did I not...?" she stammered into adorable silence.

"You did very well." He brushed a lock of her hair behind her ear. He didn't want to tell her it was the best he'd ever had as that seemed a far too dangerous thing to admit.

She opened both eyes again and sniffed the air. "Is that breakfast?"

"It is. We missed dinner last evening."

"I'm sorry, I suppose that's my fault." Philippa stared longingly at the poached eggs, toast, and a pot of marmalade.

"No, it was entirely mine." Beau set the tray on his lap so she could sit beside him and prepare a plate. "I waited for you to join me at dinner. When you didn't come down, I told Stoddard to send up some food for us."

Philippa's hand paused as she reached for the toast. "But then we..."

"Yes, and we didn't hear the footman knock."

"Oh dear. They know then about this? About us?"

"I'm afraid so. But you must not worry. My staff is loyal. They will tell no one."

She bit her bottom lip. "When I return to service, they will remember this. It could follow me back to Lennox House if they do decide to talk and what if...?" She stared up at him. "What if I am with child?"

Beau almost cursed. He hadn't even thought about that. Normally he sheathed himself in a French letter, and he was used to his mistresses having their ways of helping to prevent conception as well. But Philippa was a virgin and he lost all control and thought last night. He alone was to blame if any babe had been conceived. He was the one who knew the ways to prevent a child and his impulsiveness had put Philippa at risk.

"If you did conceive, I will take care of you and the child. You need not worry. It's not guaranteed that you will be with child after just one night, yes it is still possible, but it is not for certain."

She frowned, but after a moment she relaxed and prepared an egg and toast. She tapped the egg with the spoon, cracking the shell before she peeled it off. They ate in a quiet silence, but he liked it. They did not need to speak to enjoy one another's company. He offered her a soft smile as they finished eating and she returned it.

"Well, as much as I would like to stay here with you, we must pay calls today. Are you up for the challenge?"

She muttered something about not having a choice.

"It won't be all that bad." He tapped the tip of her nose as he slipped out of bed and dressed. Then he leaned over and kissed her soundly, until she made a soft delighted sound in the back of her throat. Only then did he step back long enough to see the dreamy grin upon her face before he left to get dressed.

His valet was waiting for him in his room, where he shaved and put on fresh clothes. He went downstairs to his study to catch up on his affairs, but the moment his palm curled around the door handle, Stoddard sprinted up to him, his face red as he panted.

"There you are! You have received an urgent summons by His Grace."

Worry prickled beneath his skin as he tore at the letter Stoddard handed him, frantically scanning its contents.

"St. Albans knows something about Philippa. I must go. Tell her to wait until I return."

"Of course, sir."

Beau collected his hat and left the house, all but running down Pall Mall Street until he reached the duke's townhouse. He knocked and the butler ushered him in.

"This way, sir. You're expected." Mr. Jarvis escorted him straight to the St. Albans's study.

St. Albans was facing the windows that overlooked the street and did not immediately turn when the Beau was announced. He seemed focused, and yet lost at the same time.

"Your Grace?" Beau spoke after minute.

Finally, the Duke turned around and Beau stepped back in shock. The Duke was splattered with...was that blood?

"Good God! What happened?" Beau demanded.

"Sit down, my boy. *Please*," the Duke entreated.

Beau slowly lowered himself into the nearest chair.

"After the Essex ball, I went hunting for the midwife who helped Albina through the birth of Roddy." St. Albans seemed unconcerned by his frightening appearance and unharmed, so Beau remained silent.

"I discovered her name was Lucy and she lived near Monmouth's estate. I arrived after dark and found the woman on the verge of death. It is her blood, not mine. I've only just returned and haven't had the time to change. You see, what I have to say could not wait."

"Your Grace..." Beau's heart began to pound against his ribs. Whatever St. Albans was about to say, he knew that it would change his life forever, he simply couldn't fathom how.

"She said a handsome, cruel man stabbed her. I can only surmise it was Lord Sommers on another of Monmouth's errands after he failed to kill Philippa." The duke spoke her given name quietly which surprised Beau. That fact that the duke had just called the maid by anything but her surname was shocking. St. Albans was always too proper, except when it came to Beau and his endearment of using *my boy*.

"You believe Sommers killed the midwife? Why?"

"Because she was a loose end, one that had to be removed."

"What does she have to do with Philippa?"

"That woman had *everything* to do with her. I held the poor woman in my arms and her dying breath expelled one crucial word." The duke's eyes were full of pain, to the point where it hurt Beau to meet his gaze.

"What did she say?"

"Twins. My boy. *Twins*."

"Twins..." Beau's ears began to ring. He blinked as things began to settle into place. "But how...?"

"Philippa is mine, my boy. My granddaughter."

Beau's chest tightened, preventing air from getting in. He gripped the arms of the chair, his knuckles white.

"Your granddaughter?"

"Yes. Somehow she and Roddy must've been separated at birth. We must find the girl's parents, those people on Bond Street."

"Yes... The textile shop owners," Beau said faintly. He could barely process what the duke had told him. If what he said was true, then...

Beau flinched. He'd seduced and compromised St. Albans's *granddaughter*, not a servant. There would be far greater consequences for what he'd done with her last night. Not that he was enough of a cad to assume that

Philippa as a maid mattered less than her as a lady, but only that St. Albans's wrath might be harder to manage than Philippa's parents.

Hellfire and damnation. What have I gotten myself into?

"We must tell Philippa," Beau said, trying to remain calm. A duke's granddaughter, a woman who was still in grave danger, had been working as an upstairs maid at Lennox house.

"We must find her parents first. I'll change my clothes. Wait for me."

After the duke left, Beau found his legs and went to wait in the foyer. Jarvis was already there, watching him anxiously.

"Do you know what this is about, Mr. Boudreaux? His Grace has been secretive, but I worry about him," the Butler confessed.

"As do I, Jarvis. As do I. As soon as he can tell us what he knows, I suppose this will all be revealed."

"Ready?" St. Albans came down the stairs freshly dressed.

"Yes." Beau followed him outside where the coach was waiting.

"Your Grace, if she's truly your granddaughter..." Beau wasn't sure what he wanted to say.

"If she is, you and I must discuss her future," the Duke of St. Albans said without hesitation.

"Future, yes." Beau had the strange sensation that an invisible rope was tightening around his neck.

"She's been living with you for days with no chaper-one." The duke's trap shut around him.

"She has," Beau agreed.

"You know my feelings on that even when I thought she was a servant. Now that I am convinced she is my flesh and blood, you will do the honorable thing, my boy."

"Yes, yes of course," Beau replied as he pulled his neck clock. Was it overly hot inside the coach? Yes, it was very hot and smoky.

I've died and now I'm burning in the fires of hell for what I've done.

The coach jerked to a stop.

"Bloody Christ!" The duke dove out of the coach as men and women suddenly started shouting fire! Beau looked out of the open coach door to see a row of shops nearby were indeed on fire. The center shop had a hanging sign which said *Wilson's*. Beau began to run, sprinting past the other man as he reached the shop.

"Beau! Wait!" St. Albans was behind him, almost on his heels, but there was no time to wait. Beau opened the shop door and rushed inside. He lifted his arm, covering his mouth with his shirt. With his other hand he ripped his neck cloth off and covered his mouth so he could breathe past the smoke filling the air. Flames licked up the walls, eating up the large rolls of cloth displayed about the shop. A set of stairs led to another floor. Beau braced himself against the heat as he headed up the cramped steps. He found a closed door and pounded a fist on it.

"Wilson!"

"Yes?" A shout answered him over the roar of the blaze.

"You've got to come out. I can help you."

The door opened and smoke poured into the room beyond. A man and a woman were holding each other. The woman's face was streaked with tears.

"Is there a way out? We woke up and saw the smoke..." Wilson's eyes were red and his voice rough from the smoke.

"Yes, we must go now though." Beau helped them into the hallway and as they headed down the stairs, the wood around them creaked and groaned.

"Just a bit further," Beau encouraged. He put an arm around Mrs. Wilson's waist, supporting her as they dodged the flames. The roof above them cracked, fractures showing in the wood beams.

"Run!" Beau shouted. The second the ceiling began to fall, Beau shoved Mrs. Wilson ahead of him. The beams fell right behind where she vanished into the light and safety of the outdoors. The timbers blocked the only way out. He and Wilson shared a look.

"Thank you for saving my wife," Wilson called out above the fire.

Beau nodded, not knowing what else to say. They were going to die. This was it and all he could think of was Philippa. The way her eyes seemed to consume his soul as she gazed up at him moments after they'd made love. It was a moment he would carry with him always, that feeling of...completeness, of a gentle unending obsession to never lose her. And now that memory would be his last. Wilson coughed and shielded his face against the flames.

"Wait..." Beau suddenly stared at the cloth roles all around them. "Do you have wool?"

Wilson coughed and pointed to a corner opposite where they stood.

"Grab it." He and Wilson lifted the heavy bolt of fabric. "Take it to the door, unravel over the beams." They worked to roll the heavy fabric up over the pile of flaming wood beams. As he had hoped, the fabric didn't catch fire. Wool did not catch fire easily, if at all.

"Climb! Quick!" Beau push Wilson ahead of him as they climbed the unsteady, half-burned wood pyre. There was only a few feet unblocked between the top of the door frame and the crumbled ceiling beams, but he and Wilson crawled out, singed but alive.

St. Albans was there to drag him away from the shop, shaking him hard. "You bloody fool. You could have died!" And then St. Albans crushed him in an embrace. Beau coughed. He felt almost as if he were capable of breathing fire like some medieval Dragon. He bent double, his hands resting on his knees as he panted for breath.

"You saved us," a feminine voice whispered. "Thank you."

He glanced up to see Mrs. Wilson and her husband watching him. Wilson had an arm around his wife's waist.

"We owe you our lives, sir. How can we ever repay you?"

Beau shared a look with St. Albans. "With information. We need to talk about your daughter."

"Our daughter? Philippa?"

"Yes," Beau said. "Please come back to my home with me."

"Who are you, sir?" Wilson asked, not sure what to make of the request. "What's this about then?"

"Beauregard Boudreaux. I'm the man who's going to save your daughter's life."

PHILIPPA CAME DOWNSTAIRS LOOKING FOR BEAU. SHE'D taken extra care with Louisa's help this morning to wear her best day gown in a lovely hunter's green and her hair was pulled up and threaded with crimson ribbons. Even her slippers were exquisite with embroidered leaves upon the toes.

She felt beautiful and she was admittedly excited to see Beau's reaction to her. After the night they'd shared, she'd been so worried he would pull away, that the allure of bedding her had faded. But after this morning, she'd been delighted to see the intimacy between them had only grown since they first met at Castleton Abbey.

She'd just reached the bottom steps when Stoddard opened the front door.

"Oh my word, sir!" Stoddard's startled gasp sent Philippa rushing next to him.

Beau stood there, his face blackened with soot and his clothes equally as sullied. Behind him was the Duke of St. Albans and...her parents?

"Mama! Papa!" She cried out she took in their own disheveled appearances.

Beau moved aside to allow her parents to enter. Philippa rushed forward, throwing her arms around them.

"We're all right, love." Her mother assured her in a soothing tone.

Philippa stepped back. "What happened?"

Her father shared a glance with Beau. "Someone set fire to the shop. We were trapped upstairs. Mr. Boudreaux saved us, Pippa. We would have died if not for him."

She turned to Beau, her eyes filling with tears of unspoken gratitude.

He nodded at her but something about the way he looked at her made her heart still. She saw, or maybe she just wished she saw, a look of soft, tender promises that made her ache deep inside.

When Beau spoke, his voice was rusty, and he coughed. "Stoddard. Bring us a basin of hot water and fresh towels. We'll need tea and sandwiches too."

Stoddard bowed and departed as Beau led everyone to the drawing room. Philippa sat with her mother on the settee and held one of her shaking hands. The duke stood next to the fire. He was the first to break the uneasy silence.

"Mr. and Mrs. Wilson, I need to hear about how you came to have Philippa as your child."

Philippa stared at the duke. "What?"

Her parents looked uncertain how to answer him.

The duke shook his head. "The time for deception is at an end. We are not enemies of your child, as you can clearly see, but she *does* have enemies. Until we know everything, she won't be safe. So, the truth now, if you please."

"He is telling you the truth." Philippa insisted but her mother squeezed her hand.

"Hush, child," her mother said gently, then nodded at Philippa's father. "Best we should tell them, Mason."

Her father frowned. After a moment's hesitation, he nodded and cleared his throat. "Twenty years ago, Beth and I were living in the mill house near Lord Monmouth's estate. We had just given birth to a son." He looked down at his feet. "A few days after the birth, the midwife came to see us. The night had been full of storms and the skies had just cleared when she arrived around midnight."

"This would be Lucy?" St. Albans asked.

Her father nodded. "I'll never forget. She stepped into the moonlight and I was shocked. She held a newborn babe in her arms." Philippa started to shake her head as she sensed what he was about to say.

"That babe was you, Pippa. She brought you down

from Monmouth's estate fresh from your mother's womb. You were the most beautiful baby we'd ever seen."

"No..." Philippa's vision spun a little and she shook her head, trying to clear her thoughts.

"Lucy told us your life was in danger. The earl's wife had born twins... The firstborn, a son, was stillborn. And then you came. Philippa. Lucy said you were a fighter, but your father, the earl, needed an heir but had only you. He threatened to kill you that night. Lucy begged us to save you. But in return..." Her father choked on the words.

"The cost was your own son," said St. Albans. "Correct?"

Her mother nodded and took up the story. "Our poor Roddy. We wanted to be able to see our son, but the earl forbade it. We never saw our boy again after that night. The earl gave us coin to start a new life far away from his lands, so we took you and left for London. Lucy came to visit us until you were five or six, then she stopped. She didn't want the earl to know she'd stayed in contact with us lest it put your life in danger again."

"Lucy..." Philippa whispered as old memories tinted with love filtered through her mind. The woman had called her a great warrior and had brought her dolls.

"You remember the necklace we gave you at sixteen?" Her mother asked her.

"Lucy gave it to us," her father said. "It was your mother's, your true mother. She'd taken it when she'd learned

Monmouth was putting your mother's jewels and clothes in storage. He never noticed it went missing"

"But *you* are my mother," she told Beth, her throat aching as she fought back sobs.

"You have two mothers, Philippa. The one who bore you and the one who raised you, and we both love you with all we have. Your birth mother never left you. She's been here all along guiding you to the other half of your family." Beth's eyes traveled to the duke and Philippa's gaze followed.

"You are...?" But she dared not finish.

"I'm your grandfather," the Duke of St. Albans said. "I've been waiting twenty years to meet you, my child."

Philippa could see he wanted desperately to hug her, but she didn't move. This was too much. She looked to Beau. "Did you know?"

"Who you are? No," he replied. "I never could have imagined the truth, even though it was staring me in the face."

"But why take your son?" asked Philippa. "Why not remarry? Produce a proper heir?"

Philippa's father ran a hand over his jaw and sighed. "Lucy told us the earl had trouble bedding women. It had something to do with his blood flow. She said he would likely never marry again because he would not be able to produce another child. But he was obsessed with not letting his fortune and estate go to some distant cousin. Taking our Roddy was his only choice. He wanted his lands and money to go to a boy he'd raised as his own, even if he wasn't his blood."

"Have you seen him, our Roddy?" Beth said with broken longing. "We've only heard a bit early on from Lucy."

"Yes. He's a good lad, kind and intelligent. There's nothing of Monmouth in him, thank God. I see now there's only the both of you in him," St. Albans assured them. "He's a sunny young man with a bright smile and a warm heart. I'm proud to consider him my grandson still. You should be proud as well."

Beth's lips quivered. "I wish we could see him."

"Perhaps, once this is all over," Beau said. "But for now, our priorities must be focused. Monmouth must be made to account for what he's done. If we can have him arrested, everyone will be safe."

"Until that time," St. Albans added. "Mr. and Mrs. Wilson as well as Philippa will move into my residence."

"Oh, we couldn't," her father said.

"I insist. We're family now, even if it is rather unconventional."

Beau watched Philippa as she blushed. Leave him? Could she do that after everything they'd shared? She didn't want to; of that she was certain.

"What do we do now?" Beth asked.

"We set one last trap, one that will force Monmouth into the light. Something public, something important where he fears we will unearth his secrets for the *ton* to see."

"What would that be?" Mason pressed.

Beau looked to Philippa. She stared back at him, confused by the sudden determination in his eyes. When he spoke, his words sent her world spinning.

"A wedding...between Philippa and myself."

❦ 15 ❦

"A wedding..." Philippa echoed. The word bounced around in her head until her skull began to throb. Everyone was staring at her, expecting some kind of answer. It was too much.

She was the daughter of a long dead woman she would never know. She had a father who tried to kill her—twice. And the parents who raised her weren't her parents at all.

"No," she whispered. When she saw their confused faces, she repeated herself. "I'm sorry, my lord, but no." Then what she'd said sunk in and she was mortified. Philippa surged to her feet and fled the room. For a second she stood in the hall, unsure of what to do.

Leave. That's what she needed to do.

She was halfway up the stairs when she heard booted steps following behind her. She increased her pace, but a pair of arms banded around her waist, halting her. She struggled against the hold.

"Philippa," Beau's gentle, soothing voice made her still, despite her panic. The fight left her as he turned her around and she buried her face in his chest. She didn't want comfort from him, yet she needed it. Being around him left her feeling like she was stuck in a surreal dream, a place where wonderful things were everywhere, but always just out of reach.

"I'm sorry. We threw a lot at you just now. It's only natural to react this way." He stroked her back. She stiffened, but then she sank into him again. His strong arms gave her all the support she needed not to fall completely apart.

"Beau, we cannot marry."

"Why not? I'm rather fond of you. We get along rather well. You'd be safe, and we both know it would be wise, in case you are with child." He threaded his fingers through her hair until they reached her scalp and he began to give her the most wonderful massage.

Philippa pulled away from him so she could face him clearly and force him to listen to her. "We shouldn't marry just to stop Monmouth and Sommers, or because I might have a child." She drew in a breath, and noticed his brows knit together. A sudden hardness entered his gaze. "Marriage is an act of love, Beau. It's a union of two hearts. It's not supposed to be mercenary."

"We can have it annulled after, if you wish." Beau said

quietly, yet the suggestion cut her far deeper than the idea of marrying just to catch her would-be murderer.

"'Tis madness," she replied.

Beau continued to massage her scalp. "No, it makes sense."

"But you wouldn't want to marry me. Not without the threat of Monmouth looming overhead, or if I wasn't St. Albans's granddaughter."

"I *would* want to." Beau lifted her chin, so she lifter her face to him. "I would not tie myself to you unless I wished to. Otherwise, I would have proposed another option. My suggestion is based only out of a desire to be your husband."

There was some emotion in his eyes, half veiled, that she couldn't read. "Do you love me?" she asked.

"Do you love *me*?" he countered.

"I..." She didn't know the answer. She felt *something* for him, something deep and frightening. Something so strong that if she was to give it a name, it would perhaps give it too much power.

If it wasn't love, could love follow? Did she want it to?

"Is this truly happening?" she asked. "Am I really St. Albans's granddaughter?" If it was true, then she was the cause of every danger, the cause of Lucy's death, the cause of her parents' shop being destroyed and their lives almost taken. She was responsible for all of it. The knowledge was a punch to her stomach, and she could barely breathe with the weight pressing down upon her lungs.

"Quite certain. The midwife who brought you into this world was murdered and one of the last things she said was that you were one of a pair of twins. Sommers killed her under Monmouth's orders. We're certain of it. That the fire started at your parents' shop early this morning was an attempt to remove them as well. They knew the truth and were the last ones left with the answers."

He lifted her chin, his gaze confidant, but she reminded herself she was the granddaughter of a duke, she was not subservient to anyone any longer, not even Beau. Before she agreed to anything, she needed to so something first.

"I should like to speak to my parents. Alone," she informed Beau.

"Of course. Your grandfather and I will give you all the time you need." Beau escorted her back to the drawing room. "Your Grace, let us give them the room for a minute."

St. Albans bowed to Philippa, a sad smile on his lips. She couldn't help but think back to the night she'd dined with him and the connection she'd felt. It was as if some part of her had recognized him as kin. Once they were gone, she turned to her parents, seeing them with new eyes. They weren't her flesh and blood, but they were not strangers. They had raised her and loved her as their own. And yet...

"Philippa." Her mother opened her arms and Philippa

was frozen for but a moment, then it didn't matter. This *was* her mother.

"Mama," she cried out as she embraced her. Her father joined them, wrapping his arms around them both. They smelled like smoke, but they also smelled like home.

"Oh dear, we dirtied you." Her mother moaned, noting the ashes from the fire now coating her clean skin and new dress.

Philippa shook her head. "You're safe. That's all that matters." The reality of this morning was starting to sink in. Her parents had almost died, and she hadn't even known.

"What happened?"

"We woke to the smell of smoke." Her father's voice rose a little and was hoarse. "We opened the door but the hall to the stairs was clouded and we could see the fire. We stayed in the bedchamber where we put clothes under the door to stop the smoke but..." He paused, cleared his throat. "We would've died if Mr. Boudreaux hadn't arrived. We owe him our lives."

Philippa's eyes filled with tears. Beau had saved them.

"Father, is it true? Did I really come from Lord Monmouth's house?" She couldn't yet say that monster was her father. He wasn't, even if he had sired her.

"Yes."

"Why did you agree to it? I wasn't yours and you lost your son in the bargain."

Her father's eyes were soft as he touched her cheek.

"Your life was in danger. Beth held you in her arms and you sucked on her finger. Brand new to the world, you were. Not even an hour old and you were hungry for food and love. We were offered the means to start a new life, and we knew we could keep you safe, love you with all our hearts. It didn't matter that you weren't ours by birth."

"But your son..." Philippa could not believe the sacrifice they had made for her, a child they had only known a few minutes.

"We knew Roddy would be safe, and he would have a life we could never give him. Lucy told us he grew up to be a fine man, handsome and caring, despite Monmouth. But we didn't dare believe it until Lord St. Albans told us. He will be an earl someday. He will have money, a home, a chance to marry a woman he loves. Parents, proper parents that is, do what they must for their children. When we took you..." Her father paused. "I hate admitting that we accepted coin from that man, but we used that money to buy a life in London for you. Clothes, a good tutor, whatever we could without raising the suspicions of those around us."

"We still have much of the money," her mother said. "We were planning to use as your dowry. Five thousand pounds. We'd hoped for you to have a beautiful trousseau and anything else a young bride might wish for."

The mention of that reminded her of her marriage proposal, even if it had been an entirely unconventional one.

"Do you think I should marry Mr. Boudreaux? I understand we must find a way to lure Monmouth and Sommers out, but there must be another way to do so without a marriage."

"He has a deep affection for you, Philippa. He spoke of you as we rode here in the duke's coach and..."

Her father's face turned ruddy, and her mother continued where he could not. "His eyes lit up as he spoke of your bravery, of your sweetness. I believe he might be in love with you."

"He can't be." Philippa argued. "I know he likes me, and that he has affection, but..."

Her father chuckled. "Men often don't recognize love until they are about to lose it."

Her heart fluttered as she dared to dream that her father might be right. "I never believed marriage was to be a part of my future," she admitted.

He touched her chin the way he'd done since she was a child. "For what it's worth, I believe he's a good man and marriage to him would be a good choice."

"Love is always a risk, my dear," her mother added. "But the rewards can be infinite."

Philippa played with her skirts as she thought it over, then squared her shoulders. "Then I shall do it."

Her mother burst into a smile. "A wedding, Mason. A wedding!"

"Yes, love, a wedding." Her father agreed and pulled them both into his arms for another hug.

A wedding to Beau Boudreaux... London's most notorious bachelor.

St. Albans cleared his throat. "Beau, my boy."

"Yes?" They stood outside the drawing room, both silent until that moment. Beau felt nervous... Had he ever felt that way around St. Albans? Not that he could recall.

"Are you sure about this? The marriage, I mean." St. Albans's doubting him stung more than he expected.

"You believe I shouldn't marry her?" He was too afraid to ask where the duke's uncertainty lay, either in Beau marrying his granddaughter, or the marriage as trap to bring Monmouth and Sommers to them.

"I believe you should do what is best for her, but also you." He touched Beau's shoulder. "Marry for love, my boy, not for catching some damn villains in a trap."

"But you said I should marry her since she had been compromised because she'd been living under my roof without a chaperone."

St. Albans flustered. "Well, she is my granddaughter. My need to protect her was strong, and perhaps I reacted hastily. If you recall, I didn't feel comfortable with her living with you even when I thought she was a servant. Now I believe I have a little more say in what happens to her and that's why she and the Wilsons will move in with me."

The thought of Philippa even just at the end of the street made him feel oddly caged, like a wolf lashing out at being separated from his mate. He didn't like her being away from him and it wasn't simply because he feared for her safety. He'd become addicted to her, the feel of her in his arms, the taste of her lips, and the way she said his name as she laid half-asleep in bed beside him after making love. He didn't want to let go of that. Yet St. Albans was right.

"We can have the marriage announced tomorrow," the duke said. "We won't bother with the banns. They would take too much time. It would be best if we obtain a special license. Lord knows nearly everyone does that these days."

Beau listened to St. Albans as he made plans for the wedding breakfast to be at his home and that Philippa's mother Beth would likely try to arrange for trousseau which he would donate some money toward.

"And then there's the dowry," St. Albans mused. "I'll give you ten thousand."

"Your Grace," Beau shook his head almost violently. "I won't take even one pound. You know how I feel about that old nonsense. I have my own money and..." Beau trailed off. "Bloody hell, I need to contact Lennox. He'll wonder what the devil is going on when I announce my marriage to his maid. I don't want him to misunderstand and challenge me to a duel." He was only partly teasing.

"You'll have time for that after we leave." The door to

the drawing room opened and Philippa exited, her parents behind her.

"Are you ready to come home with me?" St. Albans asked.

"Yes, but I need to pack my things."

"Your clothes can be sent over this evening."

"Oh, but I don't wish to leave my mother's necklace behind." She blushed and bowed her head in embarrassment.

"Allow me to accompany you." Beau joined her and they walked quickly upstairs to her bedchamber. He needed a moment alone with her again.

"Have you come to a decision? On marriage, I mean?"

"Yes." Philippa walked to her bed which had been put to rights with fresh linens. It was as though last night had never happened.

"And?" He followed her with his eyes, watching her restless pacing.

She stopped and offered a hopeful smile. "Yes."

Beau smiled back, perhaps too quickly given the look of suspicion in her eyes.

"But I have one condition."

"Name it."

"I need to know if you will try to love me. I know that I am not what you wished for, that you had no desire to marry or love anyone... But would you try with me?"

It was as though she knew the one thing he feared, the one thing he couldn't agree to without it being a lie. "I..."

"*Try*. That's all I'm asking. An attempt." The need for love was there in her hopeful face and he knew he would agree. He would try. Even if it scared the bloody hell out of him.

"I can endeavor to try," he whispered in her ear and he meant it. He didn't know if love would come, or if his heart would let it, but he would try. That single promise seemed to give her the strength to turn and face him. Their lips met in a feathery kiss.

"I vow to try to love you as well," she replied. "Although I suspect I am halfway there already," she added under her breath.

Beau cupped her face and kissed her like a man possessed. He only let go when they were both breathless. He kept his forehead pressed to hers, savoring the intimate touch before he finally stepped back.

"You'd better go, before I try to keep you here against the duke's wishes."

Philippa hastily packed a small bag and rushed past him. He stayed there a moment longer, his gaze drifted to the painting of Leda and the Swan.

A god so desperate for a woman he made himself mortal...vulnerable. Beau now understood Zeus's decision. Not the outcome or the violence, but certainly the initial thought of transformation and the risks that came with it.

Beau had worked so diligently to avoid love and marriage and yet he was willingly walking into the latter and it was likely inevitable that the former would follow.

If only the shadow of Monmouth wasn't looming over this whole affair...

PHILIPPA AND HER PARENTS ENTERED THE DUKE'S HOME that afternoon as guests. The butler, Mr. Jarvis, was delighted to see them. She was shown to a bedchamber, as were her parents, and all were allowed some time to rest before the evening meal. She hadn't thought she was tired but after all the revelations from that morning, her body was heavy with exhaustion. Collapsing on the bed, she closed her eyes and drifted to sleep.

She woke some time later to the sound of the dining room gong and rushed hastily downstairs. Her mother and father were already in the Duke's vast dining room, staring at everything wide-eyed. It was easy to understand their shock. They'd never been in a house like this before, let alone a grand room with gilded portraits and fine china, or a mahogany table that could seat twenty people.

Philippa was distracted through most of dinner, answering only when questions were posed to her. It was a small relief to be left to gather her thoughts. To be an upstairs maid one minute and a duke's granddaughter the next...and she was to be married in a few days? It was a lot to absorb.

She pushed her chair back and stood. St. Albans and her father stood in response.

"I'm terribly sorry. I'm not feeling particularly well. May I go to bed, Your Grace?"

"Of course, child. Jarvis, have Mrs. Honeyweather see to her needs."

Jarvis nodded and walked with her to the stairs. He hovered politely at her elbow, making her feel a bit silly.

"Thank you, Mr. Jarvis, but I can walk upstairs. Please do not trouble yourself."

"If you have need of anything, Miss Wilson, we are at your disposal." Mr. Jarvis's understanding look made her shake a little. The duke had told his butler and house-keeper the truth of Philippa's birth, but they'd been warm and gracious before as well. Nothing seemed to have changed now that her past had been disclosed to them. It was a mark of the duke's personality that he'd selected servants who were accepting of such things. She had known of plenty of fine houses in London where the servants were just as arrogant as their masters, if not more so.

Philippa paused halfway up the stairs, her fingers resting on the mantle as she felt something call to her. She turned and, without fully knowing why, headed toward the portrait gallery. She was alone as she reached Albina's portrait, and no candles were lit for her benefit. Moon-light illuminated the woman who mirrored her in so many ways.

This was her mother, a woman who'd died giving her life and a name. When she'd been here a week before, she'd been astonished at the similarities but never could have imagined so simple a truth as being the woman's daughter. Philippa studied the Albina's features, wishing so hard that she could have known her, at least for a time.

"I'm sorry we never met," she whispered to the silent face smiling down at her.

"I'm sorry, too."

St. Alban's voice made her jump. He smiled as he joined her.

"She would have adored you. In fact, I know she did. She came to visit me when she was six months pregnant. Your father was furious with her for traveling, but Albina insisted. She stood here in this very hall, a hand on her belly as she spoke of her child with so much love."

"But she had two children." The twin brother Philippa would never know was a hollow space in her heart. She would have given anything to have grown up with a sibling.

"The numbers wouldn't have mattered. Love isn't bound by limitations. She loved both of you, even before she knew you."

Philippa wrapped her arms around herself. "Your Grace, what are we going to do? If we reveal my true heritage, Roderick will no longer be the Earl of Monmouth's heir. He will be cast out of society."

The duke clasped his hands behind his back. "I've been thinking over that problem as well. Roddy is dear to me. I love the lad as much as I love you."

His words made her gasp.

St. Albans's brows rose. "You're surprised I love the boy?"

She stared down at her slippers in embarrassment. "I'm surprised that you love *me*."

"My child, I loved you the moment Beau told me he'd rescued you, before I'd ever seen your face or learned the truth about you."

"But why?"

"Because of Beau. You didn't know him, my dear. He was lost in himself. He wasn't invested in life, but then he came to your rescue. I wish you could have seen him as he talked about you. You woke him up." The duke's bitter-sweet smile tore at her heart. "After he lost his father, he had only his mother, but then he lost her as well. After that, he closed up. He changed. But now I've seen a man with hope. It scares him, I think, but at least he has it. And you, my child, are his hope. I love you for that."

Philippa bit her lip as the duke held open his arms. She moved into his embrace, shaking as sobs wracked her.

"You will never have cause to be sad again, not if I can help it," the duke promised. "You have your parents. You have me. And you have Beau."

She wasn't sure how long she stayed in his arms, breathing in the faint scent of cigar smoke and thinking how it was strangely comforting.

"Now, dry your eyes and go up to bed. We have a full day ahead of us. Your wedding."

"You truly believe marriage is a good idea?"

"I do." The duke answered without hesitation. "Beau would not have volunteered it unless he was certain that was what he wished to do."

"But it's only to catch Monmouth and Sommers." He had denied it, of course, but that may have simply been for her benefit.

"Not at all. I believe he offered marriage because he wanted it, but he is afraid to admit it. As a man, I can admit that sometimes we avoid things that frighten us. We come up with bizarre rationalizations, and we act in ways which prove mysterious to sensible ladies such as yourself. But I promise you that Beau is a good man and he would do right by you in marriage."

Philippa looked at the wall of ancestors. Her ancestors.

"Your Grace..."

"Grandpapa," he suggested softly. "If you like."

"Grandpapa." She gestured to the dozens of oil painted figures. "Would you tell me about them?"

The duke took her arm in his and they paused at a portrait next Albina's. "I would be delighted."

"This was Marianne. Your grandmother. Devil of a flirt, she was. A lover of tea and cold winter mornings where frost patterned the windows. She never met a horse she couldn't ride."

He moved on down to the next portrait of a solemn man with silver eyes and a slightly hawkish nose. She liked his dark, brooding masculine beauty.

"And him?" Philippa noticed he wore a find doublet of blue silk and high-heeled shoes that had been the height of fashion a hundred years before.

"Alexander, a great uncle of mine. Clever fellow. Always causing trouble with ladies of the married variety but never getting caught. A delightful scoundrel, or so I've been told."

And so went the introductions to a lineage Philippa never imagined could be hers. Hanoverian princesses, master painters, dukes, infamous rogues, and talented singers. The family was a noble one with color and life. For the first time, Philippa felt she might fit in somewhere with these passionate adventurers.

❧ 16 ❧

Beau walked into Ashton Lennox's drawing room and found the typically business-minded baron playing a game of peekaboo with his two-year-old daughter.

"Where's Rose?" The man chuckled as he covered his face and then pulled his hands apart to reveal himself to the child.

"Here!" Rose squealed, kicking her chubby legs in delight. She had her father's pale blond hair which curled in natural ringlets just past her shoulders. Her eyes lit up with a sense of devious mischief.

Beau coughed politely and the little girl raised a tiny finger at him.

"Rogue!" she cried out, still pointing at him.

Beau covered his mouth to hide a laugh. "I beg your pardon?"

Lennox straightened, scooped the girl up off the couch and set her on one hip before he gave her cheek a kiss.

"Go find your mother." He set her down and she toddled off into the corridor.

"Miss Rose!" The footman exclaimed, chasing her past the doorway as she giggled wildly.

"Did you just set your baby loose in the hall on her own?" Beau asked.

"Absolutely. It keeps my footmen on their toes to chase the scamp about."

"And did she just call me a rogue?"

Lennox rolled his eyes. "It is her new favorite word. Her mother tends to call all my friends rogues, so Rose now believes any man who sets foot in this house must be one."

"I see." Beau still smiled as he followed Ashton out of the drawing room and into a study where he closed the door.

Lennox leaned back against his desk. "There have been some developments, I understand?"

"Yes, how did you know?" Beau asked, a little suspicious.

"The fire on Bond Street was a very public affair. I had a man I trust watching over the Wilsons' shop and he reported to me at once that you and St. Albans had safely escorted the Wilsons out of the flames."

"So, it is true. You do have spies everywhere," Beau

muttered. He'd heard rumors for years that he should never cross Lennox, and now he was seeing why.

"I won't apologize," Lennox said. "Now, what have you discovered?"

"To get straight to the point," Beau said. "Philippa is Monmouth's legitimate daughter. She was one of a set of twins. The other child, a boy, died. Monmouth was left without an heir, so he paid the Wilsons for their son. In exchange, they took Philippa to raise as their own. We learned this from the Wilsons, but only after we found the midwife had been killed. We believe Sommers killed her and set fire to the Wilsons' home."

"Christ," Lennox muttered, seeming to put together some larger picture in his mind. "The things men will do to hold onto a legacy... and I'm starting to wonder if there is anything Sommers *won't* do if it amuses him. The man is a monster. When will it end with these two?"

"When Philippa is dead, or they are arrested," Beau replied bluntly. "Which brings me to my next point." He paused, but Lennox did not interrupt him. "I am to marry Philippa. We are putting our announcement in the morning post tomorrow and I am to obtain a special license today."

Lennox eyed him. "Is this merely to draw the scoundrels out?"

Beau held his breath a moment. "No."

"I presume Philippa is aware of this?"

"Yes, she has agreed."

"Very well. Not that you or she need my consent, but you have it."

"Thank you."

"When is the wedding?"

"A few days from now. The sooner the better, I should think. Monmouth, and likely Sommers, will seek to act once they learn of it.

"Indeed," Lennox agreed. "What would you have me do?"

"Honestly, I don't know. Maybe have pistols present at my wedding?"

Lennox nodded thoughtfully. "And a few other precautions, perhaps."

"You don't truly think they would storm into St. George's and shoot her?"

"No...At least not Monmouth, and certainly not directly. But with Sommers, I cannot be too sure." Lennox stroked his chin and a shadow passing across his face. "One can never be sure how evil men with greed in their hearts will act, and it seems that predicting Sommers is like predicting the weather. Better to be prepared than not."

"Agreed." Beau sighed. "Well, I suppose I'm off to procure a license and see to the announcement in the papers."

Lennox crossed his arms and leaned back against his desk. "Oh, now that your circumstances have changed, are you still planning to move to New Orleans to run the Southern Star shipping office?"

Beau hadn't given much thought to his own plans in days. Not since he rescued Philippa. "I... Yes. I believe I will."

"Let me know if that changes. Our business arrangement can remain the same. I would simply need to send correspondence to New Orleans to have a manager appointed for you if you choose to remain here with your bride."

"Thank you, Lennox. I will keep you informed. Once I survived the wedding, I'm sure I will have a better sense of my future."

Beau shook Lennox's hand before he left him alone in his study.

As Beau stepped out into the wintry light of October, he couldn't help but wonder what he should do. For so long, he'd wanted a change of pace. He wanted to go to New Orleans, but she wouldn't wish to leave her family or her grandfather, not when she'd just found him. There was no possibility she would wish to move to New Orleans with him.

That meant he faced the decision himself, to stay or to go. And while his heart said no, his mind insisted that time and distance apart would keep his foolish heart safe.

THE FOLLOWING MORNING, THE ANNOUNCEMENT OF Mr. Beauregard Boudreaux's engagement and upcoming wedding to one Philippa Wilson took London by a veritable storm. Emily St. Laurent, the Duchess of Essex spread the paper out before her while she ate her breakfast with her husband, Godric.

"This is rather splendid." She read over the small but tastefully composed announcement without revealing to anyone in the *ton* that Philippa was Monmouth's daughter. She was still listed as Miss Wilson, but Emily imagined there would be a fair bit of speculation about Philippa's background now that she'd captured a notorious bachelor rake for a husband.

"What is splendid, darling?" Godric's gazed fixed on his wife and Emily blushed. Even after six years of marriage and two children, she still felt like a young woman in love whenever her husband looked at her with his bewitching green eyes.

"Beau is to marry Miss Wilson. You remember what a lovely couple they made at our ball, don't you?"

"I do. Ashton and Cedric had a bet going, if I recall. Cedric wagered it would take two weeks, Ash believed it would take two days. I never thought I would see Ash lose a bet."

Emily threw a sugar cube at her husband's chest. "You men and your wagers. You lost quite a bit of coin on me, as I recall."

Godric grinned. "True, but I don't regret it. Not even

one shilling." He brushed crumbs off his chest from the sugary projectile and politely made Emily a cup of hot chocolate, adding a fair amount of sugar to it, just as she liked it.

"Thank you." Emily leaned over to kiss his cheek, but Godric turned his face at the right moment and their lips met, giving her a scorching kiss that made Emily forget all about wedding announcements for a moment.

"I'm rather surprised Beau is marrying the girl," Godric said.

"Oh? Why?"

"He's never been one to look toward marriage. He's always been outspoken against it."

Emily perused the paper again. "Perhaps it's because of who the lady in question is."

"Who? You mean the duke's granddaughter? Beau never struck me as a fortune hunter, or social climber. He has money enough of his own."

"She's not just any duke's daughter. She's St. Albans's granddaughter." Emily reminded him. "The man is like a father to Beau. I imagine the duke is overjoyed at the prospect."

"I suppose you're right. But Ash is nervous about what the girl's father will do."

Emily perused the business section of the paper while Godric buttered some toast.

"Godric, do you think Lord Monmouth is still dangerous to her even after all that's happened?"

"Unfortunately, I do." He leaned back in his chair. "Anything that steps between a man and his money is dangerous."

"But it isn't as if no one knows. Heavens, the entire League knows because Ashton told them the story."

"Yes, darling, but if Mr. and Mrs. Wilson died, there would be no evidence left. Ashton has had men scouring the church registries where Philippa and Roderick were born. The records offer no mention of the child that died, which is to be expected. Philippa is listed as the Wilsons's child and Roderick as Monmouth's. All we have now is the word of the Wilsons against Monmouth, since the midwife who delivered all three children is conveniently dead."

Emily cringed. "And the word of a peer against two commoners, yes I see what you mean. What about Lord Sommers?"

"There's a reason that demon has never been brought to account. His hellfire club was never about worshipping the devil so much as to acquire incriminating material on a number of unsavory but powerful people. He's rumored to have ties to some of Prinny's inner circle."

Emily scowled. "The king? Oh, Godric, you must all be careful." She still couldn't forget how she'd almost lost him all those years ago to Sir Hugo Waverly. He and the rest of the League had almost died.

"We will, I promise." Godric said.

She folded up the newspaper and handed it to her

husband. "We are attending the wedding, aren't we?"

"Most definitely." He smiled, but the expression was hard and dangerous. "And if Monmouth tries anything, we will be ready for him."

Emily pushed her chair back and stood.

Godric caught her wrist. "Going so soon? The children are still a bed."

"Not at all," she replied as she settled into his lap and he wrapped his arms around her waist. "I am exactly where I wish to be." She leaned in to whisper in his ear. "I predict we have half an hour before they wake up.

Godric chuckled softly. "The last time you said that, our little angels were found awake and drawing on the nursery with chalk. The footmen were scrubbing the walls for hours."

Emily giggled. "Well, then we mustn't waste a moment." She trailed a hand on his chest and delighted in the way Godric's eyes lit up with heat and desire.

"No, we mustn't." He said and dragged her mouth down to his.

CORNELIUS SELKIRK, THE EARL OF MONMOUTH, READ the wedding announcement and his breakfast turned to ash in his stomach. Panic rose like a knot in his throat. If the girl was to marry Boudreaux, that meant she'd likely already been introduced to St. Albans, her own grandfather, and it wouldn't be long before the man pieced things together. He wasn't blind. He would see Albina in the girl and Cornelius's careful protection of Roddy's future would be in jeopardy.

"Boudreaux is getting married? Never thought I'd see the day!" Roddy exclaimed as he leaned over his father's shoulder to peer at the announcement.

Cornelius jumped. What the devil was the boy doing here? He was supposed to have stayed in the country.

"Roddy, why didn't you stay at the manor house? I left early and didn't need you to come back with me," Cornelius said.

Roddy grinned as he slid into the chair beside his father and helped himself to the breakfast laid out before them.

"I heard you had an unexpected visitor that first night after we left London. I was worried when you left the following morning. Is everything all right, father?"

Cornelius closed the paper and tried to calm his nerves. "Yes, quite all right."

The girl was to marry Boudreaux tomorrow at St. George's. A *very* public affair. This was a prelude to some kind of public revelation; he could feel it. And such a venue would make everything harder, but no doubt that's what Boudreaux and Lennox intended. Neither of them were fools.

"But neither am I," he muttered.

"Pardon?" Roddy asked.

"Nothing, 'tis nothing." He focused on his son. "I thought you were going to stay with the steward and review the accounts."

Roddy shrugged. "I spent a few days with Mr. Featherstone, and we managed a full review. Nothing to worry about. The tenants are prospering and so are we."

At any other moment Cornelius would have been proud. Roddy was everything he'd wanted in a son and heir. He was intelligent, easy tempered and despite the wealth at his fingertips, he seemed content to live well within his means. There were months where Cornelius had gone without remembering that Roddy wasn't truly his flesh and blood.

His own father would have thought Cornelius weak for resorting to buying an heir, but Cornelius only wanted to make sure his legacy went on with a man who'd earned it, a man who *valued* it. His distant cousin was a fool who spent money on nothing but clothes, women, and horses. If he were to inherit, he would drain Monmouth's estate in months, and his legacy would be ruined. Cornelius had seen too many men sell their homes when gambling and dangerously high wagers ran them onto the proverbial rocks.

"Father, *who* did come to the house that night?" Roddy asked. His usually jovial face was solemn now. "They arrived after midnight. I heard the servants in the corridor. It must have been an important guest, so why was I not informed?"

"A simple acquaintance, nothing important. He needed advice and I gave it to him."

Roddy shot him a look that most distinctly said, *I'm not a child. I know you're keeping secrets.* But he didn't press the matter.

"Well, I'd better have my valet press my best clothes if we're to attend the wedding tomorrow. Grandfather will be thrilled. He's been trying to marry the man off for years." Roddy finished his breakfast and stood. "Shall we dine at the club tonight, or will you be attending to business?"

"Business, I'm afraid." He watched his son's face fall with disappointment before he left Cornelius alone.

"I'm doing all this for you, my boy," he murmured when the door clicked shut.

Then he left the dining room and proceeded back to his study. He would call upon Sommers one last time. Taking lives seemed not to bother the man and Cornelius needed Sommers' lethal talents one last time. The man had killed the midwife without hesitation. Now there were only three loose ends. The girl and her parents. Lennox and Boudreaux knew the truth, but without the Wilsons, they had no proof.

ALISTAIR READ THROUGH MONMOUTH'S LETTER AND frowned. A wedding. Tomorrow. Boudreaux worked bloody fast, but Alistair could work faster. He walked over to a tall bookshelf in his study and reached under the edge of one shelf and found a small rough lip underneath. He pulled on the lip and the bookcase creaked and gave way as he pulled it toward him, revealing a small darkened room beyond.

Alistair lit a candle and carried it into the room with him. Then he set the candle on the table and opened a nearby glass cabinet full of various bottles. He reached for one set of bottles with matching images of snakes etched into the labels by his own hand. He set the bottles on the table and approached a wall that held a dozen daggers. Taking a small, sharp one, he placed it on the table, uncorked one of the bottles, and dipped the tip of the dagger into the bottle. When he withdrew it, he watched the liquid drip off the tip. His murky reflection in the silver blade showed his dark smile.

He would let Boudreaux marry the girl. But there would be no blissful wedding night. Alistair dried the blade with a cloth before exiting the secret room and closing the door. He tossed the cloth into the fire and tucked the dagger inside his coat. There were a few more things to set in motion today to ensure Boudreaux's doom, but they were easily done. He touched the cut still healing on his face, the pinch of pain a reminder of what that girl owed him. He didn't care if she was the daughter of the king. She would pay for what she'd done, and so would Boudreaux.

❧ 17 ❧

Berkley's, Beau's gentleman's club, was quiet in the late afternoon. Men were either reading the papers or relaxing in the smoking rooms to enjoy a quiet moment away from the bustle of the streets outside. Beau reclined in his favorite chair in the main salon, watching the men come and go from his somewhat hidden spot in the distant corner of the room.

More than one older fellow had taken to napping in these overstuffed chairs, and had he been in a better mood, Beau would have smiled at the occasional snores coming from the nearest man who had a tea cup precariously balanced on one knee whilst he slept. But Beau was far too distracted to really notice. Lennox's question about New Orleans left him feeling cornered and conflicted.

"Boudreaux?" A voice drew Beau's focus from his inner thoughts. The Earl of Lonsdale, Charles Humphrey, one of

Lennox's closest friends, stood in the doorway to the salon.

He raised his chin in greeting. "Lonsdale."

Lonsdale was just passing by the snoring older man when he grinned wickedly as he bent over and whispered something in the man's ear.

"Oi! Bonaparte is coming!" The old man bellowed as he jumped up from his chair. The teacup rattled onto the red and black oriental carpet, but fortunately did not break.

"You're about a decade too late for that, old chap." Lonsdale clapped the man on the shoulder and settled him back into his chair. "And you'd better order a fresh cup of tea."

Then Lonsdale joined Beau in a nearby chair and leaned into whisper. "Sorry, I cannot abide it when they snore here in the main salon."

Beau found himself chuckling despite his cloudy mood.

"I hear congratulations are in order. Saw the announcement."

"Thank you," Beau said, but his dark mood was now returning.

"You don't seem to be full of felicitations, my friend." Charles noted. "Did St. Albans force your hand on the matter?"

"What? No...not exactly. It was my idea."

"Then what is bothering you? Lennox said the girl is

exquisitely beautiful, kind, and intelligent. Those aren't exactly terrible qualities in a wife." Lonsdale teased, but there was an earnest concern in his gaze that made Beau wish to unburden his troubles upon the fellow.

"I don't want to...lord, this sounds foolish. I'm afraid of falling in love with Miss Wilson."

"Love is a frightening thing indeed." Lonsdale agreed.

Beau shook his head. "I doubt you understand my meaning. I do not simply wish to hold onto my bachelor-hood like some trophy of personal freedom. I've seen how wonderful love is, but I've also seen how it can destroy a person if lost."

"No, I understand. Love leaves you exposed, your heart open and easy to be destroyed. It's not a thing any person should take lightly."

"My mother," he paused as he tried to reign in his emotions. "My mother died inside the day my father was executed after the Terror. She was a living shell for years. She loved me, of course, but there was so much of her missing after she lost him. In some ways I felt as though I'd lost her long before she actually died." He looked at his friend. "That's the lesson life taught me. Love is loss. Love is pain. Love is unending sorrow."

Lonsdale leaned back in his chair and for a moment his eyes closed before he spoke.

"What a load of nonsense."

"Pardon?"

"Love is none of those things. The pain of its

absence does not define what love *is*, Boudreaux. You have to decide what you what in life. A man who risks nothing gains nothing. I never knew your mother, but I can say with some certainty that she would have preferred half a life with your father to a full life without. To reconcile yourself to never knowing love, is to live half a life, no matter how long your years are." Lonsdale stood and gently touched his shoulder. "But if you cannot be that man who loves against all odds, then set her free. Don't tie her to you without love. She deserves more."

Beau's throat tightened. He'd tried all his life to be a brave man, but he wasn't sure he could be braver than his mother. He didn't know if he could survive being a shell if he lost a wife he loved madly.

PHILIPPA STARED AT HER REFLECTION IN THE DRESS shop. The pale blue silk was exquisite and the Belgian lace trimmings cost more than she could ever dream of paying. But her mother told the modiste to spare no expense for her trousseau. Philippa turned a little on the pedestals as two seamstresses pinned parts of the gown in place.

"Ouch!" She gasped at a little flare of pain in her arm.

"I'm so sorry miss, you moved." The girl pinning her sleeve in place apologized and went on fitting pins.

"The gown will be ready this evening. We shall deliver

it to Lord St. Albans's residence," the modiste informed Beth, who observed the fitting with overly bright eyes.

"That will be perfect." Beth sniffed and then looked at Philippa. "Won't it, dear?"

"Yes," Philippa agreed.

"The rest of Miss Wilson's wardrobe will be ready for her honeymoon in two days." The dressmaker added with pride.

"Have you spoken to Mr. Boudreaux about that yet?" Beth asked Philippa.

"Mama, I scarcely had five minutes alone with him this afternoon when he came to see me."

"Well, five minutes was scandalous enough," her mother declared.

Philippa rolled her eyes. Five minutes hadn't been enough time for anything at all. Beau had simply asked after her health before the weather was spoken about and they revisited the night of Lady Essex's ball. There had been no talk of Monmouth or Sommers, or anything else of concern. Beau had been cool and distant in a way that worried her. She didn't want them to marry if he was going to change or pull away.

"Well perhaps you may tease the details out of him tonight at dinner. I'm sure he will have something grand planned for you. Perhaps a tour of the continent?"

Philippa listened to her mother speak, but after a few moments, she closed her eyes and tried to regain her calm. Perhaps Beau was just as nervous as she was. It was entirely possible he was having second thoughts. She certainly was. She liked Beau more than she should have, but was it enough? Passion faded. What if what lay between them wasn't strong enough to sustain a lifelong commitment like marriage?

By the time she and her mother had arrived at St. Albans's home, it was nearly time for dinner. They changed into their evening gowns and when Philippa came downstairs, she found Beau lingering in the foyer.

"Beau?" She walked over to him and he smiled, but the expression seemed forced.

"Good evening, Miss Wilson."

Philippa stared at him, hurt and stunned by the sudden civility that had been erected between them in the last day. If this was going to be a marriage, she couldn't let him do this. She grabbed his hand and pulled him into an empty drawing room. She closed the door, sealing them inside and blocked the way out with her body.

"Beau, we must talk. If you do not wish to marry me, then for heaven's sake, tell me now. It isn't too late. No one knows what transpired between us and..." She drew in a breath as she realized she was shaking with nerves. "If this passion is an ephemeral thing for you, please do the honorable thing and set me free."

Beau was quiet, his whiskey colored eyes intense as they bored into her.

"Is it that way for you? An ephemeral passion that wilts as quickly as it blooms?" He stepped closer, his voice lowering; her body responded instantly. What she'd felt for him hadn't faded at all.

"Of course not," she said defiantly, her body flushing with desire as he trapped her against the closed door.

"It isn't for me either," he promised, yet she saw hesitation. No, it was *fear* she saw in his eyes.

"Then why are you putting this distance between us? We left civil manners and politeness behind when we…" She dared not finish.

"Made love? Yes, I thought we had, but then I discovered you were St. Albans's granddaughter and I couldn't take advantage of you."

She put a hand on his chest, and he tensed. "But you *aren't* taking advantage." His hand curled around her wrist, but he didn't pull her palm off his waistcoat. His fingers rubbed against the pulse point below her palm.

"I am not accustomed to being a gentleman, Philippa. St. Albans would be the first to tell you I have been quite scandalous in the past."

"I don't care," she insisted.

"Oh, but you should, my darling." Beau whispered. "It's so very dangerous for you to be alone with me."

Philippa saw a tempting darkness in his gaze and for the first time, she also saw the rakehell he had professed to be. Before, he had cared for her, protected her, but now she was seeing the side that *wanted* her.

"I thought you were afraid of me," she confessed, staring at his lips.

"Afraid of you? No darling, afraid *for* you. The night I claimed you, I've been haunted by your essence. Your scent, your sweet sighs as I kissed you, the feel of you gripping me as our bodies came together in the firelight." He let go of her wrist, but only so he could curl his hand around her waist.

"A man like me has hungers. I have needs you may find too strong to be satisfied." His hand slid lower, starting to pull up at her skirts. Breathless excitement rippled through her at the thought of them having only these few minutes alone before someone would look for them.

"Aren't you afraid, Philippa?" Beau's tone spoke of rough passion beneath the alluring sweetness.

"No," she said, but in truth she was nervous. She was new to this, new to opening herself up to experiences like this.

"As my wife, you would be subjected to all my desires. I can take you anywhere I please, any *way* I please." Beau stroked his fingertips along her bare thigh above her stockings and a sudden, desperate desire made her whimper. But he didn't stop. Instead, he lowered his head to her neck, kissing up to the shell of her ear just as he rubbed at her folds with one finger. He stroked her gently, then thrust that finger into her, driving her mad with desire. He didn't stop the teasing little love bites on her ear lobe as he continued to push her to the point of pleasurable pain with his intimate caress.

"Beau, please..." she whispered.

"Please stop?" The satisfaction in his eyes confused her. He wanted her to make him stop? To be afraid of him?

He started to pull away, his hand slipping out from under her skirts, and smiled down at her as though he'd won some battle she hadn't known they were fighting. But she wasn't afraid of him or her desire. She wanted all of him if she was to marry him, but it seemed he didn't want her the same way. Pain lanced her heart, so hard that for a moment she couldn't catch her breath. She had thought he desired her and promised to try to love her, but even that had been asking too much of him now it seemed.

"I see now that you are too much of a gentleman to cry off, so allow me do it for you. You are released from our engagement and from all promises you have made to me."

The triumphant gleam in his eyes instantly vanished. "Philippa, I didn't" He stopped short, closed his eyes and then blew out a deep breath. "I am sorry."

"You need not be. I was a fool to fall in love with you. I knew from the start that you would not love me back. This is my fault. I can accept responsibility."

A new gleam grew in his eyes that was just as intense but softer somehow. "You...love me?"

"How could I not?" She choked down a bitter laugh and tried to push him away from her. He stood too close. His tall body made her yearn for things that would only break her heart.

Beau did not let her escape. He pushed her gently back against the door and cupped her face in both of his hands.

"You love me, even when I try to push you away?" he asked.

"Love is love, Beau. It doesn't obey the limitations placed upon it by others. A heart loves whom it loves, against all odds. Against all reason." She didn't want to confess this to him, but the words spilled out of their own volition.

"You truly love me? Despite my faults and foolish behavior?"

Tears clung to her lashes. "Please, don't torture me any further. Go. I shall make the necessary excuses to the duke and tell him to cancel the wedding."

Beau's sensual mouth hardened. "We aren't calling it off. You and I will stand together in St. George's tomorrow and bind our lives together."

"*No.* You said you would find another way to draw Monmouth out before, so do it some other way." She pushed at his chest, but he didn't move an inch. "I won't let you make our marriage some noble sacrifice to crucify yourself upon."

"You don't understand. Marrying you is anything but a sacrifice. In fact, I feel incredibly selfish to want you the way I do. I was afraid from the start you were agreeing to marry me out of some sense of debt you felt you owed me."

Perhaps that was how it started, but after all that

happened, she felt bound to him by something far stronger.

"It is impossible not to love a man like you, even if you are exasperating." She tried to look away, but he still held her face in his hands.

"Then love me. Let me give you my name, my life even." Beau breathed in and his words filled her heart with traitorous hope. "I made a promise to try to love you back and at this moment, that promise seems easier than ever to keep."

"No more pulling away? No more games?" Philippa demanded.

He brushed his thumbs over her cheeks. "No more games. I surrender."

"Then tomorrow we marry." She grasped his wrists and he lowered his mouth to hers, claiming her lips in a kiss that melted away all thoughts except one: She was irrevocably in love with him and that was far more dangerous than whatever dark plans her bitter father had in store for her.

❧ 18 ❧

Everyone kept exclaiming all the way to the church that it was a fine day for a wedding, but Philippa was too nervous to enjoy the warmth of the sun. Her nerves had left her exhausted and short of breath. She knew Beau was already waiting at the altar because her grandfather had winked when he casually mentioned it as she and her parents rode towards St George's. It had been discussed that her father would be spoken of as another old friend of her father's from the country and would be walking her down the aisle.

"You're looking a bit pale," her mother said and touched her cheek. "Don't fret about the wedding. They go by rather quickly."

"They certainly do," her father agreed.

The duke's eyes filled with concern. "You don't wish to cry off?"

"No, I want to marry him," she assured St. Albans. She smoothed her hand in nervous patterns over the kid gloves she had not yet put on. Once they reached the church, her father assisted her and her mother out. The duke and her mother went inside. Philippa stood alone with her father outside the church and tried to control her breath.

"You love this man?" he asked, not for the first time.

"Yes. More than is wise, I'm sure." She leaned on his arm while they walked into the church together. The murmur of voices dwindled away and soon an organ began to play as they walked down the aisle. The church was nearly full, and she spotted familiar faces in the crowd.

Then her gaze locked on the one man she never expected would be here: Lord Monmouth. She froze. He stared at her, his intense, dark eyes turning her veins to ice. She half expected him to draw a pistol there and then, but he made no move of any kind.

She knew that Lennox and Beau had expected he might attend with his son, but she had secretly hoped he would not. Her frantic gaze sought out Lord Lennox, who stood two rows behind Monmouth. Unlike everyone else in the room, Lennox was not looking at her; his eyes were fixed on Monmouth.

Lord Lennox won't let Monmouth hurt you, she tried to remind herself. Beau had assured her that Lennox and several of his friends were all armed and ready to stop Monmouth if he tried anything. She wasn't a fool. She knew Lennox was hoping Monmouth would do exactly that so they could have one more charge against him.

Philippa turned her focus to Beau, who stood waiting for her. For a moment, there were only the two of them in the gilded, ancient church. She was lost in him, lost with the vision of his whiskey colored eyes, dark hair, and sensual lips that would surely mend her shaken heart. She was caught in a sunny memory of when she'd stolen a few moments alone in the Lennox library to read a book of poetry. Byron had become her favorite and his words now floated to the surface of her memory.

"But once I dared to lift my eyes,
To lift my eyes to thee;
And, since that day, beneath the skies,
No other sight they see."

He was the only sight she could see just then. He was all that mattered. He would belong to her, and she to him, and a union of their lives would bring them closer together and perhaps...perhaps someday he would love her back. She couldn't let anything else taint this moment.

She had to trust that Monmouth would not be allowed to act against her, either now or after the wedding.

Her father kissed her cheek and she joined Beau at the altar. Her blue silk gown, trimmed with Belgian lace, let her imagine for one moment that she was the gentle born lady she'd never had a chance to be.

The clergyman conducted the service and Philippa knew she would remember very detail of the ceremony. She focused on Beau's eyes and the way the light from the stained glass played in mosaic patterns on his dark blue coat. Even the way he smiled as he slipped the ring on her finger and made his vows was forever etched in her heart. She was captivated by him as strongly as the first moment he'd stepped into the doorway of Castleton Abbey to rescue her.

And, just as her mother had predicted, it was over all too soon. Beau pressed a heated kiss to her lips that scandalized the audience with gasps from the ladies and chuckles from the gentlemen. Her head spun and her knees buckled. Beau caught her around the waist before she could fall.

"Are you all right?"

"Yes, I think so. I just need a bit of air." She nodded toward a door at the side of the church which led to a courtyard with some tombstones.

Beau walked with her as Lord Sheridan joined them.

"Everything all right, Boudreaux?" Sheridan's concerned gaze moved between her and Beau.

"Bridal nerves, my lord," she apologized. "I simply need a bit of fresh air."

"Quite understandable." He followed them out into the courtyard. "My congratulations to you both, by the way." Sheridan beamed at her before he winked at Beau. "Thanks to you, I won a fair bit of coin."

Beau chuckled and shook his head. "So, I've heard."

Philippa gently pulled free so she could walk toward the gravestones. She sat down on one of them. Feeling guilty for not being stronger today, she looked at the name etched in the fading rain-smooth stone.

Mr. Edward Morris – Who lived as he loved...greatly.

"My apologies, Mr. Morris, but I can't seem to catch my breath," she murmured to the grave. She watched Beau as he laughed and spoke with Lord Sheridan.

Married. I am married to one of London's most notorious bachelors. She smiled and shook her head at the thought.

A gentle but chilly breeze swept through the grave-yard. The fallen leaves tumbled and twitched on the dry grass until several tangled in the hem of her skirts. She stood up and bent to shake the leaves free of the frost blue satin, only to stumble as another wave of dizziness hit her. She tried to call for Beau, but something struck her hard from behind and she crumpled to the ground. Her fingers clutched the dead leaves, crinkling them as she tried desperately to rise to her knees, but she collapsed back to the ground with a whimper.

She clung to consciousness as strong arms gathered her up and carried her behind a large tomb. She rolled her head up, trying to see who'd done this, to make sense of the fuzzy chaos around her. It had to be Lord Monmouth—

"Not so clever, are they?" Lord Sommers mused, looking in the direction of Beau and Sheridan. Then he looked toward a coach parked on the street near the tomb. He carried her to it as the door opened and the footman with the pale angry scar on his face helped Sommers shove her inside. The footman held a pistol on her and she sank back into the cushions, lacking the strength to fight. The coach jerked into motion while she tried desperately to keep her eyes focused on Sommers.

"Did my father have you take me?"

"So, you know the truth now? Good. That's one less thing I have to explain. No, Cornelius doesn't know I'm here. After I took care of loose ends, he decided he no longer needed my services. The fool thinks he could hire me to do his dirty work and then walk away, but I have you now and I'll do with you as I please."

Lord Monmouth hadn't planned this?

The coach stopped a short while later and she was dragged from the coach and into a shabby looking building. Sommers gripped her wrist tightly and she was hauled up a flight of stairs and into a set of rented rooms.

"You may put away the pistol, Jean. She is unable to escape." Sommers smiled cruelly as he released her wrist. "Feeling faint headed, are we?" he asked. "Perhaps a bit dizzy? Short of breath?"

Panic fluttered inside of her as she stared at him in dawning horror. How did he know? Unless...

"Poison, my dear." He removed something from his coat pocket and held it up for her to see. It was a little blue bottle with a snake drawn upon its label.

"How?" She hadn't been anywhere near Sommers in days.

Sommers grinned as he held up an inconspicuous silver pin. "Imagine how long it would take for poison to take effect in such a small but assuredly lethal dose... If, say, you were to be pricked by a pin." He tossed the pin to the floor without a care.

"The seamstress," Philippa whispered. It had been an accident, or so she'd thought.

"Indeed. The chit was easily bought. And you thought all this time you were safe. I had planned to let you die in Boudreaux's arms in the midst of your passionate wedding night, but the more I thought of him touching you and how I'd been robbed of that pleasure... Well, I couldn't allow that. So here we are." He waved a hand between them.

"I'm not afraid of death," she said, even though she was afraid, and she was sad not to ever know what it meant to feel Beau's love in return. She'd clung to such deep hopes, but now they felt so far out of reach.

"What you fear matters little to me. But I do have the power to save you." He patted his coat pocket. "One should never create a potion that has no antidote. Accidents happen, after all."

"You have an antidote?" She lunged for him, using the last bit of her strength. But he slapped her hard, sending her reeling back to fall against the bed. Her face burned but she glared at him with all her building fury despite her growing weakness.

"The question you should be asking is what will you *do* for it?"

Philippa tried to keep her thoughts steady. Lord Sommers liked to play with his victims like a bored cat with a mouse. She needed to play along if she was to survive.

"I'll do anything," she replied, her eyes meeting his. She would too, only what he was imagining was far from what she planned. He had no idea how dangerous she could be, if only she had the strength. Too long she'd seen herself as the victim of her own life and circumstances. Now she had everything to fight for, and she would fight to the death for it.

And that death would not be hers.

"Five *hundred* pounds?" Beau exclaimed. "That's a devil of a wager, Sheridan."

Sheridan laughed. "Trust me, I have wagered on far more scandalous things at a far higher price. At least I'm not an obsessive like Brummel. That devil used to bet on raindrops running down a pane of glass."

Beau laughed. "I hadn't heard that before."

"That man bet upon the most ridiculous things, but he was a dandy and a foolish one at that. Any man who values his clothes above good sense is worth knowing." Sheridan reached into his pocket and retrieved a pocket watch. He checked the time and then glanced about.

"Boudreaux..." Sheridan paled.

"What?" Beau turned to face the courtyard and his heart stopped.

Philippa was gone.

"*Philippa!*" He ran through the yard, searching behind the large tombs and saw one of her kid gloves lying on the dead grass. He knelt to retrieve it, his gaze darting around the streets. There was no sign of her.

"How did she get taken under our nose? There was no one out here." Sheridan demanded. "Monmouth is still inside; Ash and Godric are watching him."

Beau was rooted in place, terror gripping him. She was gone. He didn't know where to find her. He was... *lost*.

Sheridan clapped him hard on the shoulder. "Pull yourself together, man. We'll find her."

"We will," he echoed, but bone deep dread was pressing down on his lungs, making breathing next to impossible.

CORNELIUS SAT IN THE EMPTY CHURCH PEW, STARING AT the altar where minutes ago he watched his daughter get married. A chill prickled down the length of his spine as he had watched her say her vows. It was as if the ghost of Albina had spoken to him through the girl.

"I vow to honor and obey, to love and cherish..." Albina said as she gazed up at him...

So trusting, so in love, and so confident he had loved her in return. She'd been drawn to him, to the brooding seductive snare he'd set and only after it was too late for retreat had she learned what kind of man he really was. Yet she hadn't called off the engagement. She'd believed he would come to love her.

He almost had.

But she'd failed him. With her dying breath, she'd given life to a girl that held no place in his home because she could not inherit. For that, he had cursed Albina and seconds later she'd been gone. The image of blood pooling between her thighs on the bed was something he could never erase from his mind. Nor could he forget how it had felt to carry the stillborn son down to the gardens and bury the babe himself. Andrew.

Cornelius hadn't cried. His grief was the kind that ate away at him, digging into his soul as he felt himself bleed out slowly over a lifetime.

Roddy had saved him, as much as that was possible. The cheery boy with a kind heart was in some ways the essence of Albina's lovely spirit, even though the child had not been born from her.

And now he was going to lose Roddy too. Lennox was hovering in the church, with the Duke of Essex just behind him. They spoke in soft whispers as they waited for him to move. He still could not fathom why Lennox hadn't had him arrested for strangling the girl. Whatever Lennox intended, Cornelius was at the end of his rope and could feel it all closing in.

"Father, we should go," Roddy said as he approached the end of the pew. "I've summoned our coach."

"Er... Yes. Thank you." Cornelius stood and collected his hat from the bench. He met Lennox's gaze as he started toward the door. But a second later the appearance of Boudreaux and Sheridan from the side yard pulled Lennox's attention away from Cornelius.

"Don't let that man leave!" Sheridan gasped as he met with Lennox and Essex in the center aisle. "She's gone!"

"What?" Lennox hissed as all eyes turned on Cornelius.

Beau had already grabbed Cornelius and slammed him into the nearest pillar.

"*Where is she?*" The fierce light in the man's eyes didn't scare Cornelius, but he shook his head.

"I don't know. I haven't..."

"Beau, what are you doing?" Roddy shoved at Beau who released Cornelius. Cornelius jerked his coat and waistcoat down, smoothing out the rumpled fabric as he scowled.

"Don't pretend you're not behind this," Beau warned and this time the unspoken threat left Cornelius very afraid.

"Father, what is he talking about?" Roddy demanded.

Cornelius shook his head. To his relief, Beau did not immediately tell Roddy about his interest in Philippa. Cornelius came to the only possible conclusion. "Sommers must have her."

"On your orders," Lennox stated.

"No, not mine. I cut my ties with him yesterday."

"We know about the midwife," Lennox said. "And the Wilsons' shop."

"Those *were* on your orders," Lennox said.

"I have admitted no such thing. I had dealings with the man, which have come to an end. But Sommers is unstable, and he's become obsessed with this woman. I would put nothing past him," Cornelius warned.

"You can dance around the truth all you like," Beau growled. "But *you* set him on this path. You put this into motion and condemned my wife to die."

"I'm sorry," Cornelius muttered, and he was. There was only one way he should have handled this. He was the only one who could have made her death quick and painless. He never wanted her to suffer, yet he had been a coward and hired a monster who would never let her have a speedy death.

"There's no time for this," Lennox said as he dragged Beau away. "We can't allow him even the head start he already has. We'll gather the others and divide our efforts to search likely locations."

Cornelius was now left alone with his son.

"Father? Please tell me what's going on."

"I do not have time to explain. You should return home and wait for me there."

"Where you going?" Roddy asked.

"Please, do as I say." His son's suspicion wounded him, but Cornelius had no choice. He had to go after Sommers. And he had a good idea where the man might go.

Cornelius fled St. George's and hailed a hackney to Rimmel Street. It was a notorious rookery, full of the worst thieves and cutpurses, where many a careless man had lost his wallet, or his life. Sommers had a set of rooms there, if he recalled correctly. Cornelius dreaded to think what the man did whilst occupying those rooms.

The coach driver looked askance at his request, but Cornelius paid him double the standard fare. By the time he reached the rookery, he was sweating. He was going to have to face Sommers and trick him into trusting him one last time. It was the only way he could do what must be done.

𝕊 19 𝕊

P hilippa sat on the edge of the bed, weary and dizzy as Sommers removed his coat and laid it over the chair. When he turned to face her, she did her best to mask her emotions.

"It is rather amazing what a person will do when they believe salvation is within reach. For example, this is your antidote." He removed a second blue bottle from his coat pocket and set it on the washstand behind him. Her eyes fixed on the bottle and his smile grew.

"I can see you planning to grab it, but you're weak. Soon you'll be barely able to breathe, let alone move. So, you had better listen, my dear."

Outside Sommers' footman stood guard, and she knew she didn't have the strength to fight them both.

"Get on your knees. I wish to see you beg, to see those

silver eyes filled with pretty tears. If you please me, I may give you the antidote."

Philippa was not one to beg, but the desire to survive removed all pride. Before she could drop down, the door opened, and Monmouth walked in.

"What are you doing here?" Sommers snapped. "Why did Jean let you in?"

"He let me in because I've paid you to kill her. I thought it would be best to witness the deed done, don't you agree?" Monmouth flipped cold eyes to hers. "Please, continue, Lord Sommers. I am but a mere presence to witness your deeds."

There was a flash of uncertainty in Sommers's eyes before he smiled cruelly at Philippa.

"Very well. Knees, my dear." He pointed to the floor. Philippa looked only at Monmouth as she fell to her knees. There had to be a way to stall him, or to get to the antidote. The wood floor hurt, and she clutched at the bed beside her to brace herself against the pain. Her own father, this terrible stranger, was condemning her to die and wished to witness it.

Sommers step forward, grinning. "Now beg," he repeated his command. She wanted to spit in his face or shove a knee into his groin but she didn't dare, not when she had to play this game better than he did.

"Please," Philippa whispered. She saw Monmouth come up behind Sommers, no doubt to get a better look at her as she faced her doom.

"Please *what?*" Sommers asked.

Monmouth opened his coat and casually removed a pistol. Philippa stared in shock as Monmouth pointed it at Sommers's back.

Crack!

Sommers grunted. His expression was stunned, confused. He tried to turn around, only to have the strength drain out of him, and then he fell to the ground at Monmouth's feet.

"What did he do to you, child?" Monmouth asked.

"Poison," she whispered.

He took time to reload his pistol. "I feared as much. I never should have hired him. This was always between you and me. I am not so cruel. I can promise it will be quick and painless." He didn't meet her gaze and that's when his words sank in. He wasn't here to save her. It was just as he'd said. He wanted to see the deed done.

Monmouth finally looked at her, really looked at her. "I wish it didn't have to be this way. Had your brother lived, you wouldn't have been facing this end. But I need an heir and you cannot be one. If only I'd never seen you that night at Lennox's house. I panicked, haunted by my own past. Lennox would never have looked into your origins. It was foolish of me to even think such a thing." He cleared his throat and guilt darkened his eyes.

"But the die has been cast. Please, close your eyes," he whispered, almost sweetly. "It will all be over soon."

Philippa didn't shut her eyes, she stared at him.

"Father, please..." she whispered, hoping that would remind him they were blood relations, that she was his daughter. That had to mean something...

"Father?" A voice from the doorway made Monmouth turn away from her. Roderick was there, his face pale as he took in the scene. "She called you father..." He moved into the room, looking at the still form of Sommers on the floor, then turning his gaze onto the pistol.

"Leave now, son. You shouldn't be here," Monmouth said. "This does not concern you."

"I think it does, far more than it should." Roderick walked toward them; his hands half-raised as he slowly stepped in front of Philippa.

"She's not my daughter. She's delirious, and dangerous..." Monmouth said. "Leave," he commanded as he raised the pistol. "I will explain later."

"Father, you cannot do this. I won't let you, no matter who she is." Roderick stood his ground.

Monmouth's hand trembled. "You don't understand. She will *destroy* you. She is the end to everything."

Roderick looked to Philippa as she leaned against the side of the bed, too weak now to move. She focused on trying to retain a grip on the bedding to avoid falling on to her back.

"I find that hard to believe, father. All I see is a man lying dead on the floor, and you about to murder a helpless woman."

Monmouth stared at Roderick. "You want the truth?

Fine. Hear this at your own risk. You aren't my son by my blood. That child died in my wife's womb. But she bore a second child, the girl that you so valiantly protect. I gave her to the miller and his wife and purchased you from them. Every moment she draws breath," he nodded at Philippa. "You put your inheritance at risk. I must deal with her."

Roderick was still for a moment. "It's too late, father. Lord Lennox and Beau know the truth, don't they?"

"But they will have no proof. I will see to that. It is my word against theirs. Once she and her parents are gone, you will be safe. Your inheritance will be safe."

"My inheritance? Paid for in the blood of innocents? No, I'm sorry father." Roderick said softly. "If you wish to hurt her, you will have to go through me."

"Damn you! We will lose everything!" Monmouth shouted. "It will all be for nothing!"

Philippa gasped as Beau and Lord Lennox appeared in the doorway. They'd found her. Beau held a pistol on Monmouth.

"It's over, Lord Monmouth," Beau said. "Your son knows the truth now. We all stand against you."

Monmouth lowered his pistol and let it drop to the floor. Beau and Lennox rushed him, slamming him into the ground, toppling the chair where Sommers's coat had been draped. Monmouth fell on the ground with a grunt, Beau on top of him.

"Find some rope." Beau called out. Lennox searched

the room. Roderick turned to Philippa and helped her onto the bed, but it was too late.

"What's the matter, what did my father do to you?"

"Not him...Sommers..." She pointed a shaking hand at the bottle on the washstand before collapsing back on the bed. As her mind sank into darkness, she thought she heard Beau shout out her name. Perhaps it was all a dream...a terrible, frightening dream.

"Something is wrong with Mrs. Boudreaux," Roderick said. "She's out cold."

Beau glanced up. "Philippa?" He called out her name, but his wife was as still as death.

"You see, you've only delayed the inevitable," Monmouth said. "Sommers poisoned her."

"Bloody Christ!" Lennox swore as he spun to face Monmouth. Beau sat up, losing his hold on the earl as he continued to stare at his wife in horror. He had failed her *again*. This time he couldn't save her. He—

Pain lanced up his arm and he looked down numbly to see Monmouth had cut him with a small blade. Monmouth shoved him and Beau fell back. Lennox moved fast, slamming the earl onto the ground again and with one well delivered blow to the man's jaw, he knocked him out.

"You all right, Beau?" Lennox asked.

"Yes, I'm fine. He just scratched me with the blade." Beau took two steps toward the bed to reach Philippa but the world tilted and he stumbled, hitting his knees by the bed.

"Lennox... I can't feel my legs," he breathed. His vision dotted and he clutched weakly at Philippa's gown that trailed off the bed. The soft fabric of the gown felt like silky water, slipping against his fingertips.

"Is it poison?" Roderick asked slowly then gasped. "That bottle! Perhaps it is an antidote!" Roddy snapped the bottle up from the washstand and started toward Beau and Philippa but Lennox called out.

"Wait! Don't give it to them. Sommers was anything but an honest man." Lennox frantically searched Sommers's body with a grim look as produced a second bottle nearly identical to the one Roddy held. He stood and rushed over to Roddy by the bed.

"Are they both poison?" Roddy asked.

Beau blinked, desperately trying to focus on what they were saying, but it sounded like he was deep underwater and was hearing their voices through the waves.

"Let me see them." Lennox studied the bottles together. "The drawings are both of snakes, but look, one is lying down, coiled. The other is rearing back, ready to strike."

"Attack and peace?" Roddy murmured. "Poison and the antidote, perhaps?"

"I think so." Lennox uncorked the bottle with the

snake coiled up and held it Beau's lips. But Beau shook his head.

"Philippa...first. *Please*...."

Lennox nodded quickly and poured a bit of the contents down her parted lips before he returned to Beau and gave him a little.

"What do we do now?" Roddy asked.

"We wait." Lennox's grim words were the last thing Beau heard as he passed out against the bed with his hand still clinching the pale blue silk skirt of his wife's wedding gown.

Hours later it seemed, he stirred groggily and found himself lying on the small bed in the cramped quarters of the room on Rimmel Street. Lennox stood by the bed, leaning one shoulder against the wall.

"Welcome back," Lennox said.

Beau blinked and licked his dry lips as his memories flooded back. "My wife..."

"Here," her soft voice came from beside him. He turned to see her lying next to him in bed. Her face was less pale, but her eyes were still a little glassy.

"Thank Christ," he sighed. All other words failed him. He looked again to Ashton. "Monmouth has been taken away by the Bow Street Runners. Sommers is dead. That is at least one small mercy."

Philippa's hand settled on his chest. "Do you feel better, Beau?" she asked.

"Yes. And you?" He saw no tension or evidence of pain on her face, only a slight weariness.

"Much." She looked gravely up at Lennox. "Sommers taunted me with an antidote to the poison. He set it on the washstand. Lord Lennox discovered that it was actually the poison and that the true antidote was in his coat. He never intended to give it to me. He also had a dagger with poison on the blade, Monmouth slashed you with it."

Beau attempted to sit up on the bed and checked his arm which had been bandaged. "But how did he poison you?"

Philippa touched her sleeve. "He paid a seamstress to prick me with a pin dipped in it during my fitting yesterday. He intended the dose to kill me on our wedding night."

"Then why did he abduct you from St. George's?" Lennox asked.

"Pride," Philippa said, though she did not elaborate. Beau did not press the matter. He was sick just thinking about what could have happened.

"What happens now?" Philippa asked.

Lennox smiled at them both. "Now, you live."

But it wouldn't be that easy... Beau had almost lost Philippa today, and he could barely think past his own fears. The pain of losing her now... It would be like losing his father and mother all over again.

"Why don't we call a coach and have you both sent

home to rest?" Lennox suggested. "We have much to clean up. Bow Street will need statements from Philippa and her parents to gather the proper evidence against Monmouth."

"Right." Beau sighed as he helped Philippa to her feet. She moved weakly and he put an arm around her waist as he helped her. But deep inside he felt like a traitor to himself and to her. He knew his path already. Once she was well and healed, he intended to leave for New Orleans without her.

He'd come too close to losing her tonight and he'd felt that fear, that hint of the empty shell that he would be without her.

I'm not strong enough to survive that. I can't stay...

✦ 20 ✦

Something was wrong. Beau was far too quiet as Philippa entered his home with him. A flood of people greeted them: her parents, her grandfather, Roderick, the Lennox family, as well as a dozen others. The wedding breakfast had been cleared and put away since no one had been able to eat it. Philippa tried to ignore the twinge of disappointment at missing such an important thing like a wedding breakfast. Lord Sommers had robbed her of her happy wedding day, but at least not her life.

"We appreciate the well wishes," Beau explained to the crowd. "My wife is safe and the threats to her life are finally at an end. I apologize that we no longer have any food or drink ready, but we will arrange for that tomorrow if you are able to attend."

The guests politely accepted this change of events and

left. Only her parents, her grandfather, and Roderick remained behind. Roderick was watching her parents... *His* parents with confused hesitation. Philippa gently touched his arm.

"Would you like me to introduce you?" she asked.

Roderick's eyes brightened. "Yes, very much so." He leaned into her, whispering apologetically. "Mrs. Boudreaux, I do not understand how you can be so compassionate after what my father did to you."

She squeezed Roderick's arm. "As I have heard many times from your grandfather, you are nothing like him. I could never judge you for his actions. You are as much a victim as I am for our change in circumstances." She looked at her parents who stared at them both with nervous hope. "You never had the joy of knowing your true parents, but you may now."

As the two of them reached her parents, Beth burst into tears and Mason embraced his wife, gently shushing her.

"I'm terribly sorry," Roderick confessed. "I didn't mean to upset the lady and—"

"It is...a pleasure to meet you." Beth gasped between choked sobs as she seemed desperate not to embarrass her son.

Roderick looked between Beth and Mason and cleared his throat. "It is an honor to meet you."

Mason's voice was rough with emotion. "The honor is ours... my son." He held out a hand and Roderick shook it.

When he looked to his mother, Beth simply threw her arms around Roderick, hugging him. Roderick was startled a moment before he relaxed and wrapped his arms around her, hugging her back.

Philippa stepped away, giving the reunited family some space. Her throat closed as she realized in a sudden rush of sorrow that she had no parents to be reunited with. Her mother lay cold in a grave and her father was in prison. Her lip trembled and she drew in several breaths as she buried the pain those thoughts caused. She reminded herself that she hadn't lost her parents. She'd gained a brother and a grandfather.

"My dear child." St. Albans spoke, and she turned to see him holding out his arms. She rushed to him, this familiar stranger who'd become so important to her in so short a time. He seemed to understand her pain and held her a long while. When he finally released her, he wiped tears from her cheeks with his handkerchief.

"There now, you've had a good cry. It's quite understandable, my dear, with the ordeal you been through. But it's over now. Why don't you go upstairs and rest? We shall meet tomorrow when you feel better."

"Thank you, Your Grace."

"Grandpapa," he reminded. She smiled, though the expression was a bit watery. He turned to the others. "Mr. and Mrs. Wilson, you and Roddy are welcome to come home with me and continue your re-acquaintance."

Her parents agreed and both came to her, hugging her

tight. Her mother kissed her cheek and her father did the same.

"Rest, my Pippa. We shall see you tomorrow." She watched them walk out the front door with their son and her heart fractured a little. One light tap, and it would shatter into a thousand shards, never to be repaired.

"Philippa," Beau murmured from behind her. She spun and buried herself in him with her fingers fisted in his shirt. She shut her eyes tight and held her breath, as everything she'd been through threatened to choke her.

"I'm so sorry, my darling. *So very sorry*," he whispered over and over. What should have been a comfort to her only seemed to drive an invisible knife deeper, because his apologies warned her that some new heartbreak was on the horizon.

"You need to rest," he said.

"So, do you."

Beau flashed her a charming smile and kissed her forehead. "Let us go to bed, wife."

Wife. The word sounded so strange to her, although it was her path now. A wife to a gentleman. She was no longer a maid, no longer bound in service. Part of the world walled away from her had been opened up, but it had come at a great cost. Her husband was keeping his distance from her. Her true parents were gone and the parents who'd raised her had their true son back. She would lose her friends in service and must learn to live a new life to which she was unaccustomed.

My wish for freedom and adventure has become a curse.

Philippa kept silent as Beau escorted her to the Leda bedchamber.

"This is your home now. Your chambers will always be here," Beau said as they stepped inside.

"We will not share a room?" She hoped he would break from tradition in that respect.

"You wish to have one set of rooms?" he asked in clear surprise.

"Don't you?"

"I...had not given it much thought. I assumed you would like privacy, as most ladies wish to do."

Philippa tilted her head. "Since when have I ever been like most ladies?"

He chuckled. "A fair point. Very well. Which chambers do you prefer?"

"I like this room very much, but I suppose I would prefer your chambers."

Beau shrugged. "Why don't we stay here this evening? We can decide fully tomorrow."

She sank onto the bed and stared at him, unsure of what to do. As a maid she had so many duties she'd rarely had a moment to breathe, but now she was a woman of leisure and had far too many moments of *nothing* to do. Overcoming a sense of being lost, she looked to him.

"Philippa, are you all right?" Beau came to her and cupped her face in his hands.

"I'm fine," she whispered. "Truly."

He stared deep into her eyes. "There is nothing wrong with *not* being fine. Talk to me."

"I feel...lost." She spoke the words and a terrible pressure exerted its invisible force upon her chest.

"Lost?" Beau echoed.

"Lost. I've lost so much and because of it, *I* feel lost." She rubbed her eyes as they welled up with tears. The last thing she wanted to do was cry but at the moment, it seemed inevitable. The weight of her emotions was simply too much to withstand.

"You haven't lost anything. You have St. Albans and your parents."

He didn't understand and she was too tired to explain.

He bent his head to hers and, as exhausted as she was, she welcomed his soft, warm lips upon her own. It felt so good to have him kissing her. He gently lifted her off the bed to stand close to him as he continued to kiss away her loneliness. His heartbeat was strong and measured against her chest as she pressed closer to him and wound her arms around his neck. She had missed this since their first and only night together. The connection between them hadn't been lost as she'd feared. It was right here, like a dozen invisible yet gossamer fine strands binding them together into one heart, one soul. He murmured soft sweet words against her lips and stroked a loose curl of her hair that had come down from her coiffure.

"Feeling better?" he asked.

"A little," she admitted. His kisses seemed to have a healing affect upon her weary heart.

"Good. I should go in a moment and see that Stoddard has taken care of everything. You need time to rest, I'm sure."

"I suppose..." She'd secretly hoped he would stay here with her, cuddled up in bed, the two of them just comforting one another.

Beau continued to watch her, worry creasing his brow. His dark hair gleamed in the light coming in from the windows behind her. The faint laughter lines around his eyes and mouth enhanced his handsome features. Those lines reminded her he was a man who had lived far longer than her and had seen and suffered much, to the point where he knew that this path he was on was the very one he wished so desperately to avoid.

Yet he belonged to *her* now, as much as another person could, at least under the law of man and God. But she didn't own his heart, didn't own his soul, not in the way he'd come to own hers. Her love for him had crept up on her so slowly. She'd been afraid of it, yet she'd known it would come in time and she would not have a weapon with which to fight it. Now it was too late. She loved him with all that she was and ever would be, but she could see in his eyes a need for distance between them.

"You don't need to stay," she said. "Separate rooms are acceptable to me."

Beau opened his mouth for a moment, but he didn't

speak. A shadow crossed his face. "As you wish. I will let you rest, but first we must speak."

A fresh wave of dread swelled inside her, making her stomach clench in anxiety. "Yes?"

"Before I met you, before any of this happened, I had plans to move to America, to manage a shipping company in New Orleans that I purchased from Lord Lennox." She didn't dare interrupt him, so he continued. "I have to leave soon, and given all that has happened, I believe it would be better if you remained here. Your friends are here, your parents, and St. Albans. I would not ask you to sacrifice the comfort and ease of your life for my sake. My home and wealth would remain at your disposal and you would have all the freedom a married lady would have."

The day had somehow turned worse in the way she hadn't even thought possible.

"You won't even ask me if I wish to come? You've simply decided for me?"

"Philippa, ocean crossings are long and sometimes dangerous." His relaxed posture suddenly became stiff. "I do not yet have my home furnished or my servants hired in New Orleans. As a man, I could survive easily enough without comforts, but I do not wish to impose that on my wife."

"How long would you be gone?" She was too afraid to ask if he would ever even come back.

"A year, perhaps," he hedged. "It would depend on how

smoothly things run before I feel it safe enough to return to England."

"You lied to me." Her tone was hollow as her heart.

"Pardon?"

"You said you would endeavor to try to love me but—" She stopped short, bit her lip and then closed her eyes. "This was always your true intention."

"Philippa, I'm sorry. I didn't plan for any of this and I don't want..." He paused, his eyes dark. "I don't want to hurt you. If I leave now, this pain is all that we will have. If I stay it will be worse."

"Worse? How?"

"I can't... I'm not strong enough to fall in love with you and then lose you. I know that pain too well, and I never wish to revisit it. I'm sorry."

He turned to leave but stopped in the doorway. "I'll leave tomorrow, after the wedding breakfast. You won't have to face me again, and you have so much to live for here. Don't let me hold you back."

But the pain she saw in his eyes was not a fraction of what she felt in her heart. "I've spent my whole life wanting something more in life. You made me think it was possible. But you are leaving me, abandoning me out of your own fears that you cannot face. You are a coward, Beau." She turned to give him her back.

"I suppose you are right," he whispered, and with the click of the closing door, her husband was gone.

❄

Philippa was absolutely right. He was a bloody coward. But he couldn't change his mind. Not now. The last thing he wanted was to be such a coward, but how could he stay? He couldn't fall in love with his brave, beautiful wife. It would destroy him if he ever lost her, and he knew someday he would. Losing those one loved was an inescapable part of life. But if he didn't love her... Losing her would be hard but not unbearable.

You are a coward, Beau.

Her words echoed in his mind, the accusation carried deeper and deeper into him. He had to leave, had to get out of the house for a few hours. He had to think.

He grabbed his hat and coat from a footman and walked the distance to Lennox House on Half-Moon Street. He was shown into a drawing room and started pacing the floor. That was how Lennox found him.

"Correct me if I'm wrong, but shouldn't you be in bed with your bride?" Lennox asked.

"Yes, but..." He stumbled on the words. "I made a mess of things. I have to leave for New Orleans tomorrow. Is the ship you sold me ready to sail?"

"The *Moonlight Marvel?* Yes, I can send a message to the captain. He was to set sail in three or four days, but it is an easy thing to move up to tomorrow, as they aren't taking any cargo with them."

"Good. I should like to leave before sunset," Beau replied.

"Beau…" Lennox began. "We've been friends a long time. I hope you will not be angry with me if I speak honestly."

Beau smiled ruefully. "Say what you will."

Lennox nodded to himself before he spoke. "You are running away. Not just from her, but life. You believe that you can outrun your fears whenever they draw too close, and in the end you lose more than you gain. If you abandon her, you abandon all of it."

A knot of pain lodged in Beau's throat. "I know, Ash, I know." He knew that he would be leaving behind the glories along with the sweet ecstasies, but he would escape the depths of true and darkest despair, which was what he feared far more.

"Is that what you wish for? A life half-lived? An existence only on the surface?" Lennox queried gently. His concern only made it that much harder for Beau.

"If it helps me escape the pain of loss, then yes."

Beau didn't miss the wounded look at Lennox's eyes. It was rare to see such emotion in the baron's gaze. He was carefully guarded with his emotions, but he also didn't avoid them like Beau.

You, Lennox, are far better and braver than I am, he thought.

"I wish you luck, old friend. I shall send a set of letters and deeds to various properties in New Orleans along with you. If you haven't bought a residence yet, I have one that would suit. It's only just been built, a grand house with plenty of room to expand. It's about three hours outside of New Orleans by coach."

"Thank you, I would be glad to take you up on that."

Lennox held out a hand and Beau clasped it in his.

"Thank you, for everything," Beau replied. "Especially for Philippa. You saved her life."

Lennox lips twitched. "Actually, I rather think it was you."

"But you gave her the antidote…"

"Saving a life isn't always as simple as poisons and antidotes. Sometimes it's far more. It's giving a person a home, a family, a life they dreamed of their whole lives. She was dying inside, Beau, until she met you."

"I wish I was a better man for her then," Beau whispered. He nodded once more to Lennox before he left the room. He couldn't afford to disappoint anyone else today. The pain he feared was closer than he wished, pushing at the walls of his own guarded heart.

ROSALIND JOINED ASHTON IN THE DRAWING ROOM. "Was that Beau?"

"Yes." Ashton came to his wife and pulled her into his arms. His Scottish hellion laughed in delight.

"Why didn't he stay? Is Philippa all right?" She asked him as he nuzzled her cheek.

"I fear he's leaving tomorrow for New Orleans. Philippa isn't going with him."

Rosalind drew back. "What? Why not?"

"That is a complicated question, my heart. Beau believes if he leaves now, he won't be hurt if he loses her. He thinks he can avoid falling in love."

Rosalind frowned. "But surely he knows..."

"He's the only one who *doesn't* know he's already madly in love with his wife."

"Oh Ash, we must make him see." Rosalind begged.

"More than anything, I wish I knew how. But every man comes to see his love for what it is in his own time. We can only pray that Beau will realize his mistake before he leaves for New Orleans, so that he might come straight home and beg his wife for forgiveness."

Rosalind pressed her cheek to his chest, and he wrapped his arms tighter around her. "We were not so different than them," she reminded him.

"Not much," Ashton agreed. "But I came to my senses before it was too late. Beau is running and I fear he won't change his mind."

Rosalind lifted her head, a clever gleam in her eyes. "Because *he's* running, he's not the one who needs to chase. Don't you see?"

Suddenly Ashton did see what his wife was telling him.

"Ah. Yes, yes I do, my love. And if there's time, we might yet save them both from further pain."

His wife smiled. "This, among many reasons, is why love you."

Lennox quirked a brow. "Because I meddle in the lives of others?"

"No, because you fight for love."

Ashton's heart swelled even more with love for his wife. "*Always*."

❧ 21 ❧

If only yesterday had been a terrible dream. Philippa wished that thought over and over as she pretended to enjoy her wedding breakfast. The boisterous mood of the guests in the room should have been welcome after everything that happened in the last few weeks, but she felt hollow compared to the happy, beaming people surrounding her. Her friends from Lennox House were here, as well as Beau's friends. Not one guest was unwelcome, yet Philippa could barely manage a weak smile when anyone spoke to her.

Her grandfather handed her a glass of champagne. "I'm so glad to see you're doing well."

"Thank you. We were fortunate Lord Lennox discovered the correct antidote to that dreadful poison." The entire situation had left her in a state of shock she hadn't yet recovered from. It truly felt like it had all been a bad dream, but the reality of it continued to creep in on her little by little.

St. Albans's face darkened. "When I think of you dying yesterday and none of us knew... My dear, it will haunt me forever."

Philippa's heart sunk at the look of sorrow upon his face, and she clutched his arm. "Please, grandpapa, you mustn't."

He offered her melancholy smile. "Now I see you are not enjoying your breakfast. You and Beau have barely spoken to one another."

She knew the instant her face betrayed her pain because he ushered her out into the corridor away from the other guests.

"My child, whatever is the matter?"

"It's such a silly thing," she lied. As if Beau's leaving was anything but monumental.

"What is it?"

"Beau is leaving this evening for New Orleans. He plans to live there at least a year and he doesn't wish for me to come with him."

St. Albans's brows drew together, and his mouth firmed with grandfatherly fury. "What? That's nonsense. I will speak to him at once."

"No!" She grabbed his arm to prevent him from going back into the drawing room.

"But he isn't thinking with his heart."

"I think the problem is that he *is* thinking with his

heart... the heart that was broken twice before I ever knew him."

"He's being foolish." Her grandfather muttered. "Bloody idiot."

"Yes, but that's his choice. The last thing I want is to trap him where he least wants to be." She tried to remain calm, but this entire situation was putting her on edge.

"My dear girl." St. Albans plucked the champagne flute from her hand and set it on a side table against the wall, then he took her into his arms and held her. She was to be forever in awe of this gentle man who was so fierce in his protective love for her. "Are you positive you don't wish for me to box his ears?"

She answered with a little giggle, though the feeling was tinged with sadness. "No, please. I will not have you quarreling with him on my account."

The duke's aggrieved sigh spoke volumes. "I thought he had better sense, but it seems he is as stubborn as ever."

"Why don't you go back inside? Roderick seems quite down and I'm certain he could use your support."

St. Albans nodded. "I suppose you're right. The boy's had a rather unpleasant awakening as to his father's character."

"Have you decided what to do about him?" Philippa asked. "I know we haven't had a chance to speak about any of this, but I wish for you to know my heart on the matter."

Her grandfather inclined his head and listened.

"Do not tell anyone who I am, or how Roderick and I came to be where we are now. Roderick has done nothing wrong, and I know you wish for him to be the next Earl of Monmouth."

"Are you sure?" The duke rubbed at his jaw, thinking it over. "But that would mean no one would know you're my granddaughter."

She clasped his hands in hers. "That is a small price to pay. You and I know the truth and we need not stay apart from one another now that Beau and I are married. But Roderick deserves to be an earl. He stood between me and a loaded pistol. He showed courage against the man he loved as a father against a woman he didn't know, because he believed it was right. That speaks of the caliber of his character, don't you agree?"

"I do." St. Albans's voice was slightly rough. "But I didn't wish to hurt you and cannot choose him over you."

"You do not have to," she assured him. "Let him continue to be Monmouth's heir."

"We will have to be careful not to disclose this to authorities. Your parents will need to be told to be silent on the matter."

"I will tell them."

"Monmouth missed out on you, my child. Your mother would have been so proud of the woman you have become."

Philippa blinked away tears. "Thank you, grandpapa."

She escorted him back into the wedding breakfast but before they could speak further, Rosalind Lennox gently took hold of her arm and led her back the way she came.

"Might I have a private word?" It seemed to be a rhetorical question, as they seemed destined for that regardless of her answer.

"Of course, my lady." Philippa stepped back into the corridor with Rosalind.

"I'm sorry to keep you from your wedding breakfast, but what I must say cannot wait." Rosalind grasped one of her hands. "You know how much Ashton and I care about you."

"Yes, my lady."

"And we care about Beau as well. He and my husband have been friends a long time."

Philippa swallowed thickly as she wondered what the woman planned to say next.

"I shall get to the crux of the matter. Beau told Ashton he is leaving for New Orleans. You must go with him."

It took a moment for Philippa to recover from the fact that Rosalind knew of Beau's plans to leave. "I cannot. He made it quite clear he didn't want me to come."

Rosalind squeezed her hand. "Do you love him?"

"I do. You know that. Everyone does, it seems."

"Then go with him. Trust me. When I left Ashton, I thought I didn't want him to come after me, but when he arrived at my brothers' castle in Scotland, I realized I couldn't run from my love for him."

"But what if it doesn't change anything? We would be trapped together for two months aboard a ship and in a single cabin. He might grow to despise me."

Rosalind chuckled. "My husband would be furious if he ever finds out I told you such a thing, but when a woman decides to take charge of her own desires, a man who cares about her will be unable to resist. Do you understand my meaning?"

"I'm not sure I do..." In truth, Philippa didn't follow her at all.

"I'm saying you must *seduce* your husband." Rosalind said in a low whisper. "Those two months alone in a cabin can be *very* stimulating if one knows what to do. If you show him your desire, he will want you just as badly. He cares about you and it's human nature. It's inevitable."

Philippa's face flamed. "Oh! Heavens, I don't know if I can..."

"I promise you, if you love him, you can do this. He will forget he ever wanted to be apart from you."

Seduce Beau? How could she seduce a seasoned rake like him? Surely, he knew enough about seduction to be wary of it being used against him.

"Love is worth fighting for. Beau is frightened of what he feels for you, but you cannot let him win this battle. For his sake, not just yours, you must be brave. You have survived so much already. This will be far easier than facing a madman with poison."

Philippa took a minute to think. Rosalind's warm

hands held hers as she searched deep within herself. Could she do this? Fight for her love?

Yes, I can be brave. I can fight for Beau's heart.

"I must make arrangements if I'm to leave this evening." Her trunks would need to be packed and good-byes would have to be made.

Rosalind smiled brightly. "I will help. I know the name of the ship he plans to sail on, and I will send a message to the captain informing him you will be coming along as well."

"Thank you," Philippa whispered earnestly, her heart racing. She could only pray this would was the right course of action. She knew her parents would approve, even if it meant saying goodbye. And she couldn't help but think that the mother who gave birth to her would have also cheered her on.

Rosalind led her back into the drawing room. "Now that's settled, you need to see to your breakfast and enjoy yourself."

Soon she was surrounded again by her new friends and her heart stung with pain at the thought of leaving them all behind. Her gaze drifted to Beau, who was speaking to Lord Sheridan and Lord Essex. Their eyes met and held, and she knew Rosalind was right. She had to fight for their love. She had to believe they would be happy together. The only thing holding Beau back, was Beau.

I will fight for you as you fought for me. It is my turn to be brave.

※

"Roderick, may I speak with you?" Beau approached the recently arrived gentleman. He'd arrived late to the wedding breakfast and his clothes were slightly rumpled, as though he'd slept in them.

"Yes?" His voice was weary but not unfriendly.

"How are you holding up?"

"Barely at all," the young man admitted. "I've come from seeing my father in Newgate. They are treating him well enough. He can afford it, after all, but... I'm so bloody torn about all this. He is my father. He raised me, loved me, taught me everything I know... But what he did to your wife... I can't forgive him for it."

Beau touched his shoulder. "I cannot imagine the conflict you must be feeling."

"He never... Beau you must believe me. He wasn't a monster like that, not always." He shook his head. "I'm not expressing myself well. What I mean to say is that I do not beg forgiveness for him, but I need you to know that he wasn't always this way. The man was capable of love." Roderick was quiet a long moment before he looked at Beau with surprising fear. "What if, because he raised me, I will travel down a similar path? What if the dark seed that started all this was planted within me as well?"

"I understand your concerns, but you stood between my wife and a loaded pistol. That's the farthest thing from a path of darkness I can see," Beau assured him. He had no doubts about the purity of Roderick's character. The fact that the man even worried about it showed his conscious desire to be good, unlike the man who raised him.

Roderick looked across the room and spied Philippa. "How is she? We haven't spoken much since..."

"She's healing, a little shaken still, but she is strong and brave. I believe she will come through this well enough."

"I'm glad to hear that," Roderick said. "I thought she might not wake up and I feared for the worst. Then you collapsed..." Roderick shuddered. "Lord Sommers was..."

"In many ways he was far worse than your father," Beau said quietly. "At least Monmouth acted out of his affection for you. Sommers was simply a madman who treated life and death as a game only he was entitled to win."

"You're a better man than me, Beau," Roderick said. "If that had happened to my wife..."

Beau looked over Philippa as he had done a dozen times in the last half hour. Something had changed. This morning she'd barely spoken to him. She'd been polite but so reserved, as if wishing to hide from the world in secret shame. Yet now she was holding her head high and her eyes were bright. She looked strong, if that was the right word. Had she accepted his decision to leave for America? The idea of her moving on from him so quickly stung more than he wanted it to.

You put this distance between you. You wanted this, he

reminded himself.

"Roderick, I'm leaving for New Orleans soon. I hate to ask this of you, but will you watch over her while I'm gone?"

Roderick looked puzzled. "I would be honored of course, but why must you leave?" For a moment Beau had forgotten the man was only twenty.

"I must see to a new business venture and I do not wish to deprive my wife of her newfound family and friends."

"Er, yes, of course. It's rather curious. Philippa is not my sister by blood, but I feel bound to her now, much like a brother. She brought me back to my parents, and for that she has my gratitude and loyalty until my dying breath."

Beau smiled, in part because she'd had the same effect upon him. She drew people to her. Her steady, faithful heart and brave spirit were irresistible. Even now, she'd insisted her servant friends from the Lennox house be permitted to come to this morning's breakfast, and all the guests present had assumed the servants, who were dressed in their Sunday best, were acquaintances of Philippa's from the country.

It didn't bother Beau one bit. He rather liked Philippa's noble heart and would gladly set tongues wagging among the gossips as long as Philippa was happy. And he knew he would miss this. He would miss her. It was all the more reason he had to leave.

By the time breakfast ended, he'd made his final preparations for departure. His trunks were already on the way to port and his valet was on board preparing their cabins. Since they were traveling on a fine merchant vessel, they would have excellent accommodations for the entire journey. The thought should have comforted him, but he knew the cabin would be a very lonely place. Perhaps he could assist the crew to keep himself occupied somehow during the journey?

"Sir, what else may I do?" Stoddard asked. When Beau had shared his desire to depart, he'd seen the sadness in the butler's eyes. They'd been together for so long. He would miss Stoddard and Mrs. Gronow, but he needed them to continue to run his home for Philippa. It wasn't as if he would be gone forever. Perhaps after a year, he would find the courage that he lacked now to fall in love with his wife, but that was assuming his wife would even still have him. He shouldn't let himself think of that now, not when he had much to do in New Orleans.

"I believe that is everything, Stoddard. Is my wife upstairs?"

"Er... No, sir. She left shortly after the breakfast."

"Left?"

"Yes, sir."

That was odd. "You know where she's gone?"

"I do not. She did not tell anyone where she was bound when she departed."

Beau stared down at his boots and bit his lip. She was

gone, and he had no time left to say goodbye. He'd spoken to St. Albans earlier that day and barely survived that discussion. The duke was furious with him for leaving and he'd known that would happen. And now he wouldn't have a chance to see Philippa again for a year or more.

"Sir, you should go if you wish to have time to settle yourself on the ship."

"Right... Well..." Still he tried to find a reason to delay, but he knew he couldn't wait for Philippa to return, no matter how much he wished he could.

He took his hat from Toby the footman and headed out to his waiting coach. The docks were busy in the early evening as men loaded goods on the ships. The sun was now a red sphere dipping into the horizon. He felt bad for asking the captain to make such a late departure in the day, but he'd not wanted to wait another moment.

Beau climbed out of the coach and walked the long wooden dock toward his ship, his steps becoming heavier with each second. He couldn't let his guilt stop him; he was doing what was best for him and for Philippa. In time she would understand.

At the gangplank, he met an officer on the ship who informed him that his luggage was stowed in his cabin and that his valet was on board and ready to depart. He thanked the man before he walked to the railing and rested his palms in the wood. He stared out of the darkening skies over the water.

The boatswain next to Beau stopped coiling a bit of rope. "Everything all right, sir?"

"No," Beau replied honestly. "Not in the slightest."

The boatswain blinked, startled by Beau's blunt and honest response. "Anything I can do to help, sir?"

"Answer me this," Beau said. "When a man's life changes dramatically and he's afraid... Afraid of losing all that he holds dear, what should he do? Should he run, should he stay?"

The boatswain abandoned his coil of rope and joined him at the railing.

"When a storm rises on the open sea, and the wind changes, a man must decide to brave it or try to avoid it. Either way, the man has but to adjust his sails. It's the only way to keep his ship from becoming lost." The man eyed him solemnly. "That's not to say wrecks don't happen, sir. Ships can be lost, despite every sailor's efforts to stay above the water, but a man can still survive the storm. He can cling to the wreckage until he finds a way home. The question you have to ask yourself is whether you're brave enough to adjust your sails when you see the storm coming. Are you brave enough to face the storm, come what may, and hold dear to whatever survives the waves and wind?"

The sailor then bent and retrieved his rope, finished coiling it and walked back down the deck, leaving Beau alone to contemplate what he said and wonder if he would ever be brave enough.

Beau braced his arms on the rail and watched the sun sink further down the horizon. All he could think about was what he was losing by walking away from Philippa. He would miss the way she wrinkled her nose when she laughed, and the way she danced, and the way St. Albans eyes lit up whenever he looked at her and Beau together.

I let everyone down. Everyone that mattered.

A sudden breeze rushed along the deck of the ship and chased the sails up the mast, puffing them out slightly.

"A man has but to adjust his sails," he said to himself.

Philippa would have liked that saying. He wanted to tell her and see what she thought. He wanted...

His heart gave a painful jolt as the realization hit him.

He was never *not* going to miss her.

Because he was already in love with her.

Despite his best intentions, all of his careful plans... Somehow, he'd fallen in love without realizing it. Christ, he'd probably been in love since the waltz at the Essex ball. He could almost see his father in his head, laughing at Beau for not seeing the obvious.

Beau was suddenly seized with panic. If he left her now, he would only suffer the pain of losing her for the next year, the very pain he had wanted to avoid. And in a year's time, after how he'd treated her, he feared her feelings for him would ebb away, and rightly so.

He was already facing the storm. He saw that now, clear as the skies before him. Leaving Philippa would wreck him, drown him. He had to get off the ship...he had to get his wife back. He had to win back the broken heart of the love of his life.

"I'm a bloody fool!" He cursed and ran toward the quarterdeck. "Captain?"

The captain leaned over the rail from the deck above. "Yes, Mr. Boudreaux?"

"Could you wait? I need to disembark. I will not be going to New Orleans after all, at least, not yet. I need time to gather my things." He raced down the stairs into the interior of the ship. He had to get his valet and trunks off the ship at once.

He flung open his cabin door and froze. A figure stood by the window as the last rays of the setting sun made her silhouette glow. The figure slowly turned, and a candle illuminated Philippa's face.

"Beau, I'm going with you. You cannot have me thrown off this vessel. Lady Rosalind sold her shares in the shipping company to me. As such, I own part of this ship now and—"

Beau didn't give his sweet wife another chance to speak. He crossed the room between them and dragged her into his arms, kissing her soundly. He had no idea how she got here, but by God he was thankful she was. She gasped when he finally broke their kiss, half giddy as she touched her lips.

"Well that's not the reaction I expected," she said.

She felt wonderful in his arms and his eyes burned as he fought off a tide of emotions. He never wanted to let go of her again. "What did you expect?"

"I expected you to be furious," she said. "And go off on some long rambling speech about how you were leaving for my own good."

He leaned in, touching his forehead to hers. "I was coming down here to have my trunks packed and sent back home. I realized I couldn't leave you, because I'm in love with you and leaving you was already cutting my heart out of my own chest."

"You changed your mind?" Her eyes welled up and he brushed the tears away with his thumb as they shared a lingering gaze full of silent promises they'd both been too afraid to make before now.

"I've been so blind, so afraid. How can you forgive me, love? How can you not hate me?" His voice broke. "I... thought I could just leave. That it wouldn't hurt either of us. But thinking about it now feels like I'm breaking apart inside." He was rambling in desperate sentences.

She placed a fingertip on his mouth silencing him. "You said you loved me?"

He nodded and she lowered her hand to his chest, playing with the buttons on his waistcoat. "I loved you for a while now. I've merely been too blind to see." He held her tight then eased back to gaze down at her.

"How did you come to see it?" She looked at his chest, her lashes fluttering as she tried to remain calm.

"It occurred to me that I was already missing you, and that was only going to grow the longer we were apart. A year away from you would feel like a lifetime. That is part of what love means to me. My heart longs for you, burns for you. I kept thinking of all the things I wanted to tell you, the things I wanted to hear you speak about. If I left that would all stop and I couldn't stand the thought. I know that isn't all love is." He sighed. "It's so much more than that, but once I realized that, I knew I couldn't leave. I had to come home...I had to come back to you."

Philippa raised her eyes to his and his knees felt strangely weak. He'd never believed it when the poets spoke of that quiet, fervent fire of love that burned through one's body and left them so weak and yet strong in other ways. The feeling was indeed frightening. Now that he'd tasted love, he wouldn't give it up for anything in the world.

"I never imagined I would have a life like this, or you," Philippa said. "But now that you're mine, I can't imagine my life without you." She smiled sadly. "I suppose I have my father to thank for at least one thing. If he'd never tried to kill me that night at Lord Lennox's home, I never would have met you."

She teased her fingers into his cravat, and then pulled his head down to hers for another burning and impossibly sweet kiss. He'd been holding back for so long, avoiding love and all along he'd missed the truth. Love was always worth it. With every risk of pain and heartache, it was still infinitely more than he ever could have imagined.

"We need to tell the captain we're both leaving," he murmured as he held her close, breathing in her scent.

"No. We're going to New Orleans," she said, surprising him.

"What? But your family and your friends..."

"They know my choice to leave London. Grandpapa is coming to visit us after he has his heir brought to London to start handling his affairs. My parents are going to spend time with Roderick. I've had their love for twenty years; it's his turn now. I made my farewells to everyone at the breakfast and Lady Lennox helped me arrange arriving here before you."

Beau chuckled. "I was looking for you to say good-bye. Stoddard said you didn't tell anyone where you went."

Philippa laughed. "I hope you aren't upset, but I asked Mr. Stoddard and Mrs. Gronow to move to America with us. Half of the staff agreed to come as well. They are to follow us a week after Stoddard has the house closed. Your steward will manage your estate."

"You accomplished all of this in one day?" He couldn't believe it.

Philippa grinned. "With Lady Lennox's help. We divided and conquered."

Beau rubbed his hands down her back. "Do you truly wish to come to New Orleans? I wouldn't force that upon you. I would happily stay in London."

"I *want* to go. All my life I've wanted adventure,

wanted something more. I didn't know what destiny had in store for me until I met you."

Beau's heart tightened at her words. "Then I vow upon the path of our stars that you and I shall have adventures together, always."

Always. The single word contained all the things he ever wanted to say to her.

"Sir?" A sailor stood at the doorway. "The captain wants to know if you need help leaving the ship?"

"Tell him my wife and I are staying aboard and we're ready to set sail whenever he sees fit." Beau looked at Philippa and she nodded in agreement.

"Very good, sir." The sailor politely closed their cabin door, leaving them alone.

"Fifty days is a long time alone together," Beau mused as he played with a lock of her hair.

"Oh, it is," she agreed in mock solemnity. "You know, I had a grand plan to spend those days seducing you and convincing you that you could not live without me."

"Were you now? I would be happy to play the cold and unfeeling husband if you still wish to seduce me," Beau suggested and grinned rakishly down at her.

Philippa giggled and shoved him onto the bed. He stumbled and fell arse down on the mattress. She hiked her skirts up and straddled his lap so she could kiss him. He moaned in delight as it put their bodies in a perfect position to make love.

"I thought perhaps I would start with this..." she said

coquettishly as she rocked against him.

"Christ... Yes." He reached between their bodies, struggling with his clothes until he freed himself from his trousers. She continued to kiss him, laughing when he cursed as he struggled to remove her underpinnings. Then he was sliding into her and it felt like he was home the instant their bodies connected.

Philippa's grey eyes flashed silver with passion and he held her close. Their mouths dueled for dominance as he guided her into a gentle rhythm upon him. The pleasure built up slowly but to ever greater heights until their release came and he felt every bit of his body and heart shatter along with hers.

He'd been such a fool to fear love, and he'd almost lost it before he'd even realized how wonderful it was. He nuzzled her neck, kissing her skin and tasting the faint sweat mixed with her natural sweet scent. She regained her breath, panting softly in his arms. He felt cut open, raw, and yet with her there with him, somehow he wasn't afraid any longer.

"I was afraid of love," he confessed against her ear as he simply basked in the joy of holding his wife. "But I should have been afraid of never having loved all."

She stroked his jaw and their gazes locked. "You don't have to be afraid. You are loved beyond imagining."

His eyes burned and he kissed her back, this time fiercely as he wrapped his arms tight around her. "As are you, my love. Now and forever."

EPILOGUE

New Orleans, three months later...

Philippa stood at the far end of a long dirt road that led to a white columned manor house. It had been almost completely ready for them to live in when they'd first arrived. Ashton Lennox had prepared for whoever was coming to manage the shipping line. Ahead of her, Beau stood next to a tall man with fair hair, one of the architects that Beau had recently hired to help build onto their new home. They were both devoid of their coats due to the warmth. The winter in New Orleans was far fairer than in England. Between them, they carried a wooden beam that would soon form part of the new nursery on the back of the house.

Philippa placed a protective hand on her stomach as she walked through the avenue of tall oaks that lined the road to their home. The wind moved through the tunnel of foliage, providing a cool breeze, and the nearby river lent more breeze off the water. She liked it, this tunnel of trees that seemed to channel all the elements of nature while guiding her back to the house.

They'd only arrived in New Orleans one month ago but already she felt like this was home. She could picture generations of children and grandchildren running through the house and grounds, dozens of Boudreaux descendants who looked like Beau with dark hair and whiskey colored eyes. It was a destiny she was certain would come to pass, perhaps even centuries from now.

Philippa held a letter in her hand as she finally reached the plantation house.

"Beau?" She called out.

Her husband came at once, wiping sweat off his brow with a handkerchief. "Everything all right, my love?" He embraced her gently, nuzzling his face against her neck.

"We have a letter." She held it up. He grinned as he recognized the heavy wax seal on the back. The St. Albans crest.

"Have you opened it yet?" Excitement danced in his eyes.

"Not yet."

Beau scooped her up in his arms, carrying her over the threshold like a Celtic bride and deposited her on the settee in the drawing room. She broke the wax seal and read the letter's contents.

· · ·

Philippa and Beau,

I'm delighted to tell you that I'm on my way to New Orleans. In fact, there is a small chance I'll arrive shortly after this letter. I've taken care to leave my estate in order and plan to remain with you both in New Orleans for some time.

All my love, Thomas Winthrop, His Grace, the Duke of St. Albans.

"He's coming so soon?" Beau joined her on the settee. "By God, it will be good to see his face again."

"Indeed, it will." Philippa looked out the window and saw a coach coming up the long drive. Surely, they weren't so lucky that St. Albans would actually arrive right after his letter.

"Stay here," Beau rushed out to meet the coach, but Philippa ignored him and followed him to meet the arriving vehicle.

"My boy!" St. Albans cried out as he burst out of the coach.

"Your Grace." Beau hugged the duke. His joy reflected Philippa's own at the sight of her grandfather.

"Ahh, my child." He drew her into a hug.

"Careful, Your Grace. She's in the family way." Beau interjected actively.

"Oh, hush. I'm only three months along. I'm not some delicate creature." Philippa reminded her husband, but he did not look even the slightest bit apologetic.

"Congratulations!" St. Albans hugged her again and she knew in that moment she was complete.

"How are my parents, and how is Roddy?"

"Wonderful. They plan to sail out in the spring to see us and return to England after a month."

"It's a good thing we are building more rooms to the house, then." Beau waved at the home.

"Good thinking, my boy. Well, show me around. Let me see what you've been up to."

St. Albans entered the house after Beau, and Philippa laughed to herself with joy. She knew her grandfather was here to stay. His heart, like hers, belonged with family. The three of them belonged together. Each of their broken hearts had found healing with one another.

Beau turned to her in the foyer, holding out a hand. "Darling, come along." Philippa ran to catch up. She saw the look upon her grandfather's face, an expression of quiet but endless content. It seemed all was well with the world when one could be with those they loved with all their hearts.

She twined her fingers through Beau's, and he pressed a kiss to her lips before they escorted St. Albans to the drawing room.

She beamed at him. "Welcome home, grandpapa."

"Thank you, my child. Now, it seems you both have settled in?"

"We have," Beau said proudly. He'd been working tirelessly on the house and it showed.

"Well, what made you come around to love, my boy? I can see you finally realized you loved my granddaughter." St. Albans gentle honest question caught Beau and Philippa off guard only but a moment.

Philippa peered up at her husband from beneath her lashes, curious to see what he would say. Beau raised her hand to his lips and pressed a kiss there that drew forth a blush.

"I realized my heart was already broken the moment I decided to leave her in London, Your Grace. I changed my mind and found her waiting for me in my own cabin aboard our ship. She'd outsmarted me, and I was delighted to inform her that I was no longer afraid of love. I learned that loving someone beyond imagining is the greatest gift a soul can have, and that I'm gifted beyond measure." Beau paused, his voice softened and his eyes brightened as he continued. "I never believed in fate until I met her. But it was fate from the moment we met. Life finally blessed me in a way I could never have dreamed."

Philippa's heart clinched tight as she looked at Beau. Fate had blessed them both. They'd both been afraid of love, afraid to love and lose. They'd both been so very wrong. Fate had brought them together and given them everything.

"And you, my dear?" St. Albans voice became slightly rough with emotion.

Philippa smiled. "It is as if I was destined to love him... Always."

. . .

THANK YOU SO MUCH FOR READING *BOUDREAUX'S Lady!* I hope you're interested in checking out the contemporary series by Kristen Proby that inspired this story! Turn the page to read the prologue and first chapter of *Easy Love*, the first in the series by Kristen!

The next story in the League of Rogues series is *Escaping the Earl!* A cute novella that includes Rafe playing a reluctant matchmaker to two of his friends. Be sure to stay signed up for my newsletter HERE so you won't miss it when it releases!

EASY LOVE BY KRISTEN PROBY
PROLOGUE

Eli-

E "You work too hard." The voice comes from behind me. I'm standing behind my desk, gazing out over the French Quarter and the Mississippi River from my fifty-fourth floor office windows in New Orleans. The sun is blazing already. It's only eight in the morning, but it's a stifling eighty-six humid-filled degrees out there, much hotter than the cool comfort of my office.

It seems all I do is watch the world from this office window.

And where the fuck did that thought come from?

"Earth to Eli," Savannah says dryly from behind me.

"I heard you." I shove my hands in my pockets, fingering the silver half-dollar that my father gave me when I took this position, and turn to find my sister standing before my desk in her usual crisp suit, blue today, her thick dark hair pinned up and worry in her hazel gaze. "And, hello, pot, I'm kettle."

"You're tired."

"I'm fine." She narrows her eyes at me and takes a deep breath, making my lips twitch into a half smile. I love getting her riled up.

It's ridiculously easy.

"Did you even go home last night?"

"I don't have time for this, Van." I lower into my chair and motion for her to do the same, which she does after shoving a banana under my nose.

"But you have time to stare out the window?"

"Are you trying to pick a fight today? Because I'll oblige you, but first tell me what the fuck we're fighting about." I peel the banana and take a bite, realizing that I'm starving.

Savannah blows out a deep breath and shakes her head, while mumbling something about pigheaded men.

I smile brightly now.

"Lance giving you problems?" My hands flex in and out of fists at the idea of finally laying that fucker flat. Savannah's husband is not one of my favorite people.

"No." Her cheeks redden, but she won't look me in the eye.

"Van."

"Oh, good, you're both here," Beau says, as he marches into my office, shuts the door behind him, takes the seat next to Savannah, steals my half-eaten banana out of my hand, and proceeds to eat the rest of it in two bites.

"That was mine." My stomach gives a low growl, not satisfied in the least, and I give a brief thought to asking my assistant to run out for beignets.

"God, you're a baby," Beau replies, and tosses the peel in the garbage. My older brother is taller than my six-foot-four by one inch and as lean as he was in high school. But I can still take him.

"Why the fuck are you two in my office?" I sit back and run my hand over my mouth. "I'm quite sure you both have plenty to do."

"Maybe we missed you," Savannah says with a fake grin and bats her eyelashes at me.

"You're a smart ass."

She just nods knowingly, but then she and Beau exchange a look that has the hairs on the back of my neck standing up.

"What's going on?"

"Someone is stealing from us." Beau tosses a file full of spreadsheets in my direction. His jaw ticks as I open it and see columns of numbers.

"Where?"

"That's what we don't know," Savannah adds quietly, but her voice is full of steel. "Whoever's doing it is hiding it well."

"How did you find it?"

"By accident, actually," she replies crisply, all business

now. "We know it has to be happening in accounting, but it's buried so deep that the who and how is a mystery."

"Fire the whole department and start over." I shut the file and lean back, just as Beau laughs.

"We can't fire more than forty people, most of whom are innocent, Eli. It doesn't work like that."

"There has to be a paper trail," I begin, but Savannah cuts me off with a shake of her head.

"We're paperless, remember?"

"Oh, yeah, saving the fucking trees. Are you telling me that no one knows what the fuck is going on?"

"It's not a huge amount of money, but it's big enough to piss me off," Beau says quietly.

"How much?"

"Just over one hundred G's. That we've found so far."

"Yeah, that's enough to piss me off too. They're not just stealing post-its out of the supply closet."

"And it's not predictable. If it was a regular amount, on a routine, we could find it no problem. But I don't want to cause mass hysteria in the company. I don't want everyone to think that we're looking over all of their shoulders every damn minute."

"Someone is stealing, and you're worried about the employees' feelings?" I ask with a raised brow. "Who the fuck are you?"

"He's right," Savannah adds. "Having the co-CEOs of the company on everyone's asses isn't good for morale."

"What about having the CFO do it?" I ask, referring to Savannah, who shakes her head and laughs.

"No, I don't think so."

"So, we just sit back and let whoever the fucker is use us as his own private ATM?"

"Nope." Savannah smiles brightly, her pretty face lighting up. "I want to bring Kate O'Shaughnessy in."

"Your college friend?" I glance at Beau, who has no expression on his face whatsoever. Typical.

"This is what she does for a living."

"She looks over people's shoulders for a living? She must be everyone's favorite person."

"You're on a roll today," Beau says quietly.

"Kate works with companies who are dealing with embezzlement. She comes in as a regular employee and blends in, investigating on the down-low."

"Can she actually do the job? It won't work if she doesn't know what she's doing."

"She has an MBA, Eli. But I want to put her in as an administrative assistant. They see and know everything, and they talk to each other. She's likable."

"Okay, works for me." I glance at Beau. "You?"

"I think it's the way to go," he agrees. "None of us have time to do it ourselves, and I don't trust handing this off to anyone else. Like Van said, people talk. I'd like to keep this quiet. Kate will sign all the necessary non-disclosure agreements, and from what I've heard, she's excellent at her job."

"One thing," Van says, and leans forward to stare at me, the way she does when I'm about to be in deep trouble. "You're not allowed to mess around with her."

"I'm not an asshole, Van..."

"No, you're not allowed to get your man-whore hands on her."

"Hey! I am not—"

"Yeah, you are," Beau says with a grin.

I sigh and roll my shoulders. "Not having the same date twice doesn't make me a whore."

Van simply raises a brow. "Leave her be."

"I'm a professional, Van. I don't sleep with the employees."

"Is that what you said to that assistant that sued us a few years back?"

"Anymore."

"God." Van shakes her head as Beau laughs. "She's a nice woman, Eli."

Instead of replying, I simply narrow my eyes at my sister and swivel in my chair. Kate's a grown woman; one I'm most likely not attracted to anyway.

It's been a few years since much of anything has held my interest for long. That would require feeling something.

"Call her."

EASY LOVE

CHAPTER ONE

Kate~

"Hello?" I ask breathlessly, as the cab I'm in whizzes down the interstate, heading directly for the heart of New Orleans.

"Where are you?" Savannah asks with a smile in her voice.

"In the cab on the way from the airport. Are you sure I shouldn't check into a hotel room?"

"No way, Bayou Industries owns a beautiful loft that we'll pretend you're renting while you're here. Come directly to the office. I have a meeting, so I won't be able to greet you, I'm sorry."

"It's okay," I reply and bite my lip as the cabbie cuts off another motorist and my stomach rolls. "I'm hoping to make it alive. I might not survive the cab ride."

Savannah chuckles in my ear, and then I hear her

murmuring to someone else in her office. "I have to go. Eli will meet you."

"Eli? I thought I'd meet with Beau—"

"Eli's not as scary as we've all led you to believe. I promise." And then she's gone. The cab swerves again, and I send up a prayer of thanks that I didn't eat breakfast this morning as I use my hand to fan my face.

It's darn hot in the Big Easy.

During all the years I went to college with Savannah and her twin brother, Declan, I never did make it down here to visit them, and I can't wait to explore the French Quarter, eat beignets, have my tarot cards read, and soak it all in.

Of course, I'd rather soak it all in while not wearing so many clothes. Who knew it would be so hot in May? I shimmy out of my suit jacket, fold the sleeves over so they don't wrinkle, and watch as above ground cemeteries, old buildings, and lots of people zoom by.

Eli is the one Boudreaux sibling I've never met. I've seen photos of the handsome brother, and heard many stories about his stoic, tough, playboy ways. Van says the stories are exaggerated. I guess I'll find out for myself.

Well, not the playboy part. That's just none of my business.

Finally, we come to an abrupt stop. There's a red cable-car on one side and mountains of concrete on the other. I stumble out into the hot Monday afternoon, and sweat immediately beads on my forehead.

It's not just hot. It's sticky.

But I smile despite the discomfort, tip the reckless cabbie, and roll my suitcase behind me into the blessedly cool building, where a woman sits behind a long, ornate desk, typing furiously on a computer while speaking on the phone.

"Mr. Boudreaux is unavailable at this time, but I'll put you through to his assistant, one moment." She quickly pushes a series of keys, then smiles up at me.

She's very smiley.

"I'm Kate O'Shaughnessy."

"Welcome, Ms. O'Shaughnessy," she says, holding that smile in place. "Mr. Boudreaux is expecting you." She types furiously and begins speaking into her phone again. "Hello, Miss Carter, Ms. O'Shaughnessy is here for Mr. Boudreaux. Yes, ma'am." She clicks off efficiently. "Please have a seat. Can I get you some water?"

"No, thank you."

Miss Efficient simply nods and returns to her ringing phones. Before I have a chance to sit, a tall woman in black slacks and a red sleeveless blouse walks out of the elevator and straight to me.

"Ms. O'Shaughnessy?"

"Kate, please."

"Hello, Kate. Mr. Boudreaux is in his office. Follow me." She smiles and offers to take my suitcase, but I shake my head and follow her into the elevator. She doesn't ask me any questions, and I'm thankful. I've learned to lie well in this business, but I don't know what she's already been told. I'm led past an office area and into the largest office I've ever seen. The massive black desk sits before a wall of floor-to-ceiling windows. The furniture is big and expensive. Comfortable. There are two doors, each on opposite sides of the room, and I can't help but wonder what they lead to.

"Ms. O'Shaughnessy is here, sir."

"Kate," I add without thinking, and then any hope of being able to think at all is tossed right out of those spectacular windows, when the tall man standing before them turns to look at me. The photos didn't do him justice.

Yum.

The door closes behind me and I take a deep breath and walk toward him, hiding the fact that my knees have officially turned to mush.

"Kate," I repeat, and hold my hand out to shake his over his desk. His lips twitch as he watches me, his whiskey-colored eyes sharp and assessing as they take a slow stroll down my body, then back up to my face. Jeez, he's taller than I expected. And broader. And he wears a suit like he was born to it.

Which, I suppose he was. Bayou Enterprises has been around for five generations, and Eli Boudreaux is the sharpest CEO it's seen in years.

He moves around his desk and takes my hand in his, but rather than shake it, he raises it to his lips and places a soft kiss on my knuckles.

"Pleasure," he says in a slow New Orleans drawl. Dear God, I might explode right here. "I'm Eli."

"I know." He raises a brow in question. "I've seen photos over the years."

He nods once, but doesn't let go. His thumb is circling softly over the back of my hand, sending my body into a tailspin. My nipples have tightened, pressing against my white blouse, and now I wish with all my might that I hadn't taken off my jacket.

"Please, have a seat," he says, and motions to the black chair behind me. Rather than sit behind his desk, he sits in the chair next to mine and watches me with those amazing eyes of his.

A lock of dark hair has fallen over his forehead and my fingers itch to brush it back for him.

Calm the eff down, Mary Katherine. You'd think I'd never seen a hot man before.

Because I have.

Declan, the youngest of the Boudreaux brothers, is no slouch in the looks department, and he's one of my best friends. But being near him never made my knees weak or made me yearn for a tall glass of ice water. Or a bed. Or to rip his clothes off his body.

Whoa.

"Did Savannah fill you in on what's happening?" Eli asks calmly, his face revealing nothing. He crosses an ankle over the opposite knee and steeples his fingers, watching me.

"Yes, she and I have talked extensively, and she's emailed me all of the new-hire paperwork, as well as the NDA's, which I've printed and signed." I pull the papers out of my briefcase and pass them to Eli. Our fingers brush, making my thighs clench, but he seems unaffected.

Typical. I don't usually inspire hot lust from the opposite sex. Especially not men who look like Eli. Which is fine, because he's my boss and my best friends' brother and I'm here to work.

I clear my throat and push my auburn hair behind my ear. With all of this humidity, it's going to be a curly mess in no time.

"That's a beautiful ring," he says unexpectedly, nodding toward my right hand, still raised near my ear.

"Thank you."

"Gift?"

He's a man of few words.

"Yes, from my grandmother," I reply, and tuck my hands in my lap. He simply nods once and glances down at the papers in his hand. He frowns and glances up at me, but before he can say anything, his office door swings open and Declan walks in with a wide smile on his handsome face.

"There's my superstar." I squeal and leap up and into his arms, and Dec squeezes me tight and turns a circle in the middle of the wide office. He finally sets me on my feet, cups my face in his hands, and kisses me square on the mouth, then hugs me again, more gently this time. "You okay?" he whispers in my ear.

"I'm great." I gaze up into Dec's sweet face and years of memories and emotion fall around me. Laughter and tears, love, sadness, affection. "It's so good to see you."

"Have you done anything fun since you got to town?"

"I almost lost my life in a cab," I reply with a laugh. "I came straight here."

"I'll take you out tonight. Show you the French Quarter. I know this great restaurant—"

"That won't be necessary," Eli interrupts. His voice is calm. He's standing now, his hands shoved in his pockets, his wide shoulders making the large office feel small. "You have a gig tonight," he reminds Declan.

"I can take you out before."

"Don't worry about Kate this evening," Eli replies, still perfectly calm, but his jaw ticks.

I feel like I'm watching a tennis match as my head swivels back and forth, watching them both with curiosity.

"You know what Savannah told you," Declan says softly to Eli.

No response.

Declan glances back down to me. "I really don't mind calling the gig off tonight and settling you in."

"I'll be fine, Dec." I grin and pat his chest. "Where will you be playing?"

"The Voodoo Lounge."

"I might just show up." I push up onto my tiptoes and kiss his cheek.

"I don't want you wandering around the French Quarter after dark."

"I'll take her," Eli offers, earning a speculative look from Declan, who then gazes down at me and kisses my forehead softly.

"I'll save a seat for both of you then," he replies with a happy smile. "Have a good afternoon. Don't let the boss man run you ragged." He winks at me and grins at Eli, then slips back out the door.

"You and Declan are close," Eli says when I turn back around. His hands are still in his pockets as he rocks back on his heels.

"Yes. He, Savannah, and I were sort of the three amigos in college."

"Are you planning on fucking him?"

"Excuse me?" I feel my jaw drop as I stare at the formidable man before me. I prop my hands on my hips and glare at him. "That's none of your darn business."

He purses his lips as though he's trying not to laugh. "It's none of my *darn* business?"

"That's what I said."

He tilts his head and looks like he's about to say more, but then he saunters to my suitcase and pulls it behind him, as he gestures for me to follow him.

He's kicking me out?

"Miss Carter, I'll be out the rest of the day. Reschedule my appointments."

His assistant gapes at him and then sputters, "But, Mr. Freemont has been waiting..."

"I don't care. Reschedule. I'll see you tomorrow." Eli calls the elevator, his eyes never leaving me as we wait for the car to arrive. "Do you have a change of casual clothes in here?"

"Yes. The rest of my things are being shipped down and should arrive tomorrow afternoon."

He nods and motions for me to lead him into the elevator.

"Eli?"

The air literally crackles around us as he glances down at me and raises a brow. He's barely touched me and my body is on high alert and my mind is empty.

"Where are we going?"

"To your place."

"You know where my place is?"

"I own it, *cher.*" He sighs and finally reaches over and tucks my hair behind my ear, making me shiver. "Are you cold?"

"No." I clear my throat and step away from him. "If you'll just give me the address, I'll take a cab to my place."

"I wouldn't dream of endangering your life again," he replies with a half-smile, and every hair on my body stands on end. Good Lord, what this man can do with a smile.

I need to get my hormones under control. It's simply

been too long since I got laid, that's all. And I'm not going to scratch this particular itch with this particular man. He's my boss. My best friends' brother.

No way, nohow.

"You coming?" he asks.

Yes, please.

I realize the elevator has opened and he's standing next to me, waiting for me to go first.

"Of course."

"Of course," he chuckles. "We can walk it…it's not far, but it's hot out, so we'll drive."

I nod and follow him to his sleek, black Mercedes, which he expertly drives down the narrow streets of the French Quarter. I can't help but practically press my face to the window, trying to take in everything I see at once.

"It's so beautiful," I murmur.

"Have you been here before?"

"No. I can't wait to walk around and soak it all in."

He parks less than three minutes after we set off, and kills the engine. "We're here."

"Already?"

"I told you, it's not far."

"I could have walked that, even with the heat."

"It's not necessary to make you uncomfortable," he replies simply and climbs out of the car, gathers my bag, and with his hand on the small of my back, leads me up to a loft that sits above an herb shop called Bayou Botanicals. I can smell sage and lavender as Eli unlocks the front door and ushers me inside, where I stop on a dime and take in the beautiful.

The outside of the building is well kept and beautiful with worn red bricks and green iron railings, but the inside is brand new and simply opulent.

"I'm staying *here?*"

"That you are," he confirms, his accent sliding along my skin like honey. "You'll consider this your home while you're with us. Here are your keys." He passes the keys to me, then turns his back and leads me to the kitchen, which boasts brand new appliances, dark oak cabinets, and matching granite countertops. "The bedroom is through there," he continues, and leads me into a beautiful room with a four-poster bed. "The linens are clean and fresh. The bathroom is there." He points to the left, but my eyes are stuck on the doors that lead out to the balcony, which offers a beautiful view of the street below and Jackson Square just a block away.

"There are times that it gets noisy with music and people, but there's never a dull moment in the French Quarter."

I nod and turn back to him. "Thank you. Shall we go back to the office?"

"It's mid-afternoon, Kate. Take the rest of the day to settle in."

"Oh, but, I'm here to work. Surely, I could—"

"It would look odd to bring on a new hire in the middle of the day, don't you think?"

Of course it would.

I smile sheepishly and nod. "You're right. I'll work from here." I toss my jacket onto the bed, pull my laptop out of my briefcase, and walk briskly into the kitchen. "It's going to be a process."

"Kate, I don't want—"

"I'm not going to be able to just dig in and start investigating. Van's right to give me an assistant position, but that's going to be even tougher." I tie my hair back off my face and lower into a kitchen chair as I talk briskly. If I talk about work, I won't be ogling him, and thus losing more brain cells.

"Kate."

"I'm going to have to play by the rules for a while, a couple weeks at least. I need people to trust me, so they'll open up to me."

"Kate."

"I—"

"Enough," he says sharply.

For more information please visit Kristen Proby's website: https://www.kristenprobyauthor.com/boudreaux

ABOUT THE AUTHOR

Lauren Smith is an Oklahoma attorney by day, author by night who pens adventurous and edgy romance stories by the light of her smart phone flashlight app. She knew she was destined to be a romance writer when she attempted to re-write the entire *Titanic* movie just to save Jack from drowning. Connecting with readers by writing emotionally moving, realistic and sexy romances no matter what time period is her passion. She's won multiple awards in several romance subgenres including: New England Reader's Choice Awards, Greater

Detroit BookSeller's Best Awards, and a Semi-Finalist award for the Mary Wollstonecraft Shelley Award.

To Connect with Lauren, visit her at:
www.laurensmithbooks.com
lauren@laurensmithbooks.com

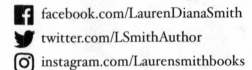

facebook.com/LaurenDianaSmith
twitter.com/LSmithAuthor
instagram.com/Laurensmithbooks

Made in the USA
Monee, IL
01 July 2021